PASSION WITHOUT PRETENSE

The setting was sublimely romantic—the beautiful garden of the Earl of Leafield's country hideaway.

"I was right in thinking this garden a proper setting for you," the earl murmured. Flora's hat fell to the ground as he took her in his arms, pressing his mouth against hers in a deep, desperate kiss. She moaned softly, and he held her closer still.

Pulling away, Flora asked breathlessly, "You brought me here for—for this?"

"And a great deal more," the earl affirmed. With all the sensual skill of his renowned amorous expertise, his hand left Flora's waist, trailing slowly and deliciously upward to cup her breast. Standing like this made her feel faint, and he took advantage of her impaired state to kiss her again. "Now that I've seen you in my garden," he said softly but firmly, "I want to see you in my house. In my bed."

As an actress, Flora had to admit the stage was set for love. The earl was playing the part of the ideal lover to the hilt. And it was all too clear in what role she was perfectly cast. . . .

TOAST
OF THE
TOWN

by

Margaret Evans Porter

A SIGNET BOOK

SIGNET
Published by the Penguin Group
Penguin Books USA Inc., 375 Hudson Street,
New York, New York 10014, U.S.A.
Penguin Books Ltd, 27 Wrights Lane,
London W8 5TZ, England
Penguin Books Australia Ltd, Ringwood,
Victoria, Australia
Penguin Books Canada Ltd, 10 Alcorn Avenue,
Toronto, Ontario, Canada M4V 3B2
Penguin Books (N.Z.) Ltd, 182-190 Wairau Road,
Auckland 10, New Zealand

Penguin Books Ltd, Registered Offices:
Harmondsworth, Middlesex, England

First published by Signet,
an imprint of New American Library,
a division of Penguin Books USA Inc.

First Printing, April, 1993
10 9 8 7 6 5 4 3 2 1

Good my lord, will you see the players well bestowed?
Do you hear, let them be well used, for they are
the abstract and brief chronicles of the time.

Hamlet, II. ii.

Prologue

London, 1807

A curtain of mist lay over the city, and Drury Lane was a tunnel of darkness in which streetlights, carriage lamps, and linkboys' torches glowed eerily. It was March, a two-faced month when wintry weather frequently marred the gentle greening and timidly colorful displays of spring, and the damp and chill in the air urged pedestrians to hurry along the famous thoroughfare, driven by a desire to take shelter from the elements.

The presence of two unescorted ladies was unremarkable in this part of town, the traditional haunt of wantons, pickpockets, and stage performers. But if they were making a harlots' progress, it was destined to be unsuccessful, because the older woman's expression was more forbidding than encouraging to the male passersby, and however shapely the younger lady's figure might be, it was concealed by a long cloak.

With each brisk, purposeful step, her hood slipped back, permitting the crossing sweeps and chair men who loitered on the greasy pavements to admire her heart-shaped face and dark curls. As they began to call out lewd compliments, the middle-aged female reached over and replaced the hood, dispelling the impression that she was a local bawd displaying her lovely protégée.

Paying no heed to her unruly admirers, Flora Campion walked on. Her pink lips moved as if in prayer, and she clasped and unclasped her gloved hands in nervous accompaniment to her whispered soliloquy. "Oh, sir," she said softly but audibly, "I will not be so hardhearted, I will give out divers schedules of my beauty. It shall be inventoried, and every particle and utensil labeled." The woman plodding along beside her made no reply, nor did she seem disturbed by being thus addressed. After a thoughtful moment, Flora added, "I think that's correct."

"Well, to be sure, ma'am, I don't rightly remember."

"Over a year since I've played the Lady Olivia." Turning bright green eyes toward her chaperone, she asked, "But where, Margery? Was it at Chichester that we last performed *Twelfth Night*?"

"Portsmouth," corrected Margery, once more adjusting Flora's hood.

"Both," said the actress positively. "I must try and find a copy of the playbook when we reach the theater—I'm hopelessly rusty. Still, I suppose it's something," she went on, "this chance to play a principal role again. I can scarcely believe it."

Margery's plain face was set in stern lines as she announced grimly, "What *I* can't believe is how Mrs. Ellis waited the whole day before deciding she wouldn't play tonight. You could've done with a bit of rehearsal."

"It doesn't matter. If I become muddled, I can always go back to Shakespeare's original text. Ben didn't alter the play too much, thank heaven."

But Flora's thankfulness was tempered by her displeasure, despite being the recipient of that stroke of fortune every understudy yearned for. A leading player had been felled by illness, but if only it hadn't been at the last minute, she fumed. However fond she was of her employer, who was her mentor and benefactor as well, returning to the theater was most inconvenient; she disliked going without dinner. And in all likelihood the play would not be repeated, which only added insult to the original injury of surrendering a favorite role to Mrs. Ellis when, at the first of the year, the company had come to London. After Benedict Forster had pointed out the necessity of subordinating one's personal ambitions for the common good, Flora had regretfully relinquished Olivia and Ophelia, Kate Hardcastle and Lydia Languish, roles she had long considered her personal property.

Her destination this foggy night was a minor theater tucked into an obscure corner of Drury Lane. It was not, as many mistakenly supposed, named for a member of any royal family, past or present, but had originally been the Saracen Princess, a popular but semi-disreputable tavern. After a damaging fire a century ago it had been rebuilt as a playhouse, and a succession of managers had struggled to make it go. The Princess had languished in the shadow of older, more illustrious theaters down the street and had long been a venue for musical burlettas and spectacles, the only offerings legally permitted the non-patent playhouses. And then she had been rescued from obscurity by fate and a determined fellow named Forster.

Flora hoped his bold venture would succeed, for remaining in one place was an unaccustomed luxury. During her six years with the troupe of players, she had lived as a vagabond, picking up and moving every few weeks.

In her eagerness to reach the warmth of the green-room fire she quickened her pace, leaving the slower Margery behind. Familiar habit had already replaced annoyance, and by the time the stage-door keeper closed the portals behind the actress and her faithful servant, Flora had quite forgotten that she'd deserted the same dilapidated building barely two hours before, in happy anticipation of a night of unaccustomed liberty.

1

'Tis beauty truly blent, whose white and red
Nature's own sweet and cunning hand laid on.

Twelfth Night, I.v.

In the fashionable district of St. James's, three well-dressed gentlemen emerged from the sacred precincts of White's Club. Two of them were actively engaged in a debate and paused on the rain-slick paving stones to continue it. When the youngest man stated his desire to visit the theater, the eldest shook his head in adamant protest and extolled the merits of a particular bottle of spirits he'd been saving for just such a night as this.

They made an appeal to the third gentleman, who towered over them. His brown hair, worn longer than the prevailing fashion, framed a patrician countenance which was both proud and noble. In a low and well-modulated voice, he informed his companions that although he had no preference for one plan over the other, he would appreciate a quick decision, as the damp was slowly but inexorably permeating his garments. In fact, he added, he would await the outcome of their discussion in his carriage.

His retreat prompted them to settle their argument. The youth called out the direction to the coachman, and issued a triumphant order to the footman at the door of the vehicle. He climbed in and announced to its owner, "I've sent your man ahead to secure a stage box, Trevor. You can sample Rupert's cognac *after* the play."

Trevor John Cotterell, 3rd Earl of Leafield, directed a smile at the gentleman seated across from him. "Well, I suppose if your fine spirit ages for a few more hours, it can only be to our advantage."

"Just so," agreed Mr. Rupert Harburton. "But I doubt our young friend has any intention of passing the evening with what lies in my cellars."

Turning to the youth, Trevor asked, "Didn't your last experience cure your partiality for opera dancers?"

Lord Edgar, taking instant exception, bestowed a disdainful glance upon his friend. "I'm ages wiser now, and I won't have you teasing me about my—my—"

"Backstage friendships," Trevor supplied.

"Well, yes. But it's no opera dancer this time. She's an actress, a leading actress—but Rupert knows. Tell him about Louise."

Bowing to the young man's insistence, Mr. Harburton said languidly, "Louise Talley, for whom this stripling has conceived a grand passion, is a featured comic actress at the new theater which has caused all the furor of late. But Baron Allingham is also laying siege to the lady, and I'm afraid the odds are decidedly—and quite naturally—in his favor. Haven't you looked into the betting book at the club lately, my lord?"

Lord Edgar's eyes blazed. "I ought to call you out for that, Rupert—by God, I shall!"

"On what pretext?" was his friend's damping reply. "No insult was intended, I was merely stating a fact. Allingham is precisely the protector La Talley has dreamed of since the day her dainty foot first trod the boards. Young, handsome, reasonably rich—"

"But he's engaged to be married," the youth protested, causing the other two gentlemen to exchange glances yet again.

Mr. Harburton shook his head, and his eyes were faintly contemptuous. "It's money and a carriage and jewels she wants from him, not a wedding ring."

"And noblemen don't marry actresses," Trevor pronounced coolly, in case Lord Edgar had failed to mark Mr. Harburton's subtle warning.

He regretted his words, because the young man immediately embarked upon a catalog of every nobleman who had ever wed a lady of the stage, as though he'd spent the past week studying the subject. Such idealism was refreshing to one who had attained the sophisticated and somewhat jaded heights of his early thirties. Without having set eyes on Miss Talley, Trevor knew she would be exactly like the jolly little opera dancer who had spurned the lordling's advances to bestow her favors on a gentleman with a fortune rumored to be one of the largest in the realm.

The crush of traffic in Drury Lane was impossible to avoid, so the gentlemen chose to abandon the earl's carriage near the top of the street and walk the rest of the way. With hours of dramatic entertainment before him, Trevor was glad of the opportunity to stretch his legs.

"Edgar is young yet," Mr. Harburton reminded him, "and a fellow is expected to cut his milk teeth on a playhouse wench."

"But not to marry her," Trevor said.

The playbill affixed to a front column of the theater informed him that the main offering was to be *Twelfth Night*, and the loud ovation from within heralded the conclusion of the curtain raiser. He would have preferred a night of drink and conversation to the proposed entertainment, having outgrown any enthusiasm for attending the play long ago.

Inside the theater, prostitutes paraded along the shabby corridors and lurked in the corners of the box lobby and saloon, their gowns barely concealing their abundant charms, while pickpockets tried to blend in with the crowd, sharp eyes and itching fingers at the ready. The Princess was prime hunting ground; her manager's unpopularity in political circles had cost him the services of Bow Street Runners, who warned the playgoers at other theaters to mind their pockets. Those persons unable to procure a box at either Drury Lane or Covent Garden had chosen the rival theater by default; the gallery was nearly full, and the exquisitely dressed bucks and dandies crowded the pit.

The earl's footman had taken possession of a stage box with worn chairs and chipped gilding. When the new arrivals took their places, the fashionable young damsels gazed hopefully at his lordship, sighing over the chiseled lips and square chin with its hint of a cleft, and noting how the chandeliers burnished the waving brown hair with a coppery brilliance.

The hazel eyes which figured so prominently in the debutantes' innocent heartburnings fell upon the coterie of married society ladies in the adjacent box. All were friends of Trevor's former mistress, whose irate spouse had removed her from town in an effort to avoid an incipient scandal.

He glanced down at a smudged sheet of paper Lord Edgar had pressed upon him, and after reading the titles of the pieces to be acted that night, he let it waft to the floor to join those left from the last night's performance. He was not altogether pleased to learn that the manager had the funds to produce a triple bill.

Trevor had heard of Benedict Forster, for he had been a popular topic of discussion ever since announcing his intention of producing the legitimate forms of drama denied to all theaters except Drury Lane and Covent Garden, which held royal patents. At first no one had placed any confidence in his plan, for without a license he couldn't open his decaying playhouse. No magistrate of Westminster, the domain of the Theatres Royal, was likely to support a possible rival.

But the provincial manager was more clever than anyone had guessed. It turned out that the Princess sat outside of the boundary separating Westminster from the adjacent borough of Holborn and therefore fell within the jurisdiction of a different magistrate. Forster was also fortunate in having several influential well-wishers so eager to have a third legitimate theater in London that they had prevailed upon the Lord Chamberlain to interpret the Licensing Act more liberally than his predecessor. Armed with a special dispensation to produce serious drama for a probationary period of one year, Forster was regarded as a miracle worker by the public, but his disgruntled competitors viewed him as a threat, for he'd made an unprecedented breach in a long-unbroken theatrical monopoly.

Trevor looked toward the stage as the talk of the town marched out from the wings to deliver the prologue in a powerful and highly trained voice. The green curtain rose, the play began, and he was able to judge for himself the charms of the creature who had so inflamed his friend's youthful ardor. Louise Talley was a round-faced girl with ginger hair, a high-pitched warble, and the habit of directing her speeches to the stage box containing the predatory person of Baron Allingham. When she made her exit at the end of the scene, she gave the nobleman a final, melting glance, as if inviting him to follow her into the wings. This caused a murmur in the pit; the bucks nudged each other knowingly as the odds in Allingham's favor rose even higher.

Louise appeared next in masculine dress, a shirt and breeches that revealed her greatest assets, a full bosom and shapely legs. Trevor understood why she was so popular, even though her speaking voice was barely adequate and she possessed no remarkable degree of beauty, but still he was confounded by Lord Edgar's penchant for her. Evidently it was common to all the young men, for Miss Talley's every appearance was greeted with calls, whistles, and stamping feet.

The audience roared its approval of the stock comic characters, Sir Toby and Maria, Feste the Clown and Sir Andrew Aguecheek, but nothing had the power to amuse the earl, who sank deeper into his chair and wished he dared close his eyes. The various Forsters acquitted themselves nobly, but Miss Talley was the weakest link; her meager talents didn't meet their uncommonly high standard. Hoping to be diverted by Benedict Forster's portrayal of the obsequious steward, Trevor lifted his head when Malvolio and the Lady Olivia made their entrance. And when his numbed brain finally accepted what his eyes told him was only too true, he joined in the collective sigh of appreciation that rose from the crowd.

The actress who had caught his attention—and held it—had the face of an angel, and the figure revealed by her blue gown would be envied by any courtesan. Her hair was lustrous and black, arranged in long curls, and her veil of delicate, spidery lace trembled as she moved across the stage.

He leaned forward, resting one arm on the edge of the box as Shakespeare's poetry was spoken in a clear, musical voice which carried across the proscenium. Its possessor displayed a very real gift for acting, to the extent that he wondered what manner of person lay beneath the meticulous characterization. Unlike Louise Talley, who was in all probability the strumpet she seemed, this actress gave no hint that she was anything other than the melancholy Olivia, her sorrowing heart closed off to mortal man.

But Miss Talley's coarser charms had won the hearts of the gentlemen in the pit. Impatient for her return, they shifted in their seats and talked over the dialogue. The scene ended, far too quickly in Trevor's opinion, and after the lovely lady glided off the stage, he looked down for the bill of the play he'd discarded so carelessly.

Mr. Harburton, guessing his purpose, saved him the trouble and indignity of sorting through the debris by handing over his own. "She must be the understudy," he whispered. "Mrs. Ellis is advertised as playing Olivia, but she's forty if she's a day. That girl is no more Mrs. Ellis than I am the Prince of Wales. Lord Edgar might be reduced to jelly by La Talley, but to my mind, there is more to admire in the dark lady's performance."

Trevor's eyes glinted with amusement and something more. He murmured, "There is more to admire in the dark lady's person, her performance aside. Who the devil is she?"

His friend shrugged unhelpfully. "I can't say, but our friend Skiffy Skeffington must know—he rubs shoulders with every actor in London."

"Quiet!" came a pained request from the other side of the box. Lord Edgar was sitting as stiffly upright as Trevor had been a few minutes earlier: once again Miss Talley had claimed the stage.

When the curtain fell, marking the first interval, the Earl of Leafield joined in the ebb and flow of humanity as playgoers went in search of refreshment and paid visits to friends seated elsewhere in the auditorium. As he maneuvered his way across the lobby, he avoided the beauties from the adjacent box, and passed by the hopeful mamas and their offspring without a glance.

As he approached a group of dandified *literati* who visited the London theaters every night, a thin gentleman in a rose satin coat and white silk breeches waved his quizzing glass and greeted Trevor in an affected drawl. "I was just telling Jones here that it's been an age since Leafield was seen in the environs of Drury Lane—the street as well as the theater." Lumley St. George Skeffington, crony of the Prince of Wales, sometime playwright, and devotee of matters theatrical, tittered at his own wit and stroked the distinctive side whiskers that were often held up to ridicule by the caricaturists. "Accompanying young Fleming, I perceive. Certainly he has been a regular visitor of late."

Trevor wasted no time in coming to the point, and asked his foppish acquaintance if he knew the name of the young actress playing Olivia.

"Ah, yes," said Skeffington on a sorrowful sigh. "Flora Campion, poor dear. An unfair world it is, for she's only the understudy, more's the pity, and takes the part tonight because Eliza Ellis is indisposed. But there's a delightful part written especially for her in Mr. Jones's new play—Forster commissioned the piece for her. Come here, Jones, and make your bow to the Earl of Leafield." At his urging, a pasty-faced gentleman moved forward from the outskirts of the group to be presented as the author of *In Praise of Parsimony*.

"They called him Gentleman Forster down in Portsmouth," Skeffington continued, abandoning the subject that most concerned his listener, "and I'll grant you he's deserving of the title, for all he's an actor. I went to Lord Dartmouth in support of his cause, and see what has come of it! Another theater, more or less legitimate, and she the old Princess. Poor Sheridan is mad as fire and nearly cut me t'other day, and as for Kemble, he and his sister Siddons are still reeling from the Master Betty business a year or so back and don't welcome a new rival."

Master William Betty, a child actor, had once been the rage, and Trevor vaguely recalled the mass hysteria the prodigy had produced during his heyday. But the theatrical nature of the conversation was beginning to bore him, and after suffering through a spate of backstage gossip, he was glad to escape Mr. Skeffington.

Strolling across the crowded lobby, he congratulated himself on his good fortune. The lovely actress was new to London and probably had no protector as yet. Even better, she was only a supporting player, not yet so established in her profession that she would object to retiring from it for a brief period. Trevor smiled so warmly that one of the painted prostitutes in his path was emboldened to approach, but he was intent upon calculating the expense of the venture he was contemplating and therefore ignored her. It would be necessary to provide

Miss Flora Campion with clothes and jewels, and she would probably expect him to offer her a generous settlement—all in all she would be expensive. But he was a man of substance, and whatever her demands, he would satisfy them. She was more than satisfactory for his needs; she was perfection itself.

Flora Campion, observing the crowd milling about the green room, feared that the audience for *The Marriage of Feste*, the evening's afterpiece, was sadly diminished. At the final fall of the curtain, a host of bucks and beaux had swarmed into the anteroom where the performers passed their time offstage and received their well-wishers after the play.

For six years Flora had trod the path to modest prominence in country towns, and now she was in London, where actors' reputations were made. Consigned to playing secondary parts, she had been ignored by critics and public alike but had received marked attention from the young men prowling backstage, ever on the lookout for a pretty and complaisant actress. She was neither: her spectacular beauty was no mere prettiness, nor did she desire a protector.

She'd retired to a corner to wait for Ben Forster, but no sooner had he made his entrance than his supporters gathered around him and his brother, preventing her from bidding them good night. Both actors still wore stage costume, although Horatio had already removed the blond wig he wore as Sebastian and was running his fingers through his black hair.

Resigned to a longer vigil than she had expected, Flora observed Louise Talley, still clad in her form-fitting breeches. Her face was flushed with compliments and champagne, and as she flirted with her partisans she spoke hardly a word to the adoring Lord Edgar Fleming and saved all of her smiles for Lord Allingham. The baron stood somewhat apart, evidently sure enough of his conquest that he saw no need to assert himself.

How would he react, Flora wondered, if she informed him that she was his kinswoman? It must be true—mere coincidence couldn't account for the upward slant of Lord Allingham's eyebrows, or the way his hair grew from a peak on his forehead, as did Flora's and her brother's. Even if the baron's complexion was olive and both Campions were fair-skinned, and although his eyes were brown and theirs green, she was inclined to believe the family legend about shared blood. Would he be shocked to learn that he had a pair of cousins on the wrong side of the blanket? Probably not; he was no model of the virtues.

Lord Leafield, piqued by Miss Campion's obvious and intense interest in his fellow peer, waited until she was no longer distracted by Allingham's presence before accosting her.

Although she regarded him curiously, he could perceive no come-hither in her green eyes, nor did she simper or flutter her amazingly long lashes at him. "I beg leave to introduce myself, Miss Campion," he began, "for Skeffington, our only mutual acquaintance, is elsewhere occupied and I'm uncertain of the etiquette that prevails backstage. I'm Leafield."

"Any friend of Mr. Skeffington's is welcome here," she answered politely. "We are honored that you should have visited our theater."

"The honor is all mine."

The carmined lips parted in a delightful smile, showing teeth that were pearly and even. The graceful contours of her cheeks were enhanced by the rouge, and the sparkle in her green eyes was more genuine than that of the false gems she wore.

When Trevor told her how much he had enjoyed her performance, she laughed softly. "You are kind, but if I acquitted myself no more than adequately tonight, I am fortunate. Mrs. Ellis, our tragedienne, has acted the part of Olivia since our company came to London."

He expressed the certainty that no one could have surpassed her in that role, all the while wondering how to broach his business. There was no delicate way to go about it, although at the very least he could do her the kindness of waiting until they were not surrounded by a pack of interested onlookers— his friends and her colleagues.

"You may deem it presumptuous of me, as we have only just met, but I hope I have permission to call upon you tomorrow, Miss Campion. I wish to discuss a personal matter, and in privacy. I have a proposition to make—on first seeing you tonight, I was convinced that you are the very lady I've been seeking. And," he added, more to himself than to her, "the odd thing is that I hadn't yet begun to look for her."

The actress's face went white beneath its light coating of cosmetics. "Pray say no more, sir," she said hastily, "for what you ask is impossible."

Trevor hastened to correct her false impression. "No, no, it's not that sort of offer—I swear it."

She eyed him doubtfully. "You said it was something personal—what did you *expect* me to think?"

"Forgive me, I hadn't considered my words very carefully. I do come to you with an offer of employment, but not in—" He saved himself from saying "my bed" by substituting quickly, "Not in the way you supposed."

As she a drew a calming breath, the taut muscles in her neck relaxed. "My lord, I'm sorry to disappoint you, but I'm not at liberty to accept any professional engagements at present."

He shook his head. "You don't yet know what I want, and I can't explain myself fully here and now. Will you permit me to call on you?"

Flora, unnerved by his aristocratic air and the intensity of his hazel eyes, would have refused outright, had he not been someone whose influence might in some way benefit her employer and her theater. With regret, for Sunday was her only day of freedom from work, she replied, "Very well, my lord, I will receive you tomorrow. After church."

"And where does one find Miss Campion at home?"

"On Great Queen Street. On the south side near Lincoln's Inn Fields." After she gave him the number of her house, he thanked her, bowed, and withdrew. As she watched the tall nobleman weave his way through the crowd to rejoin his friends, she regretted that it was too late to rescind her impulsive invitation.

Seeing that Ben and Horatio were still occupied with their backers, she deserted the green room, her brow furrowed by frustration. She wandered along a dim backstage corridor until she came to a rickety wooden staircase. She had begun her ascent when she heard the sound of clattering heels behind her and a familiar voice calling, "Wait, Florry!"

Sally Jenkins, who played chambermaid roles with great verve, placed one hand on her heaving bosom and the other on the banister. "I'm due onstage any moment, but I had to speak to you—I saw what happened in the green room. The Earl of Leafield! I vow, Florry, if Louise hadn't snared Allingham, she'd be livid!"

"He claims his interest isn't amorous at all, merely a matter of business."

The other actress tipped her head back and a peal of derisive laughter rang out in the narrow hallway. "A matter of business—and you believed him? Oh, love, I daresay it's perfectly true, but just fancy his calling it that from the start! *Business*!"

Flushed and chagrined, Flora shook her head in vigorous denial. But Sally dashed off as quickly as she had come, still chuckling, her fingers toying with the ribbons of the maidservant's cap perched atop her bright red head.

2

I beseech you, what manner of man is he?

Twelfth Night, III. iv.

The backstage area of the Princess Theatre, a confusing maze of corridors, went unseen by the public. On the topmost level of the building a long attic with skylights had been partitioned to create the carpenter's shop and the scenery-painting room. The floor immediately below consisted of storage areas for stage properties and wardrobe, and the closetlike treasury where the evening's receipts were counted and to which the players flocked on Saturdays for the doling out of weekly salaries. Tucked into a dim corner of the same hallway was Flora's dressing room, which boasted a small window overlooking the courtyard. The effluvium of dust and cobwebs which had greeted her two months ago had been swept away, but the tiny cubicle was still grimy about the edges.

That night marked the end of a week that had seemed to contain double the usual number of days, and Flora sighed in relief as her dresser stripped the brocade gown from her aching body. As usual, the brazier in the corner failed to warm the drafty room, and she donned her own clothes in haste before sitting down at her dressing table, where a clean towel and a basin of steaming water awaited her. She began the routine task of removing her paint while Margery unpinned her elaborate coiffure and combed out the long black curls.

Within a few minutes the actress and her dresser descended to the ground level where they found Madam Forster, the grande dame of the company, occupying the stage-door keeper's humble wooden chair as majestically as she sat upon Queen Gertrude's gilded throne. An impressive and regal figure in or out of costume, she had long been a mentor and surrogate mother to Flora, and because they lived on the same street, she always shared a carriage with the younger actress.

The three women exited the building, taking care to lift their skirts as they crossed the muddy courtyard to the waiting hackney. As it moved forward, Flora peered through the dirty window and saw that Drury Lane was thronged with traffic again, a sure sign that other theaters were also emptying. The fog still hung thick and low over the city.

A yawning manservant admitted her to her abode, one of the last houses in Great Queen Street. "Home at last, Frank," she announced, removing her cloak for the final time that night. "Is everyone abed?"

He shook his head. "Mrs. Drew is in the small parlor, ma'am."

She took the candle he gave her and lit her way to the room at the back of the house. The solitary young woman seated there looked up from the book on her lap to say softly, "High time you were home."

"Don't I know it."

"I've got the key to the larder—would you like something to eat? You'd only just sat down to dinner when Mr. Forster's message came."

Esther Drew preceded Flora into the dark kitchen, and within minutes she produced a loaf of bread, a round cheese, and a bottle of wine. The house was still and silent; the only sound to assail their ears was the muffled cry of the night watchman, whose voice faded with his progress along the street.

Flora ate a mouthful of bread and cheese, chewed thoughtfully, and after swallowing said, "Tonight was our best night since coming to London—the theater was almost full. How is Hartley?"

Smoothing a stray lock of brown hair in a harassed fashion, Esther said, "Poor little man, he's resting comfortably at last, and I hope he'll sleep the night through—for his sake and mine."

"What a pity his papa isn't here to see these fine teeth that cause so much trouble."

Esther's husband and Flora's brother both served on His Majesty's Ship *Vestal*, presently stationed in the West Indies. Letters from the naval officers were infrequent, newspaper reports about their maneuvers were vague, but they were in no great personal danger and the ladies were resigned to going weeks, often months, without tidings.

"I expect our brave seamen will be returning before long," Flora commented.

"With prize money spilling from their pockets," Captain Drew's fond wife said hopefully as she cut another slice of bread.

These midnight, post-performance conversations were something of a ritual by now, and both women found solace in meeting thus across the table to talk of their very different lives and wholly dissimilar aspirations.

As Esther filled Flora's wineglass she said, "To escape my fretful boy for half an hour, I accepted our neighbor's invitation to tea."

"How *is* Julie?"

"Much better, although she's disappointed that she isn't with child again."

"I can't think why—she always complains that during both pregnancies her sufferings were far in excess of what the usual female undergoes. Madam declares she was a better actress in the straw than she ever was on the stage."

"That sounds like something a mother-in-law would say! My dear Flora, I hope someday you'll experience the rigors of childbirth—then you'll learn how very ignorant you are about the subject."

Eyes dancing, Flora murmured primly, "Why, Esther, you know I'm not that sort of girl."

"I mean when you're a married woman. Julie hasn't given up hope that you'll wed her rakish brother-in-law."

Flora set down her wineglass so forcefully that some of its contents washed over the rim. As she blotted the puddle with her napkin, she said impatiently, "That boy-and-girl nonsense between Horry and me was over years ago. Besides, I've no time for a husband."

She was perfectly satisfied with her lot. At twenty-five she was no longer prey to the foolish fancies of extreme youth, and her years in the theater had taught her not to yearn for what was impossible. Her contentment was rooted in her ability to keep a roof over her head, clothes on her back, and food in her stomach. Miles, who had sailed the high seas since boyhood and was an infrequent visitor to England's shores, accepted her choice of profession and was proud of her success.

After six years of working so closely with the Forsters, she felt as much a part of the clan as if a tie of blood bound her to them in addition to a shared past and a strong mutual affection. Her intimacy with the manager's family was a consideration that far exceeded any payment or promotion. In the months since the company had arrived in London, she'd watched with amusement as its tragedienne tried to out-Siddons Mrs. Siddons and newcomer Louise tried to scale the heights of popularity attained by the much-loved Mrs. Jordan of Drury Lane. Unlike Mrs. Ellis and Miss Talley, who emulated others, Flora was bent on making use of the qualities that set her apart from other actresses, and she hoped Mr. Jones's new work would allow her to shine.

"Have you chosen the play for your benefit yet?" Esther asked.

Flora said she preferred to wait and see how the new comedy was received by the public before making a decision. As a senior member of the company, she was entitled to a benefit performance at the end of the season; on that night the total revenue, minus the operating costs of the theater, would be hers. Her colleagues would take no salary, donating their time and talent *gratis*, in the expectation of receiving the same consideration when their turn came. But despite this do-unto-others policy, battles over the rights to a play could be fierce, and the most popular pieces in the reportory were hotly contested.

Smiling across the table, Flora continued, "Horatio, clever fellow, has already bespoken *Twelfth Night*, and for his sake I hope Louise Talley remains in the company. She may be a disruptive influence, but she's filling the theater quite nicely in the role of Viola."

"And fills her shirt and breeches, too."

"Eliza Ellis can't abide performing with her—anyone could have foreseen that. They detest one another."

Well-versed in the various backstage squabbles, Esther said,

"I don't envy Mr. Forster the job of keeping so many jealous actresses happy."

"He does his best, and Madam comes to his aid whenever necessary."

Esther put away the leftover food, leaving Flora to sweep the table free of crumbs, and emerged from the larder to ask, "Is it to be the early service tomorrow morning, Florry, or the late one?"

"Oh, Lord," the actress moaned, striking her forehead in a theatrical gesture that she would have scorned to employ onstage, "we'll have to go to the early one. I'm receiving a caller—a very illustrious caller—at eleven o'clock. Unless he forgets to come, which I devoutly hope he may do."

"A he?" Esther repeated, with strong emphasis on the pronoun.

"The Earl of Leafield," Flora intoned impressively.

Her friend failed to oblige her by falling into a faint or giving any other evidence of surprise. "Should I know him?"

"Not unless you look at the Court Page in the papers."

"Well, I don't," was Esther's matter-of-fact reply. "The paper is of no earthly use to me except when it gives details of naval battles or describes the progress of the war on the Continent, which news James expects me to communicate to him." When Flora frowned at her, she added swiftly, "But I *always* read the reviews and the theatrical gossip."

Taking up the candelabra, Flora said sourly, "Lord Leafield, whom you will have the opportunity to judge for yourself tomorrow, is an extremely well-favored gentleman of about thirty. He and that nice young lord who worships Louise came backstage after the main entertainment tonight, and he asked if he might call upon me to discuss a matter of business." She frowned as she recalled the nobleman's smile, not the least of his charms. "So I said yes, though I can't imagine why. 'I know not what 'twas but distraction,'" she quoted softly.

Esther, looking into her friend's grave face, said cheerfully, "Well, a young and handsome earl coming to our humble house! Knowing you does have its advantages."

"I daresay he's planning an evening of private theatricals,

and wants to engage a professional." When the other woman began to laugh, Flora demanded, "What's so amusing in that?"

"Just what sort of *professional* does he take you for? I can just imagine the sort of private performance a gentleman of title would expect from an actress!" Esther used her pocket handkerchief to stifle her next mirthful outburst.

"You are the most corrupt-minded female of my acquaintance, Esther Drew, and considering the company I keep, that's quite a condemnation!"

A faint cry sounded from some distant source and Esther held up her hand, tipping her head sideways to listen. She expelled her breath in a long sigh of relief. "I thought it might be Hartley."

"The kitchen cat, asking to be let in. Go upstairs, little mother, and cuddle your baby. I'll see to Puss."

She returned to the dark kitchen and opened the back door to a silent gray shadow that scurried inside. Flora's presence went unacknowledged and was clearly unwelcome at this hour, when the mice were stirring. Impervious to the snub, she made her weary way to the upper regions, seeking the warmth and comfort of the bed she'd been thinking about so wistfully ever since the final fall of the curtain.

Sunday was the servants' day off, so on the following morning the two young women helped one another dress, then hurried down to the dining room, clutching their prayer books and bemoaning the lateness of the hour.

Mrs. Tabitha Brooke, titular mistress of the household, had just finished her breakfast and was trying to coax her grandson into eating a bit of toast soaked in milk. Although her husband had been dead for more than a decade, she still chose to wear full mourning. Young Hartley Drew, fascinated by the lappets of her elaborate widow's cap, tugged at them with his chubby hand.

She stared in bemusement at the two young women frantically tying the strings of their bonnets. "Why are you in such a rush to be away?" she asked, her round eyes shifting from her lodger to her daughter.

"Flora must be home well before noon," Esther explained. "She's expecting a visitor."

Mrs. Brooke reached for her teacup, oblivious to the complicit glance the two young women exchanged. "I'll be gone by the time you return, my dears, for I promised to call upon my sister in Kensington. I mean to invite Mrs. Prescott to go with me—unless you have some objection, Flora."

"None whatever," Flora hastened to assure her. "Margery may do as she pleases."

Esther bent to kiss her son's plump cheek. When she begged him to be a good little man while she was out, he replied with a gurgle.

As they exited the house, Flora commented, "What luck that your mama and Margery will both be gone when the earl arrives! Aunt Tab would think me as abandoned as Louise Talley if she knew I'd brazenly agreed to receive a strange gentleman after no more than five minutes of conversation with him."

Esther reached up to clutch her bonnet as a fierce gust threatened to blow this highly prized article from her head. "I'll play chaperone to keep you safe from the evil earl, or you can leave the parlor door open."

"I would have done anyway."

"Oh, don't be silly, Flora, I was only teasing. You're well past the age of requiring a duenna."

"Indeed, but actress that I am, I so seldom have an opportunity to observe the rules of propriety." Flora said this lightly, but her face was troubled all the same. In general she didn't waste time worrying about her reputation, but she hoped Lord Leafield didn't regard her as a loose woman.

She was aware that the public considered female stage performers to be little better than the painted creatures prowling outside the theater and decorating its lobby. Often it was true, as in the case of Louise Talley. But not even the highly respectable Mrs. Siddons was immune to the scorn her profession received, and vicious rumors had circulated when she began living separately from her spouse. Although Flora had managed to preserve her virtue, this fact didn't deter friendship with those of her colleagues whose lives were less than

chaste. During her years in the provincial circuit she had with-
stood the advances of many a backstage gallant, a breed she
judged more amusing than threatening. And as a result of her
special relationship with the manager and his family, not even
the boldest or most persistent of the actors in the company
dared to offend her by pressing unwanted attentions.

Until the encounter with Lord Leafield, her only admirers
had been harmless fops like Lumley Skeffington, or elderly
men who went no further than pinching her on the cheek and
telling her how she reminded them of some pretty actress they
had known in their salad days. Baron Allingham, everyone's
idea of the stage-door lothario, had attached himself to Louise
Talley.

She hoped the earl wasn't seeking to fill his bed, because
however comfortable it might be she had no interest in a liaison with a nobleman. Nevertheless, for a brief, titillating moment she pictured herself swathed in silks and laden with
jewels—until she realized her thoughts were most unseemly
for someone on her way to church.

When she and Esther scurried along Drury Lane past Princess
Alley, she direct a fond glance at the theater. They followed a
circuitous route, for even on a quiet Sunday morning it was necessary to avoid the disreputable alleys and side streets of Seven
Dials, the slum district lying near St. Giles-in-the-Fields.

The bells gave forth a resounding peal as the two latecomers
reached the church door. Squeezing into a pew at the back, the
ladies lifted voices in a familiar hymn about processions and
palm branches, its cheerful refrain punctuated with hosannas.
Flora's clear soprano soared exultantly as she remembered the
many things she had to rejoice about: a comfortable lodging,
money of her own, and good friends with whom to share her
joys and sorrows. And there was just enough strife at the theater to spice up an otherwise untrammeled contentment.

Yet she could not quite repress a pessimistic certainty that
something distressing would soon occur. Now that the sturdy
bark carrying her through life was moving along effortlessly
and independently, it was inevitable that the rocky shoals
ahead would show themselves, possibly with unsettling results.

3

What is to be said to him, lady?
He's fortified against any denial.

Twelfth Night, I. v.

The Earl of Leafield spent the night in a bed other than his own, the result of an encounter with a fair-haired beauty in the vestibule of the Princess Theatre. When she had confessed to him that her husband was absent from town, her azure eyes extended a bold invitation to the delights that had followed. And although he might have preferred to return to his own house afterward, Clarissa had prevented it by reminding him of her fear of sleeping alone. Presumably her husband, a portly and affable viscount, was aware of her aversion and cared not who comforted her when he was away.

Within a few hours of returning to Leafield House he set out once more, guiding his horses and phaeton out of gracious Mayfair and toward the less fashionable part of town where Miss Flora Campion lodged. A prevailing west wind had dissipated last night's fog, and there were patches of blue sky overhead. When the sun peeped out from behind the clouds at last, the neat plots of grass bounded by the town squares suddenly seemed greener and the daffodils yellower. Trevor was heartened by this sign that spring had not forgotten London after all.

Great Queen Street was a genteel thoroughfare extending from Drury Lane to the green oasis of Lincoln's Inn Fields, and the facades of its parallel rows of town houses were uniformly decorated with Corinthian pilasters. As Trevor approached the door bearing the number he sought, he heard feminine voices. Looking over his shoulder, he saw a pair of ladies coming toward him. Both were attractive, and their flowery bonnets and pastel spencers provided color to the somber street scene.

He smiled and bowed, expecting them to pass him by, but the prettier one halted, crying in dismay, "I was hoping to arrive before you did, my lord, but this morning's sermon was endless! Can it be eleven o'clock already?"

The breathless, fresh-faced creature staring up at him bore no resemblance to the woman he had accosted in the theater green room last night, and when he followed her inside, he wondered how it was possible that she could be even more beautiful than he remembered.

She introduced him to the other lady, who excused herself and went up the stairs. Trevor handed his hat to the actress, and she placed it gingerly on the hall table before removing her bonnet and tossing it carelessly onto a chair. As she led him into a front parlor, she asked if he would like a glass of wine.

"Yes, thank you," he replied, never dreaming that she would murmur something about the servants' day off, much less that she would dart from the room like a hare pursued by a pack of hounds.

Nothing about her was as he'd expected, and he didn't know whether to be sorry or pleased. He had been thrown off balance by the striking dissimilarity between his flustered hostess and the cool, painted creature of last night, to say nothing of the fact that she had actually attended matins—pious actresses were quite beyond the realm of his experience. The surroundings in which she lived and her companion's quiet respectability were equally puzzling. He wandered about the room, inspecting the prints on the walls, framed representations of crumbling Greek and Roman temples; a small but well-executed oil painting of a ship in full sail hung over the pianoforte. The silence of the house was pierced by an infant's wail, and to his great relief it was of short duration.

Flora Campion soon returned, bearing a tray and two glasses of what he guessed to be an indifferent sort of claret. In the interim she had smoothed her dusky curls and removed her spencer, thereby exposing the niceties of her figure. Hers was the smallest of waists, accentuated by the high, rounded bosom above, and she had the advantage of being so slim that she appeared taller than she really was. But her porcelain-perfect

face was her most arresting feature. The slanting brows were
as black and graceful as a quill stroke, her clear green eyes
were fringed by inky lashes, and she had an utterly entrancing
rosebud of a mouth. Trevor, who judged himself a connoisseur
of her sex, considered her one of the most beautiful women
he'd ever seen. But her apparent nervousness surprised him,
and as he accepted her invitation to be seated, it never occurred to him that he was the cause.

Flora was desperately trying to convince herself that she had
no more to fear from him than from Benedict or Horatio
Forster, the only male callers she had received since coming to
town. Unlike her actor friends, however, Lord Leafield seemed
out of place in Mrs. Brooke's parlor. He deserved a more
splendid setting, one of carved mahogany chairs and richly
colored tapestries. He would also look well mounted upon a
fine thoroughbred—he must often be outdoors, she thought,
because his skin had a warm golden tone and the waving
brown hair was lightened by the sun in places. It wasn't until
she met his hazel eyes in a glance of mutual appraisal that she
realized she was as much an object of curiosity to him as he
was to her. The strange mixture of trepidation and uncertainty
churning in her breast ebbed away, and her rather forced smile
broadened into something more genuine.

Said he, pleasantly, "The other lady—Mrs. Drew, I believe—is this her house or yours?"

"It belongs to neither of us," was Flora's equivocal reply.
"Esther's husband is away at sea, so she and her baby son
make their home with her mother. They very kindly offered to
let me and my dresser stay here as lodgers for as long as we
wish."

"How long have you been on the stage, Miss Campion?"

"Six years. I have performed at theaters in Hampshire and
Sussex, mostly in the coastal towns, and our company has
toured Ireland as well."

Her experience was yet another surprise, for Trevor had
supposed she was a neophyte. Not from any lack of talent,
quite the contrary, but because she looked so young and fair in
her flowing muslin; her face, free of cosmetics, was as appealing as a child's in its utter flawlessness. Untainted—the word

kept coming to mind, although given her profession, it was quite an illogical description. "You aren't offended by my curiosity, I hope," he said, seeking to thaw her with a warm smile.

"I've learned to expect it from strangers."

"I daresay, but I hope I won't be a stranger for very long, Miss Campion." He sipped his wine and observed her reaction to these words over the rim of the glass. She maintained her composure, and only by the swift fall of her eyelashes did she betray her agitation.

After a moment she said, "That remains to be seen. Now then, my lord, what business are you so eager to discuss with me?"

He placed his wineglass on a table. "Before I begin with explanations, I wish to know your real name."

Smiling faintly, she replied, "Is Flora Campion so very improbable? Nonetheless, that is how my parents christened me, so I can't help if it sounds like a stage name."

"It's perfectly charming," said Trevor, making a quick recovery. "To state my purpose as simply as I can, I wish to employ you as an actress, Miss Campion, and it would be a business arrangement, nothing more or less. You will impersonate a young female of quality. An heiress, to be precise."

"What is the play?"

He smiled. "One of my own creation, and it is to be enacted off the stage."

Without a moment's hesitation she answered, "I'm sorry, Lord Leafield, but I cannot help you."

"Will you tell me why? You may be quite frank."

"In the first place, I don't think I would care to pass myself off as someone I am not." When he started to speak, she held up one hand to stop him. "My profession requires it, I know, and that is precisely why I must refuse. Also, as I tried to explain last night, I am not free to accept any other work. I've signed a legal bond with Mr. Forster which stipulates that I must perform four times each week for twenty weeks, of which only half are behind me."

"But afterwards? When the period of your contract is over?"

She had to smile at his persistence, if not at the fact that her primary objection had gone unacknowledged. "Although Ben's—Mr. Forster's plans haven't been made public, I know that our company will spend the summer at Bath, where we expect to play for at least a month—with the possibility of an extension." She sat back in her chair with the air of one who had played her trump card.

The earl's request was not quite what she had anticipated, but it was almost as bad. She'd heard of such arrangements and had no desire to be party to one herself.

Some actresses made a secondary career of impersonating wife or widow, sister or sweetheart, for a handsome fee, though they sometimes risked being implicated in a minor crime, or being seduced by an enterprising employer. Prostitution usually followed, but anyone who fell that far rarely found her way back to the theater. Managers, constantly besieged by hopefuls, had replacements aplenty, and only for the most illustrious of female performers was a temporary retirement from the stage truly temporary.

Flora's first London season had been rigorous beyond guess, but she had no intention of giving it up, certainly not to help Lord Leafield play some practical joke. Lifting her chin, she said, "My lord, I fear you have wasted your time. I won't take part in this masquerade."

Apparently undaunted by her refusal or her faintly contemptuous description, he replied, "You haven't even given me a chance to explain."

She supposed she owed him the courtesy of listening, although she told him candidly, "Nothing you say can make me change my mind, Lord Leafield."

"I do hope you will," he said, "for this is a matter of great importance to me and my family, of which I am the head. Are you acquainted with my cousin, Mr. Hugh Cotterell? He is my heir and the dupe in our hoax."

She refrained from pointing out that he was taking her compliance for granted, as she had not consented to assist him. "I have not met him, but if he attends the theater he may well know about me."

"He's out of the country," Trevor reported. "And I'll tell you why, for I've no intention of concealing the truth. Hugh's character is not what one could describe as steady—quite the opposite. He is a libertine, a wastrel, and long before he came of age he had done everything in his power to drag the Cotterell name through the muck. My cousin, Miss Campion, is the black sheep of our family."

With a laugh, she confessed, "I was afraid it might be you."

"Oh? I think those who know me best would describe my wool as somewhat gray." Trevor's grin faded when he continued, "Even so, compared to Hugh's reputation mine is virtually spotless. A few weeks ago he was involved in a duel. Not his first—in fact, it was the fifth. I don't know the cause, only that it took place on the outskirts of London and the other principal was wounded in the exchange of fire."

Flora was beginning to understand why her visitor suddenly looked so perturbed. "Fatally?"

"No," he replied. "What resulted was something of a comedy of errors. Hugh's second was a gentleman reputed to be three-parts drunk at all times, Mr. Rollins, and he was foxed even at the impossibly early hour of the duel. When Hugh's opponent fell, Rollins mistakenly understood the surgeon to say the man had suffered a mortal injury. He encouraged my cousin to flee—misguided advice, as it turned out. The other fellow's wound was but a scratch, though it bled profusely."

"One can't help but feel sorry for your hapless cousin," Flora said, smiling.

"Hopeless is more like, and I feel no sympathy whatever!" he declared heatedly. "I was out of town when all this took place and knew nothing until last week, when Rollins thought to inform me that my heir is presently on the other side of the North Sea, in Copenhagen. When I learned why, I was more amused than angry. And then my visitor stopped sipping my finest Madeira long enough to make a curious and cryptic reference to Hugh's bride—he even boasted that he had been present at the marriage ceremony. From his garbled tale, I deduce that shortly before departing these shores, Hugh took a wife in flagrant violation of a codicil in our grandfather's will which stipulates that he must not marry without my knowledge and consent. If he does so—or has done so—he's cut out of the succession. By proving it, I would be able to designate another male relative as heir to my unentailed property, although Hugh would claim my title should I fail to produce a son. I'll do anything to keep Hopeton Hall and Combe Cotterell from falling into my cousin's hands—he would lose them at cards within a fortnight of my demise."

"But you do have proof," his listener pointed out, "if this man was a witness to the marriage."

"I wish it were that simple. Although he talked freely, ultimately it was unproductive because he was too drunk at the wedding to have more than the vaguest recollection of what I assume to be a hole-in-corner affair. Hugh could've been married by special license, or he may have made use of some illegal mock ceremony. That would be more in character, but I hope he did tie the knot properly. My solicitor is making inquiries, but as you can imagine, it may well require the search of every parish register in London to uncover the truth. And I will, however long it takes."

Flora, noting the stubborn thrust of his jaw, did not doubt it. "Have you considered asking Mr. Cotterell if he's wed?"

"He wouldn't admit it. I believe Rollins, who is an honest man in or out of his cups. Hugh is not and never has been. And now, Miss Campion, I come to your entrance into this sordid scene. Not even Hugh would commit bigamy, or so I hope, and by arranging his marriage to a lady of my own choosing, I'll force him to disclose the existing union."

"And to properly bait the trap, his prospective bride must be an heiress."

"Oh, absolutely. A young lady rich in money and looks, and even more important, one who rejoices in my guardianship."

"Your lordship's plan has a flaw," she pointed out, purely from a spirit of good fellowship. "Won't your cousin expect you to have designs on this paragon yourself?"

"As I am popularly believed to be a confirmed bachelor, I doubt it very much. It may be that he will confess as soon as I propose this marriage to him, in which case you would not be involved. But if I should resort to this stratagem, I depend upon your cooperation." He resumed his seat before telling her, "I have decided that your introduction to Hugh must take place out of town, at my estate in Devonshire."

"But I've already declined the honor of becoming your ward," she reminded him. "Besides, I'd never be convincing as a minor—I'm all of twenty-five." No stranger to flattery, she was nevertheless gratified when he said bluntly that she didn't look it.

"Last evening you proved that you are adept at portraying a young female of refinement and breeding," Trevor continued. "And you are no less believable now—if I didn't know better, I would swear you really *are* a—" He hesitated as a flush suffused his gold-toned face.

His implication that she wasn't a real lady was unfortunate, because Flora had begun to be fascinated by this compelling and determined gentleman. Now his condescension had soured what had turned into a thoroughly enjoyable contest of wills.

Gravely he said, "Miss Campion, you must be aware that you are quite different from—well, from Louise Talley, for want of a better example. In a variety of ways, all of which are readily apparent to me."

"You are right, I'm nothing like Louise." But she didn't elaborate on how, or ask him what he perceived those differences to be. She would not parade her virtue before this arrogant aristocrat—in all probability he wouldn't believe her, for clearly he considered every actress a slut.

Going from bad to worse, he added, "I'll pay you handsomely, Miss Campion, you have only to name your price. And I intend to provide fine clothes and a pearl necklace and all the other outward trappings of a young heiress. You may keep or sell them as you prefer. I'm also willing to use my influence in your behalf if you care to try your luck at Drury Lane or Covent Garden. I'm acquainted with Dick Sheridan, and a friend of mine is one of Kemble's investors."

Flora's patience was beginning to wear thin, and she said witheringly, "Your lordship's offer of patronage is unnecessary. I could never leave Mr. Forster, not for another theater—or for a working holiday in Devonshire. Truly, Lord Leafield, you would be wise to seek out another actress, one who might be tempted by the offer of clothes and money and such."

"As far as I'm concerned, there is no other," he interrupted. "When I arrived on your doorstep, I was prepared for either of two outcomes: that you would jump at the chance to earn a tidy sum for very little trouble on your part, or that you would not. One thing you will learn about me, ma'am, is that I do not easily despair, and I trust you will permit me to discuss this matter with you again when you've had sufficient time to consider it."

"My refusals will always be stronger than your entreaties," she maintained, "so it would save us both a great deal of time if you would accept my decision as irrevocable. I have three roles to make perfect by the week's end and will therefore have no opportunity to concern myself with your lordship's difficulties."

She was relieved when he abruptly abandoned his efforts to sway her and brought his visit to an end. At least he hadn't had seduction in mind, she thought, surreptitiously watching his departure from the parlor window. The high-stepping bay horses moved forward, drawing the phaeton and its handsome occupant out of sight.

Now that the sun was showing its face, the broad street was crowded with Sunday afternoon pleasure seekers making for Lincoln's Inn Fields. Eager to join them, Flora let the curtain fall and went upstairs to discover if Esther was interested in accompanying her.

4

I warrant thou art a merry fellow and carest for nothing.

Twelfth Night, III. i.

Early in the week Flora had believed there was ample time to put the finishing touches on *In Praise of Parsimony*, but as the days slipped quickly by she had to wonder if the play would succeed. Tumbling into her bed at night, exhausted from a late rehearsal, she sometimes remembered Lord Leafield and his bizarre proposition, but work was her primary concern. Even in her dreams she could hear the callboy's constant refrain: "You're wanted onstage, Miss Campion."

On the day before the first performance, Flora reached the theater early, neither fully rested nor completely refreshed by her Easter holiday. She sent Margery off to inspect all the seams of her new costumes, a necessary precaution ever since a memorable moment during *The School for Scandal*, when she'd drawn breath for her opening speech only to be rendered mute by a dozen pins poking into various parts of her anatomy.

She'd learned a great deal during her years on the stage, she thought, adding a few coals to the green-room fire. Backstage conversation was frank, spiced with phrases that would have horrified her sailor brother. Bawdy songs and jests abounded, drunkenness was common, but she quickly learned to accept these facts, and so much more.

Shortly after joining the company, she'd had visible proof that actors lived by a different code than most mortals. One day she had entered a deserted wardrobe room and found a couple entwined on a makeshift bed of cloaks and robes. When the nature of their enterprise had dawned on Flora, she had slipped out unnoticed, but for some time afterward she worried that she hadn't been as shocked as a decently raised young woman should have been.

At nineteen, the world had seemed so full of exciting possibilities, and she'd often imagined how it might feel to lie with a man. There was a deeper meaning to those lofty speeches she heard onstage each night, and she looked forward to the time when she, too, would experience the all-consuming passions described by the playwrights and poets.

She sat down at a scarred wooden table, spreading out her "lengths," pages of foolscap on which were written her cue lines and each of her speeches. Her study of the playwright's latest revisions was broken by the entrance of a gentleman whose dark good looks and bold movements proclaimed him a Forster.

"Hullo, Florry," he greeted her, and though his voice was a trifle husky from the earliness of the hour, it retained its rich resonance.

"Hullo, Horry." She acknowledged the actor's presence by offering her cheek for the brotherly kiss it was his practice to bestow every day.

"Jones has made *more* changes?" Horatio Forster asked sympathetically, collapsing into the empty chair beside hers.

"Yes, and all of them in the final scene. Why doesn't he ever alter the beginning? Then we'd be over the hurdle at the start of the play, instead of having to endure agonies of uncertainty all the way through to the last act."

"If you hold off learning your new words for a few hours, you'll save yourself a lot of bother. He's sure to change everything back to what it was." After discharging this advice, Horatio took up one of the pages and read it over, humming a tune under his breath.

Flora, her eyes glued to the sheet before her, said severely, "You're ruining my concentration, you know."

"That was my object," he returned, with a notable lack of contrition.

She looked up, frowning, and his red-rimmed eyes and heavy-lidded aspect told her how he had passed his evening. Flora was all too familiar with the unfocused stare that indicated a night of carousing, and she was dismayed to see the flush brought on by a bout with the bottle. But unlike some of their colleagues, Horatio had never forfeited her respect by appearing onstage in a drunken state.

"Does my appearance give you pause?" he asked. "And after I wore this coat—your favorite, is it not?"

"You were wearing it yesterday."

He dropped his jet-black head into his hands, heaving a deep sigh. "Ah, well, the truth is that I never went to bed. But don't fret, love, 'twas nothing more than a bit of holiday merrymaking and no harm done."

"I do wish that before you indulge yourself that way you'd think of me. You know what I must undergo as a result of *your* excesses! Julie will come dashing over to our house and beg me on bended knee to reform your character."

"I did think of you—longingly," he said, grinning. "My busybody sister-in-law isn't the only one who hopes you'll make an honest man of me. What say you, my mouse of virtue? It only takes a word."

"Never!" she cried, returning to the pages of dialogue.

Horatio's tone was wickedly suggestive when he murmured, "A new pantomime opens at Sadler's Wells tomorrow, *Jam-Ben-Jan, or Harlequin and the Forty Virgins.* Why don't we attend this promising spectacle, and consign Ben and the rest of 'em to the devil?"

The notion of deserting on their own first night made Flora smile. "Can't you just see his face if we did? He'd give us the sack! Or murder us."

"If our poor effort is damned by the public, never to be repeated, I'll take you to Drury Lane on Wednesday to see Monk Lewis's latest melodrama, *The Wood Demon.* Michael Kelly wrote the music, always a recommendation."

"Even if we could go, I wouldn't. Whenever I attend a play, someone always seems sadly miscast, or a clumsily staged tableau catches my eye, and I take no pleasure in it." When Horatio stretched out in his chair and closed his eyes, Flora judged it safe to return to her work.

Five years ago Benedict Forster had made a move counter to theatrical tradition and paired his wild brother with the virginal Campion lass in *Romeo and Juliet,* letting youth play youth. To the astonishment of the entire troupe, the hero and heroine began keeping company off the stage as well.

For a whole summer the two were inseparable, sitting only a whisper's distance from each other in the green room, romping together between rehearsals. They walked unchaperoned along the shingle beaches near Portsmouth, the romantic backdrop for a succession of kisses, eager on Horatio's side, shy on Flora's. Because his experience of life and love far exceeded hers, he wasn't long satisfied with so tepid an affair, so out of curiosity and a strong desire to please him, Flora permitted liberties she had denied to other swains. But even though she felt positively weak when he touched her breast or stroked her leg above her garter, she always stopped short of that great sacrifice he demanded as a proof of her love. Not even an offer of marriage could persuade her to give in; Flora had no real desire to be his or any man's wife, and told him so. They quarrelled, bringing the three months' idyll to an abrupt end. She was regretful but wiser, Horatio was resentful, and the other Forsters were vastly relieved.

There followed a period of coolness, during which Flora devoted herself to her work and Horatio consoled himself with drink and lively Sally Jenkins. Less than a month after claiming his life was blighted, he moved into lodgings with the redhead. Despite his many subsequent liaisons, he never failed to refer to Flora as the single great love of his life, making no secret of the fact that in his mind, at least, their rift was temporary.

With the passing of time they had established a less volatile, more secure friendship, but it was only marginally less physical than their short-lived romantic attachment. Flora never failed to offer her embrace as consolation for failure or disappointment, or to reward a success. He would often pat her cheek in delighted response to a joke, and during the first reading of a bad play, they kicked at one another under the table like a pair of ill-behaved children.

The dozing actor, roused by the babble of voices in the courtyard, sat up and said, "Lord, but I'm glad we're finally done with *Twelfth Night*."

"Why is that?" Flora asked absently. Other players were filtering into the room, and she still had four long speeches to memorize.

"Because Sebastian is an idiot and a fool. And I'm sick of that damned blond wig that's supposed to make me a twin to Louise. Won't you play Viola for my benefit, Florry? We match so well that I could dispense with the blasted toupee!"

"Louise is the one who can guarantee you a full house. And I won't play breeches parts."

"You could if you wanted," he said. "Even Madam played her share of 'em when she was younger." Both Forster sons referred to their mother in this respectful fashion, even when speaking to her directly.

"It's Ben's rule for me: no male characters, no Viola or Rosalind, or even Peggy in *The Country Girl*. He promised Miles never to display my nether limbs onstage."

"'Fess up, Florry, it's really because beneath your skirts you've got crooked legs, with knock knees and thick, ugly ankles."

"There's nothing wrong with my legs and you know it," she flared.

"Watch your tongue, madcap—you'll give everyone the wrong impression. What should a rake like myself be knowing about the legs of the proper Miss Campion, now?"

"Wretch!"

"Prude!" he shot back, for this was an infallible provocation.

"Wastrel!" she cried wrathfully, shoving at him.

"Gypsy!" And so they continued until both became bored with the exercise, much to the disappointment of their amused audience.

The callboy, whose title was belied by his advanced age and thinning gray hair, hurried into the room. "You're wanted onstage, Miss Campion, Master Horry," he wheezed through a pair of lungs that had inhaled the dust of old theaters for many a decade. "Mr. Jones has arrived with the revisions for the opening scene, and Mr. Forster is ready to begin rehearsal."

With an exchange of martyred glances, the actor and actress left the comforts of the green room hand in hand, and followed the rheumy messenger toward the scaffold of duty.

* * *

The master of Leafield House sat in a comfortable chair in his handsomely appointed study, reading the London news and occasionally looking out the window to watch the boys at play in the square gardens.

According to his paper, the actors of the Princess Theatre—Forster's Folly, as it was described—would perform a new comedy tomorrow evening. A week and a day had passed since Trevor's visit to Miss Flora Campion, and in the interim he'd often recalled that brief, inconclusive interview.

Her cool dignity surpassed that of Lady Derby, the former Elizabeth Farren, who had once trod the boards of Drury Lane in fine-lady roles. Derby's first countess was hardly in her grave when he married his longtime mistress, and from the moment he placed the ring on the actress's skinny finger, she'd wiped the past from her mind. Nowadays her ladyship held herself aloof from all but the highest in the land and looked down her long nose at anyone of lesser rank, as if she'd been born into the nobility. These actresses, Trevor thought with amusement, never seemed to give over playing a part. According to the strict standards of his class, Flora Campion, with her precise diction and elegant manners, was no lady; the trappings of respectability with which she surrounded herself were meaningless because her profession negated them.

Undaunted by her refusal to assist him, Trevor intended to persevere. He envisioned a pleasant association with Miss Campion, one not entirely founded upon business, for no doubt the lovely player had other talents than those she displayed in public.

Folding up his paper, he set it aside and reached for the letters on the table beside his chair. Now that Easter was past, the social Season had begun in earnest, and London's hostesses had showered gilt-edged cards upon him weeks in advance of their entertainments. Many of his fellow peers employed a secretary to take care of all but the most personal correspondence, but Trevor preferred to read and respond to it himself. After sifting through the invitations, he found a letter bearing a Bath postmark.

His aunt's ill health restricted her activities, and communicating with him was one of her primary occupations. However disappointed to find that her latest missive was only a few paragraphs long, he was intrigued by an unusual request: that he attend a party in Berkeley Square. "It will be the very first ball of the season, on Easter Monday, and is being given by Lord and Lady Batsford, whose daughter is being presented this spring," Lady Ainsley had written. "Now, dearest, as a favor to your favorite aunt, please send me a faithful report of how Lady Caroline Lewes conducts herself."

Her reticence was remarkable, for she hadn't even described the girl. Although her greater concern appeared to be the success of her friend's party, her nephew knew better. And because he had no particular plans for the evening, he decided to have a look at—he glanced at the note to make sure of the name—at Lady Batsford's daughter Caroline. His matchmaking relative knew his tastes better than anyone, and if she felt this young lady was worth pointing out, her reasons must be sound.

A springtime crop of gently reared, innocent young misses had come to town, many of them destined to become spoiled, adulterous society wives. Season after Season Trevor had watched flighty young noblewomen discard and acquire new lovers as they did ballgowns, seeking in vain for one that would wear really well over time. And even as he dallied with them, he pitied them from the bottom of his heart.

Although his father and an uncle had died in their prime, until lately he'd felt no sense of urgency about taking a wife. The late earl, his grandfather, had lived many years—too many, the old man had opined as he'd waited for death to claim him. But the troublesome heir thrust upon Trevor by that same stubborn, long-lived gentleman was reason enough to contemplate matrimony. If he acquired a well-born bride, and the requisite male child, Hugh Cotterell could no longer plague him.

But it was difficult to concentrate on the necessity of marriage this morning, when his mind kept returning to the heart-faced lady of the stage. Advancing age must have broadened his preferences, he concluded, for there was no other way to account for his eagerness to seduce someone with midnight

locks. Formerly he'd had a taste for blondes. Not saucy Nell
Gwynne types like Louise Talley, but the flaxen-haired, rosy-
cheeked epitome of English maidenhood, which he hoped
Lady Caroline Lewes would turn out to be.

"My lord."

Looking up, he saw his butler standing on the threshold.
"Another invitation, Cochrane?" He sighed, spying a square of
folded paper on the small silver tray.

The man entered the room shaking his silvered head. "It
came from Mr. Linton's offices in the Strand."

Trevor reached for the letter and ripped the seal. The solicitor's bold, definite script leapt up at him, and the message it
conveyed was troubling. "Does the man wait for a reply? I
have none."

Cochrane cleared his throat. "My lord, there is another matter. Master Hugh is here and wishes to see you."

"Send him in at once. And," Trevor called after the butler's
stiff, retreating figure, "I've changed my mind about answering Linton. Tell his clerk that I'll call in the Strand this afternoon."

"Very good, my lord."

Trevor crossed to the window overlooking Cavendish
Square, and when a wiry young man stepped into the study he
turned around and said calmly, "Don't worry, I'm not going to
scold, there's no point at this late date, and your opponent did
survive the duel. How was Copenhagen? Did you have a
pleasant stay?"

"No, blast it!" The wiry young man flung himself into the
nearest chair. "It's a cursed unpleasant place, and Denmark is
beastly—I don't think the sun shone once in the fortnight I
was there. I didn't even mind that spell of rain last week—it
was London rain, thank God!"

"Exactly how long have you been in town?"

Mr. Hugh Cotterell ran his fingers nervously through his
brown hair, a shade lighter than his cousin's. "After Jack
Rollins wrote to say I might return, I boarded the next ship
bound for England."

"You should have visited me sooner," Trevor said. "We

may not be close, but I'm always interested in knowing your whereabouts."

"I wasn't at all sure you'd receive me—black sheep of the family and all that. After my last duel, you said I was a disgrace to the Cotterell name. I'm here because I want my allowance. It was due at Lady Day."

"And was paid. In your absence, I instructed Linton to settle your outstanding debts."

"You did *what*?" When Trevor repeated his statement, Hugh's bony face went rigid with anger. "I never heard of such a damned scurvy trick! You had no right—on what, pray tell, am I expected to live?"

"On my bounty, I should think," Trevor said wearily. "What else could I do? Linton was being dunned to death by your creditors. He's *my* man of business, yet your tangled affairs were thrust upon him when you came of age four years ago. I empowered him to do as he thought best, he did it, and you should be glad to know that you've returned to your native shores unencumbered by financial obligations."

"How can I be glad, when all I have to my name is a few shillings and a single pound note?" Hugh grumbled. "I trust you can advance me some money—I'll pay you back next quarter-day, I promise."

"By then you'll be in debt again," Trevor predicted. "You need some form of employment, Hugh. I've always thought Grandfather did you a disservice by keeping you out of the army when you wanted to join."

"Then why in God's name didn't you persuade him?"

"I tried, but he never cared that much for my opinion. He only listened to one person."

"His holiness our Uncle George, the dutiful youngest son." Hugh glared at his cousin. "I daresay my exploits have prompted a sermonizing letter or two from the vicarage at Hopeton. Lord," he said heavily, "what an odd lot we Cotterells are. There's you, the paragon. And me, the prodigal. And the parson who never leaves his parish."

"Uncle George couldn't help being the favorite. Our fathers married women Grandfather disliked and offended him further by dying before their time. George took holy orders and wed the squire's daughter and remained on the estate."

"I wonder Grandfather didn't leave him the Hall and Combe Cotterall. There was no entail to prevent it."

"He who is last shall be first in the kingdom of heaven," Trevor murmured.

"Well, our uncle is last in the succession, with you and me standing between him and the family fortune," said Hugh in a voice of satisfaction. "And our male issue would come before old George and that band of cherubs living a stone's throw from the gates of Hopeton Hall."

Trevor said mildly, "Unless you married without my consent, in which case you would inherit nothing but the title."

"I don't give a damn about all those houses and farms and investments, nor do I want some lawyer telling me what to do when Consols go up or down. All I need is a regular allowance and the freedom to do as I please."

"Well, as we both know, you inevitably fall into a scrape when left to your own devices," Trevor reminded him. "But I am willing to lend my assistance, if not my money." Trevor regarded the expectant Hugh unsmilingly and said, "You may stay at Leafield House. But in return you must tell me where and with whom you've spent the last week."

Hugh swallowed twice. "Is it so important? If you must know, I've been with Rollins."

It was necessary for Trevor to count to ten, silently, to calm himself. He knew Hugh was capable of telling falsehoods to cover his sins, but this one was outrageous. "Rollins lodges just off Piccadilly, does he not?" he asked. "Clarges Street?"

"Near there—White Horse Street, Shepherd's Market."

"And you've come directly from his house this morning?"

"Of course. It's too early in the day to call on anyone but a relative."

"Your sojourn abroad seems to have exerted a beneficial influence," Trevor observed. "You never used to be so concerned about etiquette."

"If I'm to reside in Leafield House, I'd best mind my manners, hadn't I?" his cousin retorted.

Trevor reached for the decanter and poured two glasses of wine. Handing one of them to Hugh, he continued, "As long as you behave circumspectly, I think we'll rub along well enough. I suggest you visit my tailor—at my expense—and have him outfit you with less haphazard raiment. I don't think much of Rollins's valet if he lets you go out in public looking as you do now."

Hugh glowered at him but made no reply.

"I've hired a stage box at the Princess Theatre for the remainder of its season, and tomorrow evening we'll attend a new comedy, which I trust will entertain you." He paced the length of the room, then faced his cousin. "Tonight there's a ball at Lady Batsford's, her daughter's debut. She's the sort of Bath tabby who'll report your doings to Aunt Belle, so if you're wise you'll abstain from deep play or deep drinking."

"Trying to reform my character?" Hugh sneered. "I daresay I shall be worn out by all these dissipations—visits to the tailor, a seat at the theater, society balls."

"Don't be provoking," Trevor warned.

Reading the danger in the hazel eyes, Hugh felt a frisson of alarm. "I was only jesting."

"Oh, and I must ask that you refrain from mentioning to anyone that you've been with Jack Rollins for the past week. I'm afraid he isn't very likely to corroborate your story."

Sitting up a little straighter, Hugh asked, "What do you mean?"

His cousin extracted a folded sheet of paper from his coat pocket. "I've just received some tragic tidings from Linton, who has been so busy on your behalf. Two nights ago your friend was found lying dead in an alley near St. James's."

Within an instant, Hugh's countenance was as white as his rumpled cravat.

"No foul play suspected," his lordship continued, "but he received a fatal blow. The coroner ruled that Mr. Rollins, so often in an inebriated state, sustained the injury in a fall. But the unfortunate and untimely accident does raise a few awk-

ward questions about your recent activities, to say the least."
He handed over the solicitor's note.

Hugh clutched it, his hand visibly shaking, and he stared
helplessly down at the handwritten obituary. Rollins, the one
man who knew all his secrets, would carry them to the grave.

5

I delight in masques and revels sometimes altogether.

Twelfth Night, I. iii.

The Earl of Leafield and Mr. Hugh Cotterell were among the last to enter the Berkeley Square house Lord and Lady Batsford had hired for the Season. Her ladyship was one of Bath's leading hostesses, and her London connections had served her well; if not exactly a crush, the ball had attracted a respectable mix of the fashionable, the political set, and several unattached gentlemen of title and fortune. As she greeted Trevor, he perceived the glint of triumph in her eye.

Still haunted by the disturbances of the day, he was amazed that Hugh had recovered so quickly from the shock of hearing about his crony's death. When his cousin disappeared into the library, where the card tables had been arranged, Trevor prayed that Linton and his minions could work a miracle and quietly uncover tangible proof of the alleged marriage before Hugh guessed his suspicions.

The dancing had already begun; a dozen couples were gliding about the polished floor to the soft strains of a popular tune. Trevor couldn't guess which of the young ladies was the daughter of the house, but a swift inspection told him that three could lay some claim to beauty. When the music ended, Baron Allingham's partner, a slim creature in lemon silk, hurried to Lady Batsford's side like a tiny yellow chick seeking the security of the mother hen. She was quite pretty, with chestnut curls and a slim, graceful figure. Best to begin with the papa, he thought, looking around for Lord Batsford, who would doubtless be more than happy to perform the introduction Trevor desired.

Not long afterward, he lured Lady Caroline Lewes over to a sofa, preferring to converse with her rather than join her in the exertions of a *contre-danse*. His aunt's name was sufficient to inaugurate a dialogue between them, and Trevor gently quizzed her, saying, "I suppose you find London quite different from Bath."

In a shy, breathless voice, Lady Caroline said, "Bath is also busy. And I did visit London last winter, when Mama brought me to visit her dressmaker. We didn't attend any parties then, but we went to the theater."

He thought of Flora Campion, and dispelled her recurrent appearance in his mind by focusing on the bright face across from him. Her ladyship had blue eyes and a sweet smile; a pity she wasn't blonde as well, but one couldn't have everything. "You enjoy going to the play?"

"All our family like theatricals, my lord."

"Then perhaps you and Lady Batsford will help make up a theater party some evening."

Lady Caroline ducked her head. "That is for Mama to say, but I would enjoy it very much."

He smiled. Biddable, he thought, and very well-trained. Aunt Isabelle had not erred in bringing this little miss to his attention. "You may be sure I will speak to your lady mother," he said as her next dancing partner came forward to claim her, ending their tête-à-tête.

The viscountess, whose house and bed he had frequented ever since their encounter at the theater, stood nearby with Lord Allingham, and Trevor went over to greet them. The baron, casting an appreciative glance at the young lady in yellow, commented, "Pretty chit."

"Leave her to Trevor, Allingham; you're already engaged," said Clarissa, rapping his arm with her closed fan.

"Not any longer, my dear. Haven't you heard? I was jilted."

"Are condolences or felicitations in order?" Trevor asked.

"Either or both," was Lord Allingham's diffident response.

Smiling up at Trevor, Clarissa said, "Planning a match, are you?"

"As I never met the child before tonight, the question seems a trifle premature."

"Lady Batsford doesn't think so—didn't you see her hopeful expression when you approached her cherished daughter?"

"*I* was not so fortunate," the baron interjected. "I say, Trev, was that Hugh I spied in the card room? Where the devil has he been lately?"

"Why don't you go ask him?" Clarissa suggested pointedly. When Lord Allingham had withdrawn, she said, "Poor boy, his penchant for play actresses shows no sign of abating. I wonder what made him think he was ready to marry."

"I can't imagine."

Fluttering her pale eyelashes at Trevor, she asked, "What brings *you* to so insipid an affair as this, my friend?"

"I looked in as a favor to my aunt."

"As did I, in compliance with my absent husband's request. Reggie's mama is a second cousin once removed from Lord Batsford. Or is it third cousin twice removed? I never can remember those things. Just think, Trevor, if you do wed Lady Caroline we'll be related by marriage."

"Barely, from the sound of it."

Drifting closer, she whispered, "Shall I see you later? Henrietta can let you into the house."

Trevor hesitated before answering, "Very well, but only on the condition that I need not stay till dawn."

She pouted. "Trevor, you know I loathe sleeping alone."

"I know you always say so."

She accepted the compromise, but with obvious reluctance. "As you prefer, but I never dreamed you could be so cruel. Lately I've relied upon bachelors because they don't *need* to rush away. I detest frantic, hurried encounters. Married men glance so often and so furtively at the clock that I always feel like a—" But Clarissa failed to complete her analogy, leaving it to Trevor to supply the word for himself.

The next afternoon there was a frantic, last-minute rehearsal at the Princess Theatre which left the prompter hoarse from shouting lines to the forgetful.

Flora ate her dinner in her dressing room, her head bent over a fresh set of speeches. Even for this frothy comic role, her preparation was far in excess of what was common. Most players read through their new parts once or twice at most, attended rehearsals as required, and left it at that.

Earlier in her career she, too, had viewed acting as nothing more than an endless game of charades. As a consequence she had been a failure in her first speaking role, undone by insufficient study, shattered nerves, and an audience more enthusiastic about her physical attributes than her acting ability. Chastened by the experience, she had rehearsed subsequent roles more thoroughly, but still hadn't excelled as Juliet; Horatio Forster had been too great a distraction. Only after their romance ended had she set about remedying her primary faults: a lack of stage presence and a speaking voice over which she had an imperfect control.

Madam Forster had supplied the necessary instruction, imparting the various tricks that had served her well during her long career. In time Flora was able to maintain her concentration when riots broke out in the pit, or even if an unruly crowd threw objects onto the stage. She struggled to achieve the proper placement of her voice, and learned to move gracefully yet purposefully.

The reward for her hard work had finally come, and now she was about to face a London audience in a play written expressly for her. The success or failure of Mr. Jones's latest effort depended upon her, for a mediocre script might be hailed as a masterpiece if brought to life by a Siddons, a Kemble, or a Jordan. She was determined to please as Letty Loyal, for by creating the role she made it her undisputed property. And her several hours' traffic on the stage would be more of an adventure than usual, because many of her scenes were with Louise Talley, whose joy in upstaging other actresses was no secret.

Flora was posing before the mirror in her first-act gown when flame-haired Sally Jenkins, wearing her customary maid's costume, bounded into the dressing room.

"What a row took place a moment ago, Florry," the actress cried exuberantly. "The things you miss by hiding up here instead of loitering in the green room like the rest of the common herd! I thought it best to warn you that Louise will be after you tonight—beware."

Flora began applying her paint. "Why? We've been on the very best of terms all week."

"No longer. She accuses you of going behind her back to

Mr. Jones. Wouldn't you know, our illustrious playwright locked himself in a closet this afternoon to do a bit more slashing, and it was Louise's part that suffered the most. I gathered from the way she was shrieking that he's whittled it down quite a lot."

"Oh, Sal, no."

"Oh, Florry, *yes*! That scene in the third act, when you confess your love for Horatio, has been altered. Jones has altered that bit completely. Your humble servant, and I mean that literally, is now the recipient of the speech. Letty Loyal addresses it to her maid, not Selina. When Mr. Jones told Louise, she started screaming and threw her fan at the poor man— missed him by yards, but the fan hit the wall and broke to bits, which only made her more furious. She went on and on about what a scheming little hussy you are, and how Jones is your dupe, and to crown all she says she can't abide her costumes because they aren't new like yours. Ben is with her now, trying to calm her, but I wouldn't wager too much on his chances of success."

Flora turned back to her mirror. She dipped a hare's foot into the powder, saying, "Ben will prevail, he always does. What about our parts, Sal? They must be affected by these last-minute changes."

Sally shrugged dismissively. "The prompter is copying out our lengths for the scene right now, and they'll be brought up directly. We can read them through if you like, or just take our chances when the time comes."

Flora announced a strong preference for the former, and persuaded her diffident friend that they ought to rehearse. When a stagehand came to Miss Campion's door with a sheaf of pages still wet from the prompter's quill, the ladies sat down to commit the new material to memory.

Both were quick studies, and before long they went downstairs to the green room. The other principal players were there, huddled in small groups and discussing the recent contretemps. There was no sign of Miss Talley. When the various threats of vengeance were imparted to Flora, word for word, she felt more than the usual first-night flutter. The prospect of spending several hours onstage with a woman of Louise's uncertain temper was most unappealing.

"I told Ben that La Talley would be trouble," Madam Forster announced as she swept into the room wearing a feathered headdress which made her appear taller and more imposing than usual. She took possession of the most comfortable chair in the room, hers by right according to the rigid code of etiquette that prevailed backstage. Smoothing the puce gown she wore as Mrs. Loyal, Letty's mama, she reported, "When my son emerged from her dressing room a moment ago, he said the breakages will be deducted from her wages, which leads me to suppose that she fired a few rouge pots at him. He looked none the worse for it."

Mr. Osric Logan, the grand old man of the company, said from his place at the hearthside, "He should fine her for insubordination. That one would do better to give more attention to the substance of her part and less to the size of it."

The woman next to him murmured, "And so ungrateful, too, after all Ben has done for her." The speaker was universally, if unlawfully, acknowledged as Mrs. Logan in recognition of having borne the old actor five children, and because she had shared his lodgings and his bed, if not his name, for the past twenty years.

The pit was always crowded when Miss Talley was featured, but on this night, when new productions at other theaters competed for playgoers, it was a coup to have the galleries and even the box seats filled as well. From the moment the green curtain rose on the opening tableau, Flora forgot the audience and Louise and concentrated on remembering her lines. In the ballroom scene she flirted and fanned herself and tried not to panic when one of the speeches addressed to her by Horatio turned out to be fully three versions old.

Her next trial came in her first encounter with Louise, who played Selina, Letty's rival for Mr. Prodigal's affections. But the addition of costumes and scenery and an appreciative audience conspired to put her at ease, and she parried all attempts to upstage her with skill and not a little enjoyment.

After the final act, a weeping Mr. Jones was pushed to the

fore of Mr. Lumley Skeffington's stage box to acknowledge the crowd's noisy appreciation of his new work.

Benedict Forster bestowed a few words of praise upon his leading players, pointedly ignoring Miss Talley. As he gave orders to the stagehands about the proper assembly of the scenery for the pantomime, Louise flounced off the stage, her pert features set in a mask of rage.

"Never mind her," Horatio whispered in Flora's ear. "It's your play entirely."

They dodged a group of dancers tricked out as Harlequins and Columbines for the pantomime, and Flora said, "She hates me. And Eliza Ellis hasn't spoken to me since I took her part of Olivia a few weeks ago. It was bad enough when the two of them were at each other's throats, and now I'll be the target of their malice."

The green room was redolent of savory roast beef and pastries hot from the oven of a nearby chophouse, and the actors were eagerly partaking of the first-night supper. As Horatio led Flora through the crowd blocking the doorway, he said, "Ignore them."

Flora didn't care for the constant bickering that characterized backstage life, but to stand silently by and let herself be abused was equally disagreeable. "But that's so spiritless!"

"Oh, everyone knows you're a bold piece, for they've seen you ripping up at me since time out of mind."

"That's different," she said, smiling. "You deserve it. But at least you don't resent me, like Louise and Eliza."

"Only because they know you can act them into flinders. You've got more in your left eyebrow than Louise has in that precious body she's always flaunting in front of Lord Allingham's box. And as for Eliza—well, she improves with age, but Siddons ain't got nothing to fear. Why, when I made that blunder in the ballroom scene you scarcely batted an eye, and before I knew what you were about, we were bowling right along. So for that, Miss Campion, you deserve at least one of these lovely cheesecakes before they're devoured by this pack of starving rogues and vagabonds."

They filled their plates with much more than just the cheesecakes and sat down with Sally Jenkins, whose current sweetheart was at that moment sawing away on his violin in the orchestra pit.

Flora suddenly discovered she was ravenous. Although she was usually in a rush to get home, tonight she lingered, assuaging her appetite and joining in her friends' cheerful discourse. When Horatio suggested that everyone repair to a tavern to continue their revels, she realized that it was high time she removed her costume and paint and made her way home.

As she bounded to her feet, the actor caught her hand. "What, won't you join us?"

"When have I ever visited those disreputable cock-and-hen places you frequent? I haven't the strength to carouse, and if you want to drink ale and sing ballads till sunup, it's your own affair." When she tried to jerk her hand away, he pulled her down to sit on his lap and planted a smacking kiss on her mouth.

"Give over, love," he crooned, "and come along."

"Horry, let me go—you're crushing my new gown!" Flora squirmed in his embrace, but upon discovering that she was trapped she joined in the laughter.

Her levity was short-lived. Conscious of an uncharacteristic silence in her companions, she looked up to see the Earl of Leafield standing before them. When she met his hazel eyes, she flushed from her crown to her toes, embarrassed to be found sprawling across a man's lap like some common trull. Horatio released her, and she was thankful that at least he had refrained from slapping her on the backside as he so often did.

Lord Leafield bowed. "Miss Campion, I predict that the critics will hail you as the latest sensation."

"And I hope they keep a rein on their enthusiasm," she replied with outward calm, although her pulse was fluttering. "A sensation seldom lasts in London, I have heard, and lives on only to be reviled by the very public that created it. I'm surprised to see you tonight, my lord. During our last conversation I received the distinct impression that you're not a habitual visitor to the theater."

"Ah, but that was before I made your acquaintance," was his smooth reply. "Didn't you see me sitting in my box? I would swear you looked up at least once during the play."

With damping frankness, Flora told him that she took very little notice of the individuals in the audience, adding, "It is their collective response that concerns me. And I have so few friends in town that the likelihood of my recognizing anyone is very slight."

"Well, that puts me in my place," he observed. Holding out his arm, he said, "Permit me to enlarge your London acquaintance by making you known to someone who desires an introduction."

She let him lead her over to a young man standing in the corner, whose sharp features were oddly familiar to her. One swift upward glance at the earl's similarly aquiline profile was enough to support her suspicion.

His next words confirmed it as truth. "Miss Campion, here is another member of my family who admires your many talents. My cousin, Mr. Cotterell. Hugh has lately been visiting Denmark."

"How interesting," Flora murmured, both surprised and pleased that he'd apparently given up his elaborate plan to pass her off as his wealthy ward. The young man, who didn't appear to advantage beside his cousin, had a lean and hungry look. Of medium height, he had brown hair somewhat lighter than Lord Leafield's; his eyes were darker and set under heavy lids.

"You are fortunate indeed to be able to go abroad, sir," she said. "With the Continent in such disarray, few people have the opportunity to travel."

Hugh Cotterell's lip curled, and his tone was unpleasant when he replied, "My journey wasn't made under circumstances which I would describe as fortunate."

Momentarily at a loss, Flora decided that Lord Leafield had not exaggerated when he'd described his heir in an unflattering light; he might even have erred on the side of kindness. In fact, she was inclined to dismiss the likelihood of Mr. Cotterell's secret marriage on the grounds that no female could possibly consider him an agreeable prospect for a husband.

His lordship turned to her and asked, "Do you have a desire to travel, Miss Campion?"

She detected the mischief in his expression and was instantly on her guard. "No more than the average person," she said stiffly.

"I wish I might introduce you to the beauties of Devonshire. I have an estate there, Combe Cotterell—I believe I mentioned it the other day? Alas, it is too far, but perhaps you will permit me to show you some of the pleasant views to be found nearer London." Then he flashed his most winning smile, the one Flora could not resist, and said he hoped he might have the honor of driving her to Richmond Park in his phaeton.

The refusal was forming on her lips when she became aware of Horatio's jealous presence. He was glowering, an unsubtle indication that he didn't approve of her consorting with gentlemen other than himself.

Determined to give him a much-needed lesson and with no thought for the possible consequences, she shifted her gaze back to Lord Leafield, forgetting her earlier determination to resist him. Smiling back at him, she gave a reply that Horatio would be sure to hear: "I would be delighted to accept, my lord, and look forward to the engagement with all my heart."

6

Trip no further, pretty sweeting,
Journeys end in lovers' meeting.

Twelfth Night, II. iii.

Several days of rainfall encouraged Flora's hope that there
would be a postponement of the proposed expedition to Richmond, but on Friday a footman arrived on the doorstep with
his master's brief note, which fixed the hour. Saturday dawned
gloriously fair, sealing her fate, and she prepared for her ordeal by bathing in a tub of rose-scented water, wishing she
could remain there all day. To be at home was to be at peace,
for the atmosphere at the theater was strained at best, bellicose
at worst.

As Horatio had predicted, Miss Talley and Mrs. Ellis had
joined forces against her. They united in giving her the cold
shoulder in public; when there was no danger of being over-
heard, they sneered insults. But because they behaved circumspectly during performances, she made no effort to retaliate
and suffered their snubs and sulks in silence. Louise continued
to upstage her whenever possible, but Flora was experienced
enough to turn this ploy against her, and often the other actress
was the more discomfited.

She was soaping her arms when Esther barged into the bedchamber, holding a newspaper aloft. "You're mentioned in the
theatrical review!" she cried triumphantly.

Flora's sense of modesty was greatly diminished after her
years in the common dressing room, but she drew up her knees
to cover her bare bosom.

Her friend climbed upon the unmade bed and spread out the
paper. " 'The Princess Theatre, often called Forster's Folly by
those with pretensions to prognostication—' "

"Spare me the long-winded rhetoric," Flora intervened

hastily, "I've already heard it *ad nauseum*. Every paper in town has joined in the endless debate about whether our theater should be licensed, and Sheridan has mounted a fierce campaign against Ben. The insults and broadsheets are flying thick and fast the length of Drury Lane. What does the reviewer say about the *play*?"

" 'With his new work, *In Praise of Parsimony*,' " Esther read, " 'Mr. Jones marks the return of comedy in its genteelest form. On Tuesday last the play was received with approbation by the faithful worshipers at the Temple of Thespis.' He goes on to describe the plot—I shan't bore you with that bit—but somewhere he mentions the actors. Oh, yes, here it is: 'Mr. Horatio Forster, in the role of Prodigal, exhibits those qualities of person and performance that must delight the fair sex and be not unacceptable to the discriminating playgoer. Mrs. Forster, having won the admiration of provincial audiences, bids fair to enjoy a similar reputation in the Metropolis and shines as Mrs. Loyal . . . Mr. Logan, in a genuinely comic performance . . . Miss Talley as Selina, the coquette, has the unfortunate habit of dropping her character at the end of the scene.' "

"Only when Lord Allingham is present," Flora said fairly, resting her head against the rim of the tub. "Go on."

" 'As Letty Loyal, Miss Campion demonstrates not only her histrionic talents, but also a naturalness of expression and movement. She excels in the role of the lady of quality as has no other since Miss Farren retired from the boards a decade past to wed into the Peerage, thus continuing her onstage roles in the Play of Life. Miss Campion satisfies; nothing in her performance is distorted, and laudable consistency appears to be her watchword. It is to be hoped that the Management of the Princess will continue to feature this lovely lady in future works of comparable merit.' " Esther started to fold the paper. "That's all."

"How gratifying."

Esther puckered her mouth in a moue of displeasure. "I think he might've been more enthusiastic. I was at the theater on Tuesday, and it seemed to me that the play was a considerable success."

The actress expelled a long sigh. "Oh, the critics will ever regard tragedy as the very pinnacle of dramatic art. The best a comedy can hope for is, 'All very well in its way,' or, 'a fine effort, for a comic play.' But the managers know that the surest crowd-pleaser is some vulgar burletta or spectacle, like the ones at Astley's or Sadler's Wells. Give the public a dancing horse, or a dog that saves a drowning female from a tub of water, or a precocious boy like Master Betty in an adult role, and you'll have a success in the theatrical realm of London."

"What will you wear today?" Esther asked, folding up the paper.

"I don't know," Flora replied gloomily, and she sank deeper into the water as though to escape what lay ahead. "I wish I dared to send his lordship word that I've succumbed to an ague and am too ill to join him today."

"You'd look mightily foolish if he happened to visit the theater tonight and saw you playing Letty Loyal."

"True," she acknowledged regretfully as Esther peered into her wardrobe.

"This sprigged muslin walking dress with the scalloped hem and blue underskirt is vastly becoming."

"He's only taking me to look at some trees and flowers, not to call upon Her Majesty the Queen."

The young matron eventually managed to rouse the indifferent actress from the tub. Flora put on the muslin gown as suggested, and a matching blue spencer, and let Esther select a fetching hat. Despite her extravagant show of unconcern, the sudden thump of the door knocker caused her to give a little jump, and shriek that she wasn't yet ready.

"He's frightfully early—by nearly half an hour," was Esther's comment as they hurried downstairs.

But Frank had opened the door to someone far more welcome than Lord Leafield, and Flora, seeing her employer standing in the hall, took the last steps at a skipping pace. "Here's a pleasant surprise!" she cried. "I hope there's no trouble at your house, Ben."

"Oh, no," Benedict Forster replied as she ushered him into the parlor. A stockier version of his swarthy younger brother, his graying temples and the faint lines at the corners of his shrewd, dark eyes attested to the fact that he had spent his forty years busily. "I'll not stay long, for I understand that you're expecting a visitor."

"Did Horry tell you so?"

"Yes," Forster said, taking a seat. "And my better half persuaded me that the news I have for you couldn't wait." His mouth twisted humorously.

Flora smiled. "Julie wanted you to act as her spy, and sent you here in the hope that you and Lord Leafield would collide on the doorstep. Apart from her curiosity, what brings you across the street this morning?"

"Theater business," he announced promptly. "Our management committee held its weekly meeting last night. I've made some necessary changes in the distribution of roles in *Hamlet*. Madam has given up Queen Gertrude, pleading fatigue, and Mrs. Ellis will replace her."

"But you're playing Hamlet, are you not?" When he nodded, Flora said on a choking laugh, "Yet you and she are much the same age."

"It will be no more singular than other such pairings in the history of our profession. When we begin rehearsals on Monday, you'll resume your former role of Ophelia."

"But why *Hamlet* so soon? I thought *The Critic* was to come next, with the tragedy to follow."

Her visitor struck a pose that she recognized as his cunning Richard the Third. "So it would've been, but I changed my mind in order to deliver a mortal blow to that damned cur Sheridan. He'll be offering a comedy at the Lane next, and after that, according to my spies, he's mounting Monk Lewis's new tragedy. I'll present the opposite: a tragedy followed by a comedy. By the by, did you read that scurrilous piece in the paper?"

"Which one?" she murmured. "I believe the latest called for you to be placed in the public pillory, and suggested that Forster's Folly be closed down immediately."

"I published a notice of my own yesterday, offering a hundred pounds to anyone who came to me with the identity of the author of such a foul libel. And what do you think was the result? Old Sherry comes 'round to the Princess, as cool as could be, to confess that he wrote it himself! Worse yet, the scoundrel demanded payment on the spot!"

Poised between dismay and high delight, Flora asked, "And did you give it to him?"

"What else could I do?" he replied testily. "Well, for all he has no head for business, he's got a deal of charm. I hope he'll use the money to pay his actors—they go whole weeks without their wages, poor devils—but it's more likely he'll lose the whole sum at cards or on some wager, or spend it all on drink."

She didn't believe for an instant that her employer was anything other than vastly proud of his quarrel with the great Sheridan of Drury Lane.

"I'll have my revenge on him for libeling me, Florry, you see if I don't," he declared. "By providing a counterpoint to his next two plays, I'm assured of making a stir—and I'll regain my hundred pounds at his expense. Even better, he wrote *The Critic* himself, which will make my triumph all the sweeter. You're to play Tilburina. Louise will be Tilburina's Confidante, and she can try to upstage you with a vengeance, because that's her character."

"So I must go mad and rave on and on about wildflowers in both plays, the tragedy and the farce. Lovely," said Flora with gentle sarcasm.

"I want you to spoof Mrs. Siddons in your portrayal of Tilburina. Madam my mother will undertake to instruct you; she knows the woman well." He rubbed his hands together and said gleefully, "It'll be a slap in the face to those damned Kembles at Covent Garden—I'll knock their long noses out of joint, see if I don't. And then, after we've made them uncomfortable, we'll retire to Bath. London is a theatrical desert in the summer, there's no getting 'round it, and I won't waste my investors' money on the four most useless months of the year. In the autumn, I'll return to take on the two patent theaters in a head-to-head contest on their own ground, I will, and it'll be a three-way race, you mark my words."

He kissed her cheek at parting, and took both of her hands in a firm grip. "You're not too much troubled by that pair of spiteful vixens at the theater, I hope? Oh, yes, Horry keeps me informed about all the doings in the green room. I prefer not to meddle in my actors' affairs so long as they appear onstage as expected, in a more or less sober state, but if matters get out of hand—"

"They won't," she said positively. "Horry, like all Forsters, is overprotective. Do you think I could have survived so long in this profession if I couldn't take care of myself just a tiny bit?"

"I suppose not. Remember, my Julie will have her nose pressed to the parlor window all morning, waiting to see this earl of yours. Have a pleasant time, my dear."

"I'll try," she promised.

The two occupants of the open carriage said very little to one another as it traversed Piccadilly and passed through the turnpike gate near Hyde Park Corner. Trevor was concerned with his restive horses, but they calmed down on the Fulham Road, preferring market gardens and pasture to city traffic.

Glancing over at his passenger, he saw that the long ribbons of her wide straw hat streamed behind her, and offered to slow the pace if she preferred. "I'm afraid that I tend to give them their heads as soon as they're clear of the crowded streets," he explained.

"I like traveling along so briskly," Flora told him, clutching her headgear. "It's a novelty for me, as I've never ridden in a phaeton before today."

"Mine is honored in being the first. Is that the reason you accepted my invitation? At the time I had the impression you did so to pique one of your fellow performers, the one who plays Mr. Prodigal."

"How the devil did you guess that?" Instantly regretting her unladylike exclamation, she said contritely, "I must remember to mind my tongue when I'm not in the green room. But yes, I *was* trying to put Horatio in his place."

"I look forward to future opportunities to assist in that effort," he replied.

Flora chose to leave this hopeful remark unanswered and said hastily, "I wish you'd tell me something about Richmond, for I'm as ignorant of what lies outside London as I am about the city itself."

She was relieved when he embarked upon a monologue in which he detailed the town's associations with royalty, pausing long enough to show his ticket to the keeper of the Queen Elm Gate.

When he told her how the grieving King Richard had razed the Palace of Sheen after his first wife's tragic death, Flora said, "I played his second queen once, in Chichester. Not a large part, for it's very much a man's play. The Duchess of Gloucester has the best of all the women's speeches, the one beginning, 'Finds brotherhood in thee no sharper spur?' Madam Forster was most impressive, and so was Mr. Logan as old John of Gaunt." As the phaeton drew up before the Star and Garter, an ostler hurried forward to take charge of the temperamental bays.

"You must know the whole of Shakespeare's works backward and forward," her escort commented after they began the ascent of Richmond Hill.

"I don't think anyone does," she replied, "because nowadays managers hack and alter the texts mercilessly. In general I prefer acting the comic plays, although the tragedies are more popular with audiences. In fact, we'll be busy with *Hamlet* soon, so I shall be obliged to go mad and get me to a nunnery and all that." Eyes twinkling, she added, "Of the thirty parts I possess, a quarter of them are Shakespeare."

He asked curiously, "What does it mean, to possess a part? Are thirty a great many?"

After discovering his superior knowledge of history, she was not sorry to have an opportunity to display her own small area of expertise. Looking away from the magnificent view of the Thames, she said, "When an actor possesses a part, in theory it's his for life, unless he voluntarily relinquishes it to someone else. At the end of his career, the great David Garrick possessed over ninety."

A short time later, as they strolled through the Old Deer Park, she commented, "It's remarkable, the sense one has of being in the country, and yet we aren't so very far from London. I didn't realize how desperate I was to see fields and trees, as well as the river itself. I've never lived in a city so large that I couldn't easily escape it when I wished."

"I, too, find London wearisome," he answered. "So much so that I recently purchased a rural retreat at Twickenham. It can't compare to Combe Cotterell, of course—my part of Devonshire is delightful at all seasons, and the estate is near enough to the sea to enjoy a pleasant breeze on the most uncomfortable of summer days."

A smile teased the corners of Flora's mouth. "I hope you aren't about to repeat your invitation of a fortnight past, my lord. But as you have introduced me to Mr. Cotterell, I suppose that you no longer contemplate the 'fictitious ward' scheme you outlined to me."

"It seemed best to me that Hugh know you for what you are—or perhaps will be," he said obliquely. "As for proving his marriage, I'm at a standstill. Do you remember I told you about Rollins, the fellow who was Hugh's second in the duel and witness to the wedding?"

"The man who is generally three-quarters drunk."

"Well, now he is four-quarters dead." She stared at him, and he nodded. "My only real evidence against Hugh died with him. It's frustrating, to say the least, because my cousin's behavior more than hints at concealment. He is disturbed by something—whether the enormity of his deception, or Rollins's demise, I can't be sure. But I didn't ask you to come with me today to talk about Hugh."

At a turning in the path they came upon a group of deer, and Flora halted, staring at them in fascination.

"They are quite tame and would feed from your hand," Trevor told her. "In the days of the Tudor and Stuart monarchs, the deer at Richmond were hunted, but now they are left to themselves and the care of the park keeper."

When they walked on, he posed several questions about her life before she came to London. Flora set aside her usual reluctance to talk about herself and proudly informed him that her father had been an instructor in mathematical sciences at the Naval Academy in Portsmouth.

"He was not a navy man," she elaborated, "but my brother is. He serves on His Majesty's Ship *Vestal* in the West Indies.

Papa was born in Hampshire. My mother was Irish—she loved to sing and dance, and had a wonderfully expressive speaking voice. I think she might have made a fine actress."

"And how did you come to be one?"

"Mama was a needlewoman—she had been apprenticed to a seamstress—and she sometimes sewed costumes for old Mr. Forster's theater. He became quite fond of our family, and let Miles work as a stagehand during his school vacations, excellent training for a seaman, because of the ropes and knots used for the scenery and mechanical devices. I often attended the play, with my brother or my parents. Perhaps because the theater was so familiar to me, it didn't hold the same romantic fascination it does for most young girls." She shook her head over the great tides of time that had ebbed and flowed since those long-ago days when her only experience of the theater had been from the audience side of the footlights.

"Mama and Papa died suddenly of a fever," she continued. "Miles was in port at the time, and we decided to give up the house, sell the books and furniture, and invest the capital in Consols. The Forsters had offered me a home, you see, so by the time Miles received his orders to sail I was settled. It seemed foolish to live on my allowance when I could so easily earn my keep on stage, but old Mr. Forster wouldn't hear of it. But it wasn't long before Ben, the elder son, inherited the theater and employed me at eighteen shillings a week. My first professional appearance was in a crowd scene."

"What was your brother's reaction?" he asked.

"By the time he learned what I had done, he was on the high seas and couldn't do a thing to stop me. So I served my apprenticeship and worked my way up from utility performer and walking parts to speaking parts."

Her removal from the Forsters' household, the painful result of her break with Horatio, had occurred next, but she chose not to disclose this bit of her past. "Eventually I took lodgings of my own, and by then I had Margery to take care of me. She had been dresser to another actress, and one day she came to me and said, 'You're young to be taking to this work, miss, but you'll do well enough if you live as respectable as you can and keep away from face paint whitened with lead, because it's poison. Rice powder will save your complexion, you mark my words.' I invited her to be my companion on the spot."

Her tale came to an abrupt halt, and she resisted his lordship's efforts to draw her out further. "There's nothing left to tell, except to give you a catalog of performances. We actors mark the passage of time by the order of the roles we play and the towns where we appear."

While they waited for the ostler at the Star and Garter to harness the horses to his phaeton, she thanked Lord Leafield for an excursion that had been far more enjoyable than she had expected, adding, "How I hate to leave all this behind for crowded, noisy London!"

"We needn't return yet," he said smoothly. "At what hour must you be at the theater?"

"Six o'clock."

"Then we've half the afternoon left to us." He helped her into the vehicle and climbed up to sit beside her. "I know a pleasant place along the river, only a couple of miles distant. I think you'd like it very much."

In no time at all they were bowling along a stretch of road that followed the curves of the Thames. Flora sensed an urgency in him, a kind of suppressed excitement, as if he knew a lovely secret and looked forward to sharing it with her.

Their brief journey ended at a gatehouse. An elderly man, whom the earl greeted by name, emerged and took charge of the phaeton.

"We'll walk the rest of the way," Trevor told Flora as he helped her down from the high carriage.

Wildly curious, she went with him down the drive until they came to a domed white building set in a miniature park. Behind it were flower beds, a trifle overgrown but profusely colorful, and the grassy bank of the river. Taking her by the hand, he led her to the willow grove at the water's edge.

"Faith, but you're a beauty," Trevor breathed, untying the ribbons of her hat and lifting it from her head. A fringe of black curls decorated her brow, and the long ringlets, caught up on either side of her face with silver combs, fell to her shoulders. The coiffure was slightly out of date, but its simple classical lines suited her. "How everyone stared at Richmond—do you ever get used to it? When you look in your mirror, do you see what I do?"

"I'm usually too busy covering my face with rouge and powder to take much notice of how I look," she answered.

Trevor touched her cheek, her temple, then traced the curve of her ear with a gentle forefinger, murmuring, "I was right in thinking this garden a proper setting for you." She was a flower in more than name, for her skin was as white and soft as the petal of a lily, she smelled of roses, and her carnation lips were an invitation to do what he had dreamed of doing for weeks. Her hat slipped to the ground when he took her in his arms, pressing his mouth against hers in a deep, desperate kiss. She moaned softly, and he held her closer still, never thinking she meant to protest his actions.

Pulling away, she asked breathlessly, "Whose house is this? Yours?" He affirmed it with a smile. "And you brought me here for—for this?"

"And a great deal more. My caretaker assured me the painters and plasterers and upholsterers are gone for the day— lucky for us, is it not? Otherwise, it would be necessary to repair to the village inn, where the beds are so lumpy and ill-aired, and complete privacy hard to achieve."

His hand left Flora's waist, trailing slowly and deliciously upward along her torso to cup her breast, and her nipple drew itself into a bud of sensitivity. Standing chest to chest with him made her feel faint; she couldn't think properly. He took advantage of her impaired state and began kissing her again.

For a brief, mad moment she submitted, but then his questing tongue flicked against hers. Shocked and confused, she tried to break free of his embrace. "No—you mustn't."

"Now that I've seen you in the garden," he whispered, "I want to see you in my house. In my bed."

Gazing up at his eager, golden face, Flora said vaguely, "I hardly know you."

"You will. Come, let's go inside."

Flora shook her head in emphatic denial, adding, "I can't—I won't. Did you expect me to lie with you simply because I let you kiss me? If so, you were sadly mistaken." She bent down to retrieve the broad-brimmed hat lying on the grass. "Thank goodness it's not spoiled—otherwise I would have made you buy me another."

"I'll buy you dozens of bonnets," he vowed, "and gowns to go with them. Whatever you ask, Flora, shall be yours."

"I won't be taking anything from you, I don't accept your *carte blanche*," she answered. "Because I am a woman of the world, five-and-twenty years old, and an actress besides, your suggestion doesn't shock me. But I state this very clearly, so you will have no doubt: I've no intention of entering your house. If I'd known your purpose in bringing me to this all but deserted place, lovely though it is, I would never have come. I refuse to be your paramour, Lord Leafield, not even for the space of an afternoon," she declared, standing her ground as he approached her again.

"Is there nothing I can do to change your mind?"

Ignoring his question, she announced coolly, "I wish to return to London."

They walked back to the lodge gates in silence.

"Is there someone else?" Trevor asked. "On the night we met, I saw you watching Allingham in the green room—do you mean to snatch him from Miss Talley?"

"What a poor opinion you have of me, and I can't think what I've done to deserve it." She sighed, tying the bonnet ribbons beneath her chin. "I don't fancy Lord Allingham as a lover, and he interests me only because I knew his grandfather, who dandled me on his knee when I was but a child."

Trevor, disappointed by her unexpected rebuff, was relieved to know that he had no rival. "At the outset of our acquaintance, I warned you that I don't give up easily—I hope you remember that."

"*You* may regard your tenacity as a point of pride, my lord, but in my opinion, it's a most regrettable flaw of character."

Laughing at this sharp assessment, he assisted her into the phaeton.

At dusk that evening, a shabby hackney coach followed the direct route from the West End of London, halting before a vast expanse of market gardens. The passenger, a solitary gentleman, climbed out of the vehicle and said sharply, "Wait for me, and I'll make it worth your while." The driver mumbled unintelligibly and reached for a flask hidden in the folds of his greatcoat.

It was almost dinnertime; the laborers had tied up the last of the young plants and were gathering up their hoes and spades. The young man hurried along one of the pathways that dissected the garden plots, breathing in the scent of damp earth and listening to the murmurs of the menials.

A female voice called out from the shadows, "Oh, Hugh, you did come!"

"Did you doubt me, Emmy?" he asked the girl who materialized in his path.

Her worried face reminded him of the morning she had found him lying in Goodman's Fields. Half drunk he'd been, his face bruised from a fight—the usual coda to a night of carousing—and she had taken him home. She wasn't exactly pretty, for her features were ordinary and her dark hair was thick and unruly. Sometimes, when they lay together in the dark, he could strike sparks by stroking it. Her eyes were big and brown, she had a wide mouth, and even now, with so much on his mind, he was wild to kiss her.

After satisfying his urge, he asked hoarsely, "Did you bring it?"

"Is that the only reason you came? After so many days apart, I thought you'd be glad to see me."

"Glad enough to wish I could see more of you." He reached beneath her figure-concealing shawl, placing one hand on her breast and the other on the leather pouch she clutched. "You've been well? No more sickness in the mornings?"

"No, it passed. But oh, Hugh, I've missed you so!"

Hugh was too busy tipping the contents of her purse into his hand to reply in kind. "I say, Em, is this all?" He frowned down at the jumbled coins and banknotes.

"I used to think five pounds a fortune till I met you. My da's an honest working man, and a thrifty one—p'rhaps I should give it to him."

She snatched at the money, but he had closed his fingers over the cash. "It's mine now."

"And if you keep my money, you'll have to keep me as well, won't you?"

"We'll see about that." Hugh pulled her close again, and she twined her arms around his neck. Eventually he said, "I mean to settle with my former landlady, and I'll pay her enough so she won't remember either of us, if anyone comes asking. We can't continue to meet this way, Em. Trevor isn't above having one of his servants spy on me." Scowling, he released her.

"What is it, Hugh?" The girl placed a consoling hand on his shoulder. "It's not only the earl troubling you."

"Jack Rollins is dead, poor old rogue. What makes it even worse, I told Trevor I'd been staying with him on White Horse Street to cover the fact I'd been with you at my old lodgings. That was enough to make him suspicious. Of what, I can't say, but I don't like his finding out about Rollins so soon—he knew before I did."

"I can't hide my belly from Da much longer."

Hugh patted her arm. "I'll make things right with him as soon as I can, I promise. Here's one piece of good news: Trev is dangling after a pretty chit named Caroline, and he may well have serious intentions. His marriage will set me free, for he'll turn his attention to the begetting of a son and heir who'll make me redundant. Just be patient, Em, and we'll be together soon, you'll see." He gave her a swift parting kiss.

She stood staring after him for a long time. Nearly all the laborers had departed, but the few who remained eyed her so curiously that she ran blindly down one of the paths, hoping none of them had recognized her. If word of tonight's meeting, or its purpose, ever reached her da's ears, he would put a stop to her pin money. Without it, Emmy had no hope at all of seeing Mr. Hugh Cotterell again, whatever right she might have to his visits. And, she reminded herself bitterly, to his support.

7

When came he to this town?

Twelfth Night, V. i.

In spite of working in a theater where impulsive hugs, sly pinches, and playful slaps were common coinage, Flora was unable to dismiss the incident in the riverside garden as readily as she had supposed she might. Her mind often returned to that episode in Twickenham, and she was disturbed by the memory of his lordship's firm embrace and searing kisses. She'd made a mistake in accepting his invitation on such slight acquaintance, and now that she recognized the true purpose of his pursuit she would avoid him.

But he was making that difficult, and the repercussions of his regular appearances in the green room were as uncomfortable as they were unwelcome. Backstage gossip, fueled by Mrs. Ellis and Miss Talley, was so rife that the manager's wife felt it necessary to call upon Flora.

After taking a chair in the front parlor, Julie Forster arranged her fashionable draperies in graceful folds about her and turned her golden head this way and that to give her hostesses a more complete view of her white silk turban. "What do you think?" she asked.

"Charming," replied Esther, somewhat preoccupied with helping her mother hand the cups around.

"It comes from Madame Felice's establishment," Julie said grandly. "You must go to her, Florry, and be sure to tell her I sent you so she'll reduce the price of my next purchase." Leaning forward, she said slyly, "I heard that Lord Leafield is courting you."

Mrs. Tabitha Brooke gasped, her eyes round with amazement. "Oh, my, I had no idea!"

"And Sally Jenkins told me he seems positively smitten."

The widow's mouth dropped open. "You don't say," she murmured, glancing at her lodger. "Flora, dear, is it true?"

Flora assured her landlady that these allegations had no basis in fact. "Fie, Julie," she scolded the tale bearer. "You of all people ought to know better than to trust green-room gossip."

Julie pouted. "Well, you might at least tell me more about Lord Allingham and La Talley. Has he made her an offer yet?"

"Not to my knowledge, but Louise and I aren't in the habit of exchanging confidences." Flora hastened to divert her by asking, "What day has Ben chosen for your removal to Bath?" This was a successful gambit; Julie, distracted by the question, quickly forgot Lord Leafield and began describing the dresses she considered necessary for a stay at the fashionable spa.

That evening Esther Drew revived the discussion of the impending journey. As soon as Flora returned home from the theater she declared, "Ever since Julie was here, I've been thinking how much I, too, would like to exchange London for Bath, which would certainly be healthier for Hartley. My mother plans to visit Margate with my aunt, and I have no strong desire to go with them or to remain in town alone. We might take a nice house together, and I believe Mama has a friend there who can inform us about what's available at this season." They discussed the scheme at length, and after a day of departure was agreed upon Esther asked, "Was Lord Leafield at the theater tonight?"

"With a party of ladies," Flora reported sourly as she massaged her temples. "Louise, who can't keep her eyes off the audience, told me his stage box was crammed with females—a countess and a viscountess and the daughter of one or the other, I forget. She was furious, because during the first interval Baron Allingham left his seat and joined the earl's party and none of them stayed for the afterpiece."

"Your admirer didn't come backstage to pay his respects?"

"No. Thank goodness," Flora added rather belatedly, her cheeks pink.

"I think the Evil Earl is extremely clever. You'd best be careful."

"What do you mean?"

"If Lord Leafield had visited the green room tonight, you'd have forgotten all about it by morning. By not doing so, he has ensured that you will puzzle over his actions, and thus he keeps himself alive in your memory."

With unwonted sharpness, Flora declared that Bath was looking better to her all the time.

Hamlet had enjoyed a mild success, and the new production of *The Critic* was receiving even greater acclaim. It had provoked the ire of its author just as Ben Forster had hoped; vitriol poured forth from Sheridan's pen to be printed in the columns of the newspapers and theater journals. Several of Forster's most prominent performers, Flora among them, suddenly received flattering offers of employment from Drury Lane. Those who had no particular loyalty to their manager decamped for a higher salary at one of the permanently licensed theaters. Most of them remained, choosing the security of a smaller but regular weekly wage over a larger one paid out at irregular intervals. Salaries at the Princess might be less than at the patent houses, but at least the treasurer never fobbed off the players with excuses and false promises when Saturdays came around. Drury Lane was especially notorious for forcing its actors into debt, that state so familiar to its proprietor.

The comings and goings at the smaller theater were so frequent and so many that the company treasurer's ledger began to resemble a schoolboy's mussed copybook as he crossed out the names of the departed and hastily scrawled entries for newcomers. By the week of the actors' benefits, there was much consternation and speculation over who would or would not be on the roster.

Flora chose *In Praise of Parsimony* for benefit night; its cast was still intact. She placed a notice of advertisement in the newspapers and visited all the shops that enjoyed her custom, offering her tickets for sale.

The play had lain dormant for several weeks, so she bullied Ben Forster into scheduling a rehearsal on the day of performance. She set out at her usual hour, and along the way met Sally Jenkins, who emerged from the rutted side street where she lodged with her violinist.

The redhead matched her bouncing, leggy gait to Flora's even steps and with an ostentatious lift to her brows observed, "What, no watchdog Margery trotting behind you today?"

"She and Esther are packing."

Pointedly ignoring the leering drayman who flung a ribald comment in their direction, Sally asked, "Are you nervous about tonight?"

"Nervous, hopeful, fearful—the whole gamut of emotions. I'm only half awake as well, because Horatio's drunken caterwauling woke me at dawn. He must've made a great deal of money from *his* benefit—he was singing beneath my window, and later I heard what sounded like an altercation with the watchman. I don't expect to see him till tonight."

"He'll be at rehearsal, no matter what the state of his poor head," Sally prophesied. "He'd drag himself out of bed for you—or through the gates of hell."

"I fancy this morning they're one and the same." After sidestepping a burly individual, Flora turned to her friend and said, "I'm thoroughly sick of London—nothing but dirt and crowds and noise and smells from the market." She wrinkled her nose in distaste.

Sally laughed. "You can't measure the whole city by Covent Garden! I like London, it's so very gay—especially at night, when every other town comes to a dead halt." She chatted merrily until they reached the theater courtyard, when she suddenly placed one hand on Flora's arm, bringing her to a standstill. "Look," she breathed, her voice tremulous with emotion, as she pointed out the object that had so excited her.

An elegant landaulet with a coachman on the box stood in the muddy yard, its body gleaming with coat upon coat of paint and varnish, the pinnacle of luxury. The actresses watched in fascination as a spectacular vision in primrose silk emerged from the stage door and made her mincing, pouting way to the waiting equipage. It was Louise Talley, who was followed by the stage-door keeper and a liveried footman, both burdened with what Flora and Sally recognized as the personal properties and costumes that had formerly been scattered about Louise's dressing room.

While her minions stowed her belongings in the carriage,

Louise called out, "Good morning. Rather, it's good-bye," she amended, her round face taking on the quality of a feline who had been at the cream. "From now on I'll be performing at the Theatre Royal, Drury Lane. I've been engaged by Sheridan, with the assistance of Lord Allingham," she added with a simper.

A grin replaced the amazement on Sally's freckled face, and she drawled, "Is that so?" She made a sweeping, all-inclusive gesture. "And might this fine turnout be another example of the baron's kindness?"

"Perhaps." Louise lifted her dimpled chin, daring Sally to say more. Then she turned to Flora to say grandly, "My dear, I'm desolated not to be able to take part in your benefit tonight, and of course Allingham will miss it too—I'm making my first appearance at the Lane, and he wants to be there to support me. But you simply *must* come to tea one afternoon to tell me about it. I'm living in Bloomsbury now in a charming house, with servants and everything."

This was no great surprise; Flora had heard the same words many times from the lips of other actresses. And she knew that Louise had no intention of inviting an old rival to her new abode but was merely puffing off the fact of it.

Sally chortled. "The baron has been *very* kind indeed: a house, a carriage, servants, and even a job at Drury Lane. We must congratulate you on your great success, Louise. And Allingham, for I'm sure you'll be worth every penny he pays for your upkeep." Her voice was laced with sarcasm when she added, "But let me offer a little friendly advice: don't give up the stage, or if you do, be sure to put by a few pounds and shillings for a rainy day. He's reputed to be fickle, your baron, and since you've begun with him, you won't want to slide down the social scale too rapidly. Will it be a viscount next time, or only a baronet? And what will it be next year—a brothel?"

"How dare you! Why, you're nothing but a common, drag-gle-tail slut, Sally Jenkins!" cried Louise, her full bosom heaving with wrath and the effects of too-tight lacing. "Everyone knows you live with that violin player, that Fred Stafford person, so you've no cause to insult me!"

"I'm not ashamed, for I've never sold myself, and that's what makes a whore a whore. Good-bye, Louise, and good luck to you. You'll be needing it."

Watching the elegant carriage slog through the thick ooze, Flora sighed, "Poor thing, I almost feel sorry for her."

"What a stupid girl you can be sometimes," was Sally's exasperated comment as the doorkeeper ushered them inside the dim theater. "Louise chose her path and I don't condemn her for that, only for doing you an ill turn. And Ben, too. She came to him with nothing more than a good figure and a saucy manner, and he was clever enough to make her popular. Now she repays him by going over to the enemy, and I have no patience with such base treachery! *Sorry* for her? You ought to be furious, for now she won't be playing Selina in your benefit tonight. And the understudy's voice squeaks so badly that half the sense of the words will be lost."

None of the players received the news of La Talley's defection with regret, and many were heard to mutter, "Good riddance." But everyone echoed Sally's opinion: the most grievous wrong had been desertion at benefit time. Theatrical tradition decreed that all personal disputes should be set aside, and for a brief time camaraderie and general good-will reigned at the close of the season.

Madam Forster, Louise's chief critic, summed up the general feeling by predicting that the actress would soon be earning all of her living on her back and none of it on the boards. Flora's rehearsal suffered a necessary delay—a messenger was summarily dispatched to the understudy's lodgings—and her colleagues entertained themselves with gossip and tea and games of whist.

The postponement was fortunate for Horatio Forster. When he lurched into the green room, Flora was energetically rubbing a piece of bread across a white satin slipper to clean it. "Never mind," she said, interrupting his profuse apologies, "it doesn't matter that you're late. Louise has bolted—to Allingham's bed and Sheridan's theater."

"Has she now?" Horatio glanced around the room. "Then why the long faces? She won't be missed, and this means she won't be going to Bath with us, the tiresome wench."

"Suppose the people demand their money back?"

Flora's companions assured her that these fears were unfounded. The understudy arrived sooner than anyone had expected, harassed and unkempt, as if she'd been dragged from her bed, but when the rehearsal was over even Flora had to agree that Louise would not be much missed. It was far easier to work scenes with an actress who remained in her appointed place instead of constantly creeping around the stage to gain the most advantageous position.

She declined Horatio's playful suggestion that she accompany him to a tavern on Maiden Lane for a feast of oysters and ale, and returned to Great Queen Street. She found Esther in the nursery, and was describing to her the tumultuous events of the morning when Frank intruded, his arms overflowing with flowers.

"Carried here by a footman, ma'am, in a blue coat with brass buttons as large as shilling pieces," he said impressively and not without envy.

Flora, by now familiar with the blue and buff livery of the Leafield House servants, examined the bouquet. Hidden among the hothouse specimens were several white campion blossoms, and she was irrationally touched by the play upon her name. While her friend read the card that accompanied the tribute, she turned to the manservant. "Tell Mary to put these in water—there must be quite enough flowers here to adorn all the downstairs rooms." As he left the room she muttered ominously, "The earl bought up most of the box seats for my benefit."

"Can Julie be right? What if he *should* offer what Louise Talley has—a house and a carriage and—"

"You sound as if you think I ought to accept!"

"Of course not, but you can't deny that it's exciting."

With studied offhandedness, Flora replied, "I am not the least bit flustered—or flattered—by his persistence. Next week I'll be on my way to Bath, Lord Leafield will likely go to Brighton with the rest of society, and the curtain will be rung down on this bizarre episode."

On this defiant note, she swept out of the room, leaving Esther to frown over the earl's card and to inhale the sweet fragrance still lingering in the air.

Four days later, a post coach carrying four weary women and a fretful child arrived in Bath.

After two days on the road, the entire party was exhausted, particularly young Hartley, who had proven himself to be an uncomfortable traveling companion. The vehicle halted before a long row of connected residences, the trunks were deposited on the pavement, and a cook-housekeeper emerged to greet her employers. Mrs. Meeks, a stout soul with a broad, friendly face, dutifully showed them the drawing room, dining parlor, and storerooms on the ground floor. The bedchambers and linen closet were upstairs, with a garret above. The furnishings were simple, neither new nor terribly worn, and the beds were sufficiently comfortable to induce sleep almost at once.

The new day was young when Flora and Esther received their first caller. Horatio Forster found them at the breakfast table; Flora was still wearing her paisley dressing gown. He bussed her cheek, then demanded the same privilege of Mrs. Drew. "Your first day in Bath, and you haven't made your pilgrimage to the Pump Room? Our Julie is there now, you may be sure."

"I'm more interested in seeing the theater," Flora said candidly.

"Dearest one, I would be delighted to escort you to Orchard Street," he told her. "In fact, Ben is waiting for me there—the wagon carrying our properties and stock wardrobe is due to arrive this morning. Let us go at once."

His black eyes included Esther, who shook her head, saying all she cared to do was to laze the morning away and perhaps call on her mother's friend in the afternoon. Flora excused herself to change, and when she returned Horatio was describing the farewell dinner given to his brother by the management committee.

"Have you heard?" he asked Flora jovially. "We're going on holiday soon. Julie has persuaded Ben to spend a month at Brighton, and you're invited to join us."

"Hasn't she seen enough of the seaside?" Flora wondered. "We used to play at the theater on Duke Street every winter."

"Oh, our Julie was a working girl in those days," he reminded her with a broad wink. "Now she's a lady of leisure, wife of a rising theater manager, and as such will command respect at a fashionable resort."

Esther Drew shook her head, smiling at Mrs. Forster's pretensions. "I suppose she means to be very genteel while in Bath, if she's taking the waters every day and parading in the Pump Room."

This program sounded dull to Flora, but it was also the sort of nonsense that most appealed to Julie Forster, whose retirement from the stage, subsequent motherhood, and love of fashion left the two women with nothing in common but a fondness for Ben Forster.

The elegant matron had cut short her visit to the Pump Room to accompany her husband to the theater, and she greeted Flora with pleasure, casting her knowledgeable eyes over the actress's attire.

"But my dear," she declared in shocked accents, "you mustn't go about in that plain pelisse! And that antiquated fichu—really, now! That's last year's gown, too, don't bother to deny it."

"No one else in Bath will know," Flora murmured, adjusting the white neck-handkerchief tucked into the bodice. Her cambric gown was a favorite, and she was too accustomed to this sort of criticism to take offense.

"I'll take you to the shops," Julie said decisively. "Ben says you cleared over a hundred pounds from your benefit, so you can't plead poverty as an excuse for going about so shabbily dressed."

"My money is safely deposited with my banker in London, so neither you nor the Bath shops will tempt me to loosen my purse strings. A subscription to the circulating library and a new trimming for my best bonnet will be the limit to my expenditures."

"Oh, do let's go to Milsom Street! I depend on you to keep me company today—Madam is visiting old Mr. Siddons, and Ben will be here for hours yet. I can show you our house on

Trim Street—the children will love to see you. Sam asked me this morning when Florry was coming, and baby Julia is saying whole words now!"

Only five days had passed since Flora had last seen the two young Forsters, but she raised no objection. Horatio went with them, and where the pavements were narrow or too crowded for three persons, he fell behind and sauntered along in their wake. When they paused at a library so Flora could pay her subscription fee, the actor joined the other gentlemen loungers.

After touring the shops and taking tea with Julie, Flora returned to her own lodgings. Upon being informed by Mrs. Meeks that Esther and Margery were away, she gathered up some writing paper and carried it to the sitting room to compose a letter to her brother.

Because it had been many weeks since Flora had written Miles, line after line flowed from her pen. She described her recent activities, told him of the riches her benefit had provided, and even described the enmity of London's theater managers, for she invariably told him the bad along with the good. Despite this habit of full disclosure, she sat idle for several minutes, tickling her chin with the point of her quill as she pondered whether or not to tell him about her most notable admirer. In the end, she wrote only that she had encountered several distinguished persons, the Earl of Leafield and Lord Allingham among them.

The more impressive of the two titles stood out on the page, and she stared down at it with strange fascination. Had he truly been determined to prove his cousin's marriage, or had that only been a ruse to lure her to his bed? Was he presently chasing after some other, more willing female? She had no way to know. In which case, she chided herself, she ought not to care.

After she finished her letter she left it unsealed, thinking Esther might add a few lines to Captain Drew at the bottom. She reached for a pen wiper as the door knocker sounded below. Supposing that it heralded the return of Horatio, she told Mrs. Meeks to admit her visitor and send him upstairs.

A few minutes later she looked up to find a tall gentleman silhouetted in the doorway, watching her. The quill fell from her fingers. "What the devil are *you* doing here?" she cried as the Earl of Leafield executed one of his polished bows in her direction.

"From your expression, I assume that the devil would be a great deal more welcome. I actually hoped you would be *glad* to see me."

She rose hastily, outraged to find him in Bath just when she had been thinking herself well and truly free of him. Raising one hand to her head, as though she had received a stunning blow, she moaned, "Oh, no." She wavered slightly on her feet, then crumpled to the floor.

8

If you can separate yourself and your misdemeanors,
You are welcome to the house.

Twelfth Night, II. iii.

Kneeling beside the fallen lady's limp form, Trevor parted the snowy scarf tucked into her bodice. When he placed one hand on the warm flesh of her bosom, it rose and fell erratically, indicating extreme agitation, as did the strong and tumultuous heartbeat. Her face was unusually flushed for an unconscious person.

"Is this an attempt to hoax me?" he murmured before bestowing a restorative kiss.

Flora struggled to sit up. "How could you—the housekeeper might have walked in!"

He released her with a regretful sigh. "Still so cruel?"

The ready answer fell from lips still throbbing from the firm, familiar pressure of his. "Still so constant, my lord," she replied, trying to appear as cool and composed as Countess Olivia, whom she had quoted. She avoided his amused and mocking gaze as she straightened her fichu and smoothed her tumbled hair.

"You are unhurt?" he asked.

"I learned the trick of falling years ago. The only damage will be to my gown, as I don't usually expire without the carpet of tragedy." Seeing that he was puzzled by her reference, she explained, "The green baize cloth that covers the stage floor during a tragic play has a practical use: it keeps our clothes from being soiled in the death scenes. In *Hamlet*, or *Macbeth*, the bodies pile up fast and furiously, and the carpet is a necessary comfort. Costumes are costly." She twisted around to get a rear view, which eluded her. Presenting her back to him, she asked worriedly, "Did I dirty my gown?"

After a very thorough inspection of her posterior, Trevor informed her that she had not.

"I shouldn't have greeted you by falling at your feet, but I couldn't resist the temptation. I've played so many madwomen lately that my own wits have become somewhat addled." After inviting him to be seated, she gazed at him curiously. "How did you know where to find me? *My* name wasn't included in the list of new arrivals in the morning paper."

"I chanced to meet Mr. Forster—the younger one—on Bath Street today, and he gave me the happy news of your recent arrival. Hugh and I are playing a long overdue visit to our aunt, who resides on Sydney Place. A most convenient circumstance, now that you are also here." He placed one hand over his heart.

His loverlike gesture alarmed her only a little less than the kiss. In a carefully disinterested voice, she asked how long he would be in town.

"That depends upon you."

"I don't understand."

Said he, a trifle impatiently, "If you recall our discussion at Twickenham, you'll know why I've dragged myself to Bath at this benighted season."

"And if you do the same," Flora shot back, "you would remember that I was firm in my refusal." She crossed to the window, striving to maintain the frigid disinterest she'd cultivated ever since their impromptu excursion to his riverside villa, where he'd made his intentions plain. After marshaling her thoughts, she faced him again and said, "I didn't take to the stage for the purpose of parading my wares to noblemen. I'd have made it clearer to you when we first met, but I never supposed that you would carry me off to your house without a by-your-leave, as if I were a common strumpet."

"I scarcely gave your reputation a thought, not being aware that it was so much at risk."

Deeply affronted, she gasped, "What a horrid thing to say!"

"I didn't mean it unkindly." He extracted a piece of paper from his pocket and held it out to her. Smiling, he said, "Not *carte blanche*, my dear Flora, but a notice for the newspaper. I'd like you to look it over."

" 'To the young woman who contracted a secret alliance with a young gentleman, Mr. H. C.,' " she read aloud. " 'The aforementioned lady, by presenting herself at the offices of R. P. Linton, the Strand, with proofs of the marriage, may lay claim to a handsome reward, entitling her to a future of independence and security.' "

When she returned the paper to him, he told her, "That advertisement will be printed in the *Times* and the *London Gazette*."

"Both are easily had here in Bath," Flora pointed out. "Suppose Mr. Cotterell sees it?"

"The risk was one Linton and I chose to take, knowing that Hugh seldom reads the papers. Of course, his wife may be similarly disinclined. In the meantime, I've formed yet another plan to spur his confession, which requires your assistance. I offer the same terms I did last time—name your price and I'll meet it. You shall have new clothes, fine jewels, whatever you desire if only you'll visit Combe Cotterell and encourage my cousin to ingratiate himself with you."

"Are you so sure that he would try?"

Trevor's lip curled. "Married men are the most debauched fellows of all, surely you know that without my telling you. Yes, I'm convinced you can coax the truth out of him within a very short time."

"You want me to be your spy!"

"I suppose that's an accurate description," he agreed.

"I can think of others, all of them equally base."

"Oh, I don't mean for you to become his mistress," he said audaciously. "Not when I continue to cherish hopes of my own."

Flora approached his chair. "Lord Leafield, won't you *please* call a halt to these games of yours and let me be? In a few weeks I depart for Brighton with the Forsters, and until then I'll be very busy at the Orchard Street theater."

"But you won't always be working, will you? Like me, you'll surely need a pleasant diversion while you're in Bath."

"I don't want to be your 'diversion.' "

"Couldn't you be my friend?" he persisted.

"People would be bound to talk, as they did in London, and

I loathe being the subject of gossip and speculation. Don't you?"

"No one gossips about Lumley Skeffington. He haunts the theaters, and not only does he pay court to the actors and actresses, he also passes himself off as a playwright. Not," he said consideringly, "that I have any ambition to do the same. You're an intelligent and talented woman—that's just as obvious as your valentine of a face—and I happen to prefer your company to that of Mrs. Siddons."

"Mrs. Siddons could be your mother, my lord. Not a soul will say that of me, you may be sure." Placing her hands on a chair back, she continued, "You speak as if you can suddenly decree us friends and it is done, but friendships can't be forced, or ordained. They grow."

But she was already weakening. Didn't her long association with Horatio prove that a man and a woman could sustain a platonic relationship? To say nothing of the great Dr. Johnson and Mrs. Piozzi, or Mrs. Siddons and Thomas Lawrence. But perhaps the latter pair made a poor example; some mildly suggestive rumors had circulated about the famous tragedienne and the noted portrait painter, although at one time he'd been suitor to her daughters.

"Oh, very well," she said at last, "I accept your offer of friendship, but only conditionally. You must forget everything that happened at Twickenham, and you will cease to badger me about joining your summer house party in Devonshire."

Trevor stepped forward to clasp her hand, pledging himself to uphold these terms. "As you wish." She must have been satisfied, for he had no difficulty convincing her to accompany him to Sydney Gardens the next day, after her rehearsal.

When he left Westgate Buildings he made his way through the town to the graceful Florentine bridge over the Avon. Pulteney Street extended to the park, bounded on each side by Sydney Place. As he approached one of the newer houses its door was opened to him by a footman who relieved him of his hat and cane, saying, "Her ladyship is in the sitting room, my lord."

The strong resemblance between the Countess Ainsley and her nephews could be traced in the firm jaw, aquiline nose, and hazel eyes, but ill health had taken its toll of her looks. Her complexion was sallow, and her mouse-brown hair was liberally flecked with gray.

"My dear Trevor, you've been away quite a time," she observed as the earl entered her sunny sanctuary. "What have you been doing?"

"I looked in at the Pump Room, stopped at Meyler and Sons, and wandered about the Abbey Churchyard. And then," he added on a triumphant note, "I called upon Miss Flora Campion."

Lady Ainsley sat up straighter in her chair, her blue-veined hands gripping the arms. "You have come to terms with her?"

"Not yet." Lowering his voice, Trevor asked, "Is Hugh at home?"

"Heavens no, he's hardly the sort to sit with an ailing lady all day," she replied, but without a trace of self-pity. "Tell me about Miss Campion."

"She's as lovely as ever, and just as stubborn. I believe her contract with Forster expires at the end of July, and it could well take me till then to convince her to visit Combe Cotterell. At present she is contemplating a trip to Brighton instead."

"When shall I see her?"

"If you peek through your drawing-room window tomorrow afternoon, you might catch a glimpse of her. She agreed to walk with me in the gardens, and if I can overcome her inherent distrust of designing noblemen to that extent, I think we need not doubt a happy conclusion to this business."

Her ladyship's fond expression gave way to a concerned frown. "Trevor, you will have a care, won't you? The creature may be playing a game as deep as your own."

"Never fear, ma'am, the little play actress can't do me a particle of harm. I have everything to gain and nothing to lose, whereas she, poor girl, must always be on her guard against me. I have influence, I have money, and I am a man. Any one of those would be enough to ruin her, and the combination is formidable if used against her—or exerted in her favor." But he rather doubted that Flora Campion feared him, and she appeared to possess more good sense than he would have liked in his victim.

In the firm voice that was at odds with her frail appearance, Lady Ainsley warned him, "Whatever your position, it's not wise to make a policy of turning other people's lives upside down to suit your convenience. If Miss Campion won't help you, hire some other pretty actress to seduce the truth from Hugh, or alter the succession by some other means."

"How?" he asked grimly. "By proposing marriage to the first presentable female who crosses my path?"

"Well," her ladyship replied, "you might at least wait until the Batsfords return from London. I have heard that their daughter Caroline is still unattached."

By the end of Flora's first week in Bath, she was in love.

She could only suppose that those persons who had described the city as dull, staid, and gossipy were hopelessly hard to please, for she admired its architecture, from the abbey to the public buildings, and especially the terraces and crescents that draped themselves so gracefully upon the surrounding hills. London had been a hodgepodge of stone-built and stuccoed dwellings flung up beside brick ones in a mix of styles, but the buildings of Bath were characterized by a pleasing uniformity. Nearly all had been built in the last century from a local stone that gleamed like gold in the summer sun.

Lord Leafield met her on Orchard Street after her first rehearsal and escorted her across the Pulteney Bridge to the pleasure gardens on the other side of the Avon, which he likened to a miniature Vauxhall. This analogy fell short, for Flora had never visited London's famed gardens, but because she had no measure against which to judge, Bath's version couldn't suffer by comparison. It was composed of velvety bowling greens, several pleasant arbors, cool labyrinths of shrubbery, and swings. An outdoor concert was in progress, and they strolled the banks of the canal to the faint accompaniment of chamber music. Punts crammed with merrymakers glided across the water; pretty girls darted in and out of the trees, pursued by their eager swains. Lord Leafield explained that despite the spa's reputation for stodginess, its young people enjoyed a greater freedom than did their counterparts in London.

Bath was a melting pot of humanity, and no longer the resort of preference for the wealthy and titled. Merchants, half-pay officers, and professional men had settled there with their families, as had those persons whose ill health made them dependent on the medical men, mineral waters, and hot baths. Although Julie Forster searched the weekly papers for the names of new arrivals, the number of aristocrats in residence mattered little to Flora, who only hoped there were enough playgoers to fill the Orchard Street theater.

From the first night *The Rivals* played to a crowd, for its Bath setting made it popular with the locals. Flora considered Lydia Languish the most foolish of heroines, but at each performance the old theater rang with the public's appreciation of the even sillier Mrs. Malaprop and the many mistaken identities.

All in all she was content, but during one of Horatio's regular visits to Westgate Buildings, she voiced her single source of frustration.

"When will we ever be finished with this dratted play and move on to something else?" she wailed. "I'm sick to death of it, and so must you be, for I swear Captain Absolute is just as idiotic as Lydia."

"A good thing old Sheridan can't hear you!" The actor lowered the loose pages of the manuscript he'd been reading. "I'm afraid you won't like Mr. Jones's latest work any better. The author may claim that *Callista, or the Melancholy Maiden* is better than *In Praise of Parsimony* or *The Inconstant Lady*, but to me they're much the same."

She approached the sofa and Horatio handed her a few loose sheets. After a cursory glance at the speeches and stage directions, she sighed. "'If 'twere played upon a stage, I would condemn it as an improbable fiction.' But I suppose if we think it stupid, it's sure to be a hit." She flung herself into a chair. "*Must* we sit about with nothing to amuse us but Mr. Jones's masterpiece? Let's go somewhere—I'm deadly dull today."

Horatio's black eyes hardened and his deep-timbered voice lacked its usual teasing note when he said, "I was forgetting that you are accustomed to more exalted society than that of a humble actor. Should I deck myself out in pantaloons and fancy waistcoats and drag a gold-topped walking stick around every time I step out of my door? I'm not sure I can keep up to your new standard in gentlemen friends, Florry love."

"I only meant—"

"And naturally," he interrupted with his expert sarcasm, "like your other admirer, I ought to shower you with compliments and spout quizzical nonsense all the day long."

"That's exactly what you *are* doing," was Flora's acid comment. "Am I to infer from this invective that you are jealous of Lord Leafield?"

"Have I some cause to be jealous?" he asked, his voice rising with the question. "I can't help worrying, for I've always had the impression that you abhorred the sort of connection that Leafield clearly has in mind."

"You can't judge every other man by your own depraved self," she pointed out venomously. That Horry, who knew her best, should be the first to sully her new intimacy with Lord Leafield with suspicion was more than she could bear. And he had reminded her of the earl's attempt to seduce her in the garden of his villa, an incident that still figured prominently in her traitorous memory. "Why must you imagine the worst? I'm a grown woman, not some ignorant little child to be guarded from the whole bad world by a pack of Forsters!"

"Is that so? Well, I thought it right to give you a hint that some people—your *true* friends, I might add—are beginning to wonder at the curious change in your attitude," he told her, his face flushed. "And if you're not careful, you'll soon hear me say, 'I told you so.' "

Flora's wrath blazed. Reaching for the nearest object, a calf-bound book from the circulating library, she hurled it at him with all the force in her arm.

He caught it neatly. "Practicing to play Kate the Shrew?" he sneered.

"Go to the devil!" she advised him at the top of her lungs, and without another word, he stalked out of the house.

The next person to court her displeasure was Esther Drew.

When she arrived home from the theater, burdened with one of the generous bouquets Lord Leafield sometimes provided, the young matron looked up from her needlework to remark, "Isn't it imprudent to encourage this friendship that seems to have sprung up between you and the evil earl like a mushroom in the night?"

Flora, knowing that to answer one question with another was a useful device, asked coolly, "You don't like him?"

"I don't know him well enough to form an opinion, and you can hardly know him much better," said Esther. "Oh, I grant you, he's a gentleman of distinction, and very attractive, but his following you to Bath and singling you out as he does encourages gossip."

"There's no scandal in walking with Lord Leafield in a public pleasure garden and driving up to Landsdown in his phaeton. Or letting him once—only once, mind you—escort me home when we chanced to meet on High Street."

"But he stayed quite half an hour afterwards. And if you've forgotten that he visited your dressing room three times this week and sat through a rehearsal, Margery hasn't; she told me." Esther stabbed her needle into the fabric. "You seemed reluctant to receive him the first time he called on you in London. And as I recall, the day he drove you to Richmond, I could hardly get you out of the house and into his carriage. When he engaged the seats for your benefit, you said—"

"Have you been keeping a tally?" Flora interrupted, feigning an amusement she didn't feel.

"I'm sure you care next to nothing for what I may think, or what Julie thinks—and she has been very vocal on the subject, you may be sure. But what about Miles? I don't think he would be pleased to know his sister is keeping company with a nobleman who pays her dubious court—no man would. Does he know?"

"Yes," Flora answered with quiet dignity. "I have nothing to conceal."

Esther reached for her scissors and cut a thread. As she smoothed out the new seam in her son's short coat, she said, "You think I'm meddling, but I do feel very strongly that you should keep away from Lord Leafield."

"What harm can he do? If you object simply because he's a

man and I'm not, I must remind you that Horatio and I are also close."

"You and Horatio share a profession, and you have the same interests and background."

"How inconsistent!" Flora trilled. "Horry has a *terrible* reputation—he's a notorious rake."

Esther said quietly, "He wouldn't compromise you. He still loves you, as I'm sure you know."

His erratic behavior seemed to prove this, but Flora shied from admitting it to herself. "I've never set myself up as an arbiter of morals, or criticized the way others choose to behave. Now that everyone is doing it to me, and over such a simple thing, I find it most disagreeable. The Earl of Leafield is witty and amusing, and very good company. I never imagined that someone unconnected with the theater could be so—so interesting."

And before Esther could make another irritating comment, or further disparage her new friend, Flora took herself off to bed.

9

Well, I will be so much a sinner, to be a double dealer.

Twelfth Night, V. i.

A ferocious storm descended upon Bath one morning, turning the creamy stone buildings to dull gray and wetting the streets and pavements. Pedestrians hurried home for their umbrellas, and many remained there, postponing their shopping expeditions and visits to the Pump Room.

The rain continued all week. On the first day of bad weather, Flora and a sneezing Esther huddled by the fire or took turns standing at the parlor window to watch the diminished traffic below. By the next day they were resigned to indoor pursuits, and passed the time reading the latest novel from the circulating library and playing with the baby. In the evening, Flora strapped on her pattens for the short but wet walk to the theater, with Margery holding the umbrella over both their heads.

One damp afternoon Mrs. Forster's manservant brought the ladies an invitation to an afternoon party, and Flora was tempted by the promise of tea and cakes and theatrical gossip. Julie's entertainment would be no different from any leisurely hour in the green room, except that the actresses would wear their best gowns and gentlemen would be absent. But anything was better than spending another day in Westgate Buildings, so she left Esther to nurse a sore throat and walked to Trim Street.

A babel of tongues—the Scots brogue, the singsong accents of Wales, the lilt of Hibernia, and the plebian dialects of London's boroughs—battled for supremacy as her peers welcomed her. Julie greeted her warmly, nodding approval of her lemon-hued gown, and accepting Esther's regrets with a sigh. Flora had no desire to sit down at a whist table, so she paid her respects to Madam Forster, impressively attired in maroon satin and her customary turban as she held court from a rosewood settee.

The great lady was describing her recent visit to William Siddons. "Poor man, his legs are very bad, and he's completely chair-bound, with only his cats and his memories to keep him company. But I told him, 'Siddons, the world may talk, but as I see it, your separation from Sarah was the wisest decision of your life.' And do you know what he said?"

Madam Forster's audience waited, hushed and expectant, but she was too experienced a performer to give immediate satisfaction. She sipped her tea, glanced around the room, and drew a breath before saying, "He answered, 'Eulalia, thirty years of marriage is a tie that cannot be broken, but 'tis best we live apart. I am a poor thing now, and she was ever too grand a creature for the likes of me.'"

Sally Jenkins chortled. "From all I ever heard, he was a worthless husband and not much of an actor, either!" Before Madam could rebuke her, she added defiantly, "Well, he did lose a great deal of his wife's money through poor advice and bad investments."

The older woman nodded her turbaned head and agreed that it was too true. "But he has been a support through Sarah's many trials—the deaths of their daughters were the worst of them—and he stayed by her side during a scandal or two. They're on friendly terms still, for he visits her in London when his health permits, and she comes to Bath between her professional engagements."

The topic of Mrs. Siddons's marital affairs was abandoned, and other items of theatrical dirty laundry were aired. Sally, who cared little for the past, only the present, sidled over to Flora and whispered, "Never once have I heard of a marriage that didn't make me vow and swear to remain single so long as I'm on the stage! I'll not hand over my earnings to a husband, or mother his bairns all day in addition to slaving on the stage by night. Far better to live in sin, if you ask me!"

Flora pointed out the flaw in her reasoning with a reminder that the absence of a wedding band didn't preclude the possibility of motherhood.

"Oh, there are ways and means," Sally replied, her blue eyes twinkling. "Just ask Eliza Ellis if you ever need to know."

"Pooh, I can't believe any of her tricks are infallible. Actresses in keeping send for the midwife regularly; it's an occupational hazard. Think of Mrs. Jordan: never wed and she has twelve—no, now it's thirteen children—ten of them by her royal consort."

Sally said carelessly, "Mrs. Jordan is as good as married to her jolly sailor duke. It's no secret he depends on her for money, his family is so stingy and he so expensive. I suspect she'd rather retire, but because his grace of Clarence hasn't the wherewithal to provide for so many offspring, she must keep slogging away. I'll bet a guinea he has the poor soul back on the stage come September."

"Done! For I believe she has already given up acting."

When Julie took up a newspaper and read aloud an account of a splendid private party at the Countess Ainsley's home on Sydney Place, Flora's conversation with Sally tapered off. The list of notable guests and the detailed descriptions of the ladies' toilettes elicited sighs of envy from the actresses, and her mind wandered back to Lord Leafield's brief, bored reference to his aunt's entertainment, which had kept him away from the theater one night. According to the paper, he'd opened the glittering ball by dancing with Lady Caroline Lewes.

"'The young ladyship,'" Julie read in dulcet tones, "'wore white sarsenet with a gauze overdress trimmed in seed pearls sewn in a floral pattern.' It must have cost her mama a fortune!"

One bright morning the earl called on Flora with the intention of taking her on a tour of the surrounding countryside. When she exhibited reluctance, he assured her that he owned no villa in the environs of Bath and further enticed her with a description of the famous standing stones at Stanton Drew.

During the drive, Flora played with her parasol uncertainly, as though it were a new and unfamiliar stage prop. From time to time she drew her eyes from their pastoral surroundings to look over at her companion, noting how the sunshine intensified the red tints in his hair and the russet coat complimented his broad shoulders. Keeping her lashes discreetly lowered, she traced the muscles of his legs, clearly visible through the doeskin breeches. As the product of a community in which physical attributes were noticed and commented on—and bartered—she couldn't help but be aware of the face and form of a man so splendidly endowed. His motive for continuing to seek her out was still a mystery, and she sometimes warned herself that her growing fascination with him was as foolish as it might prove dangerous.

"How does *Callista, or the Melancholy Maiden* progress?" he asked while they strolled among the massive rocks rising up from the village common.

"Slowly," she sighed. "There was a quarrel between Sally Jenkins and Mrs. Logan at our last rehearsal over a bit of staging more beneficial to one than the other."

"Your friend Miss Jenkins I know, but which lady is Mrs. Logan?"

"She played Mrs. Malaprop in *Rivals*, but under a different name," Flora explained. "On the playbill she's Mrs. Walsh, but we call her Mrs. Logan."

He looked away from the tallest and most impressive monolith to ask, "And why is that?"

"Despite the fact that she and Mr. Logan have lived together forever, he already has a wife in Ireland, and because he belongs to the Roman Church there is no possibility of a divorce. So Mrs. Logan is actually Miss Walsh, being a single lady, but we call her 'Mrs.' as a professional courtesy and 'Logan' for the sake of the children. They have five."

His hearty laughter made some of the grazing sheep move nervously away. "It's a wonder you can keep it straight. Not many of your colleagues are wed, are they?"

"Mrs. Ellis is, though I think she'd rather *not* be," Flora said frankly. "And Ben. Sally prefers not to marry into the profession, and like poor Mrs. Logan, who would if she could, she must live by a different code of behavior."

"And what is your code?" he inquired, no longer smiling.

"To give my best performance, and make Ben proud," she answered promptly.

* * *

Hugh Cotterell paced his aunt's parlor impatiently, desperate to know the outcome of his cousin's drive into the countryside. He'd remained at Sydney Place all afternoon in the expectation that Trevor would return as an engaged man, for his courtship of Lady Caroline had progressed to the point that this was entirely possible. Lord and Lady Batsford were giving a party at their Grosvenor Place mansion on that very night, a perfect opportunity to announce their daughter's forthcoming marriage.

Hearing his cousin's tread, he stuck his head into the hallway and called, "Come have some brandy, Trev, and tell me about your outing. Did you have a pleasant drive?"

"Quite," Trevor answered as he entered the parlor. "Miss Campion had a fancy to visit the Druidical stones at Stanton Drew."

"Miss Campion," Hugh repeated dully. "But I thought—damn it, Trev, what kind of game are you playing?"

The earl's face was impassive as he picked up the brandy decanter, and his voice was cool when he said, "I'm not sure I know what you mean."

"Lady Caroline Lewes, Miss Flora Campion, and Mrs. Martha Harris. You've danced attendance on all three of 'em since we arrived in Bath. If your intentions toward her ladyship are honorable, I can't fathom why you go to the widow's house every night, and continue to chase after that black-haired wench from the Orchard Street playhouse."

"Miss Campion is damnably elusive," Trevor replied. "So I have taken advantage of my unstructured but long-standing arrangement with Mrs. Harris."

Hugh shook his head in disgust, and a stray lock of hair fell across his brow.

"Do I detect censure in your countenance? Where the fair sex is concerned, *your* reputation can hardly be described as stainless, Hugh."

The younger man glared at him before charging out of the room.

If Hugh only knew the truth, his cousin thought, he would be even more confused.

Trevor had learned to value the chaste friendship he had sought so selfishly, for Flora Campion was an ideal companion—bright, entertaining, and capable of discussing weighty subjects as well as frivolous ones. She spoke her mind freely and never balked at expressing an opinion—not even when it ran counter to his—and he found her frankness appealing and attractive. But greatly though he admired her strength of mind and character, he was amazed by her devotion to her work, and the demands it placed upon her.

In the past, watching a play from the comfortable distance of a box seat, an actor's life had looked easy. He'd dismissed the popular stories about Mrs. Siddons fainting in the wings after a performance as apocryphal, the puffery of a greedy manager anxious to fill his house. But lately he had seen Flora's colleagues stagger off the stage, stunned by fatigue, concerned only with changing out of their costumes and returning to their lodgings for much-needed rest. Others, full of energy and exhilarated by the performance, would laugh and chatter away, and they usually repaired to the nearest tavern for food and drink and good fellowship. Trevor could never predict to which group Flora would belong on a given night. Sometimes when he met her in the green room she could hardly hold up her end of a conversation; on other nights she seemed quite unaffected by her labors.

During one visit to her tiny dressing room, he had shifted one of her costumes from a chair, a blue gown so heavy that he asked how she could wear it for nearly four hours. "No wonder poor mad Ophelia is dragged down to a watery death," he had commented. "This must weigh a full stone."

"By the end of an evening it seems like more!" she'd answered. "Ben has been infected with Kemble's passion for historical accuracy, and we players suffer in our velvets and brocades and stiff petticoats. Margery haunts the secondhand shops and hoards every scrap of interesting or antique material she can find. But the more trimming a dress has, the greater the likelihood that something will come loose or fall off. She earns her wage, you may be sure."

It troubled Trevor that Flora should feign insanity and death night after night, and though he could only guess at the effort required for the part of Ophelia, he suspected that there was an emotional toll as well as a physical one. But she joked about the mad scenes, and in reply to one of his queries she laughed and said, "I quite enjoy my funeral in *Hamlet*. While I'm stretched out on Ophelia's bier and Horry and Ben are dueling over me, I usually decide what I'm going to wear the next day!"

Ironically, the life she led was a sheltered one, the very antithesis of the wild romp he had once supposed it to be. And though Trevor coveted both the daytime and the evening hours she spent on Orchard Street, at the same time he had a contradictory desire to further her career, to help her reach the pinnacle of success that he believed to be the sum of every player's dreams.

After puzzling over the matter for some time, he finally decided upon the perfect scheme, one that had the added advantage of placing her in his debt.

Very early one starry summer morning, the Earl of Leafield and Horatio Forster exited one of Bath's popular taverns, arm in arm and laughing uproariously.

Grasping a lamppost to steady himself, the actor asked, "Where to next, m'lord?"

"Bed," was Trevor's reply.

His companion responded with a wicked grin. "If any man can find a brothel in a town as stuffy as this one, it's me. But you must swear not to mention it to my Florry, because I hope—because she might—well, you can't say anything to her," Horatio concluded sheepishly.

"I'm not going with you. I just remembered," said Trevor in a voice of wonder at having forgotten, "that I've got an appointment in the Crescent."

"Which Crescent? Bath has scores of 'em," the actor called after him.

The walk and the night air failed to improve his disordered senses, but Trevor managed to reach the heights of Lansdown Crescent without any mishap. Removing a key from his waistcoat pocket, he let himself into one of the terrace houses and ascended its curving staircase slowly and unsteadily, relying on the handrail and overcompensating for the height of the risers.

A blonde female in a nightgown of nearly transparent material waited for him in her candlelit bedchamber. As she guided him toward the bed, he mumbled an apology and stretched out, his heavy eyelids shutting out the revolving walls and furniture.

Several hours later, Trevor was roused from slumber by a shove. He turned unfocused eyes upon the person bending over him—not the dark-haired beauty who had figured in his fevered dreams. Her dressing gown gaped open, and while Trevor waited for his vision to clear he inspected her voluptuous charms dispassionately.

Evidently she'd received the wrong impression, because she shook her head, saying, "There's no time for that, my lord. I'm expecting visitors, and if you meet them on the doorstep, you'll ruin my reputation, you will."

Trevor knew it was too late for his hostess to harbor concerns of that sort. How his head ached—it was all Horatio's fault, damn him. "What's the time, m'dear?" he muttered.

"Something past ten." The lady sat down at her dressing table to brush out her honey-colored hair. "I thought it might be best to let you sleep it off."

"Was I very drunk?"

"I've seen worse."

Too late he realized that it was most ungallant of him to admit that he couldn't recall what had or had not occurred in the widow's curtained bed.

He left Landsdown Crescent in a hackney, wincing as its wheels met each rut in the uneven street. His discomfort went beyond his throbbing temples and parched mouth; he couldn't rid himself of the suspicion that he'd treated someone abominably last night, perhaps several people, himself included. He had failed his mistress by visiting her in an inebriated state. The wisdom of keeping a mistress in so gossipy and insular a place as Bath was questionable, particularly during his courtship of Lady Caroline Lewes. As for Flora Campion—he tried to convince himself that she was the only person he hadn't betrayed, but the effort made his head ache all the more. He needed to see her, to explain—but somewhere between High Street and Laura Place he decided it might be wiser to let someone else deliver the happy news that had prompted last night's celebratory excesses.

10

But come what may, I do adore thee so
That danger shall seem sport, and I will go.

Twelfth Night, II. i.

"I plan to accompany Julie to the Pump Room this morning,"
Flora announced when she joined Esther at the breakfast table.
"Why don't you join us?"

The young woman raised shining brown eyes from the letter
she had been reading. "James expects the *Vestal* to return in
September—isn't it wonderful? He's been at sea a year and a
half, he hasn't even met his son! And he's bringing back prize
money, for they lately seized a French privateer and a pair of
American vessels."

"What news of Miles?" Flora asked eagerly.

"My husband slanders him terribly, accusing him of having
flirts in every port. Apparently a Barbados sweetheart has been
supplanted by a pretty planter's daughter in Jamaica. I wonder
if anything will come of it?"

"Not if they're sailing for England—my brother inevitably
makes a clean break before weighing anchor."

Their conversation ended with the arrival of Mrs. Benedict
Forster, splendidly attired in a jonquil bombazine pelisse and a
feathered bonnet.

Many residents were required by their physicians to take a
glass of tepid, sulphurous water in the morning, so the Pump
Room was bustling even at that early hour. Flora was thankful
when Julie wearied of promenading and edged toward an alcove with some chairs strategically placed for viewing the assembly, though the music coming from the orchestra gallery
overhead hampered conversation.

"There's that dreadful Mrs. Harris—they say she sometimes
receives a certain nobleman with whom you are acquainted."

The same disturbing rumor had reached Flora earlier in the week. Eliza Ellis, jealous of her success as Ophelia, had been the first to inform her that Lord Leafield had a mistress.

"Here comes the Countess of Batsford with her daughter, Lady Caroline Lewes," Julie announced. "There was a grand ball at their house on Grosvenor Place this week; did you see the notice in the *Chronicle*?"

Flora murmured a negative reply before asking, "Which is Lady Caroline?"

"The one dressed all in white. Such a lovely complexion, and the prettiest chestnut curls! I saw her in a millinery on Bath Street the other day, trying on hats."

Flora's eyes sought the lady so described, a fragile fairy figure in foamy gauze. Did the earl consider this acquaintance to be one of those boring social ones he often joked about? She couldn't imagine what a worldly, sophisticated nobleman found intriguing about a chit still in her teens, however pretty. As she watched the frail, elegant Lady Ainsley greet Lady Caroline, her spirits plummeted even further. Was Leafield thinking of marriage?

Suddenly the spacious room seemed more crowded than it had been earlier, crammed as it now was with ladies connected to the earl: his aunt, his reputed mistress, his prospective bride, and herself. And for the remainder of the morning, she devoted herself to the task of assuming a casual and impartial interest in the parade of humanity.

She returned to Westgate Buildings in a reflective state, and was rescued from looming melancholy by a visit from her employer.

Ben Forster gave her one of the warm and affectionate smiles he reserved for her alone, saying, "I swear you grow lovelier by the day, my dear."

"Alas, no," she replied in mock despair. "Would that it were so. I've reached an age where I can expect each day to diminish my looks, not enhance them. What do you want from me, Ben?"

He flicked her cheek with one finger and admitted that he had, in fact, come to discuss his plans for the forthcoming season in London. "I mean to open with a new production of

Romeo and Juliet." Ben paced the length of the room, and she recognized from his knit brow and unsmiling countenance that he was about to make another meaningful pronouncement. Turning slowly and deliberately, he intoned, "You're ready for Juliet."

"But Eliza—"

"Will play Lady Capulet," said Ben firmly. "She's too old to act the heroine and you know it as well as I. Now hear me out, Florry. Romeo and Juliet gives us the opportunity to shine. There are processions and dances and sword fighting— oh, it'll be a damned fine display! New scenery and costumes, all the trappings." He crossed his arms over his broad chest and nodded several times. "Yes, I rather fancy you in a blood-red gown for the crypt scene. Velvet, of course."

"Of course. Will I have the same Romeo?"

"Horry has a fancy to play Mercutio."

"Perfect," Flora murmured. "He is Mercutio."

"Well, what do you say?"

Flora hesitated, uncertain of how best to explain what was in her heart and mind. "I'm flattered, and I do hope I'll prove worthy of your trust in my ability."

"I have no worries on that score," he said, patting her shoulder. "I expect you to study your playbook while you're in Brighton, and Madam will be happy to school you if you ask her." He ran one hand through his dark, gray-streaked hair. "She and Julie and the children will go to the seaside as planned, and Horry with them, but I must return to London. The preparations for a production of this magnitude cannot be delayed." Beaming upon his protégée, the manager predicted, "The critics will hail you as the greatest Juliet of this or any age, better than Susannah Cibber, better than Bellamy, better than Anne Brunton. Your success will be the certain means of saving the Princess Theatre."

A frown of annoyance flitted across Flora's face. "Be careful how you coax me, Ben. I'm no Louise Talley, and I won't court the kind of public attention she craved."

"You'll reap the benefits as surely as any of us." Sitting beside her on the sofa, he took her hands in his. "Only think of the acclaim, the prestige you might win for yourself." When he detected no sign of enthusiasm, he added, "And money—you'll have that too. I'm granting you a share of our profits next season."

She stared at him, letting her breath out in an awed exclamation: "Profit shares!" That mark of honor was reserved for performers of the first rank and importance.

"Lord Leafield, the newest member of our management committee, has proposed it, and I seconded wholeheartedly."

"Lord Leafield!" she echoed.

"He has purchased some of my shares in the Princess, enough to warrant his sitting on our committee."

"You sold your own shares?" This was perhaps the most shocking of all his news.

He replied gruffly, "How else could I suddenly afford *Romeo and Juliet?* We needed another investor, fresh blood—blue blood—and Leafield came forward at just the right moment. Never fear, Horry and I retain the controlling interest. We've been meeting together at the White Hart for several days now, and last night the agreement was concluded, drawn up, and signed. From the way my brother looks today, I gather he and the earl had quite a celebration after I left them."

"He has mentioned none of this to me—Lord Leafield, I mean."

"I believe he'll prove quite useful to us," Ben continued. "Because he sits in the House of Lords and has some influence politically, I'm encouraging him to sponsor a third theater bill in Parliament next year. If it passes, we can continue playing at the Princess, but without it we'll have no theater come January. The earl would be a formidable ally, so I want you to cultivate your friendship with him." When confronted by Flora's shocked face, he hastened to say, "I wasn't encouraging you to lie with him! I regard you as a sister—I expect you will be before much longer. Horry is a good deal steadier these days, for which some credit goes to you."

"I'm sure it's only because Bath offers fewer dissipations than London." Avoiding the subject of Horatio, Flora asked, "If the bill fails, what then?"

"The provincial circuit has grown wearisome after all these years—and to you, I know it well. I want a permanent home for my little band of players, preferably in London, but Bath is frequented by the gentry and would be an acceptable alternative. I've considered purchasing the Orchard Street theater."

"With Lord Leafield's money?" she asked bluntly.

He nodded. "So keep him well amused, my beauty. Cater to him in those innocent ways you women use to keep us gentlemen dancing on a string. Mind you, I like him well enough, but I'm not above exploiting him. And you shouldn't be either."

Flora's reading of the situation was that she was the one being exploited, and by both gentlemen. "You are utterly ruthless when it comes to having your way, Ben. Just as *he* is," she added bitterly.

Puffing out his chest, he said proudly, "I was born into this profession. You saw how my father spent his life toiling and scrimping, plowing every penny and shilling into his company and his theaters. Even so, he never got to London. I did, and I'm determined to stay there as long as I can." Ben retrieved his hat from a table, then faced her to say, "Julie and Madam and Horry share my dreams, and I hope you do too. I can't achieve them without your help."

His stage performances had never failed to elicit her strongest emotions, and he was no less effective in a shabby sitting room, with an audience of one. In answer to the appeal in his dark eyes, she gave him her hand. "Yes, Ben, I am with you. How could I not be, after so many years and everything the Forsters have done for me?"

After her next rehearsal, when Lord Leafield met her at the stage door, she was tempted to cut him dead. Instead, she tersely informed him that she was cognizant of his arrangement with Ben.

"Well, I didn't exactly swear the Forsters to secrecy," he replied unabashedly, placing his hand beneath her elbow to lead her around a puddle in their path.

She jerked her arm away. "I won't have anything to do with proving your cousin's marriage, so you can save yourself the trouble of asking me to go to Devonshire."

"That wasn't my intention."

"Do you mean to say that ensuring my compliance wasn't your primary object when you entered into this partnership?"

With a smile and a shrug, he admitted, "Not my primary object—more like a secondary, even a tertiary one. The theater has become my hobby of choice, a harmless diversion from the unvarying round of London seasons, Brighton summers, autumn shooting parties, and winter hunts."

Flora paused in the middle of the pavement and turned accusing eyes upon him. "How can I believe you? First you came to Bath, knowing I would be here. Then you edged your way into my circle of friends, and now you have become one of my employers."

"I was afraid you'd construe my motive as unalloyed self-interest—that's why I postponed telling you about my pact with Forster."

"What I cannot accept," she raged, "is that you used your new powers to raise my status in the company. By granting me a share of the profits, you've placed me under an obligation that I consider as burdensome as it is distasteful. I can guess what sort of favors you'll demand in return!"

She was sadly aware that the years of stage training had taught her the arts of unleashing emotion, not how to control it. To argue with him in the middle of a public thoroughfare was as rude as it was foolish, so after a pithy declaration that she was perfectly capable of reaching her door without assistance, she stalked off.

Trevor knew better than to follow.

That evening he obediently escorted his aunt to a party in the Royal Crescent, and although no new or interesting faces met his jaded eyes, one of them seemed out of place. Baron Allingham explained his sudden and unprecedented visit to Bath with a jest about escaping importunate creditors, but Trevor didn't believe him. Nor did he fail to note that his friend seldom strayed from Lady Caroline's side, to the obvious consternation of Lady Batsford. Trevor cared very little about this development; his interest in the young lady had already waned. In London she had appealed to him because of her looks, her pedigree, and his aunt's long friendship with her mother, but now that he knew her better, he was less inclined to seek her company. He didn't examine the reason for this change, and chose to believe it was because she was too young for him.

Bored with his well-born flirt and his overly obliging mistress, Trevor was increasingly aware of Flora Campion's superior attractions. His mind was so full of her that he could muster no desire for Martha Harris, whose warm body and eager caresses would not soothe the sting of the actress's sharp setdown. The violence of her wrath worried him; he feared that he'd forfeited her esteem. Would he ever discover the source of that passion Flora exhibited on the stage? He had ample proof that she was not as pure and virginal as the ingenues she portrayed, for she spoke freely about subjects that would prostrate most females with shock, and on several occasions he had seen her romping backstage with Horatio Forster like a hoyden.

He left the party early, but instead of going to Landsdown Crescent, he returned to Sydney Place with his aunt.

During the drive, Lady Ainsley made an observation about Caroline Lewes to which her nephew agreed in a voice so devoid of expression that she said, "Why, Trevor, I thought you liked her, and at the risk of provoking you, I'll add that I'd hoped it was so."

The gentleman leaned back to rest his head on the upholstery. "There was a moment—perhaps several moments—when I thought I might have met my fate, but the feeling passed quickly. I'm reluctant to wed a charming face only to cut Hugh out of the succession. I've said so all along."

Fingering the fringe of her velvet cloak, she asked, "Did you see that wild-looking young baron buzzing about her tonight?"

"Allingham? The Batsfords could do better for her, but they could do much worse, so long as they don't object to the occasional actress or opera dancer."

"That reminds me of something I've been meaning to ask you, Trevor. When we travel down to Combe Cotterell, will it be ourselves and Hugh, or does your friend Miss Campion go with us?"

"I haven't the faintest idea."

His aunt gave him a sharp look. "Indeed? This is the first time in the thirty-two years I've known you that you've admitted being less than certain about anything. I'd like to meet the woman who has reduced you to so pitiable a state."

"Does that mean you are willing to receive a play actress?"

"Lud, the Siddons woman has been everywhere, from Windsor Castle on down. Why should I object? Tomorrow I'll send a note to Miss Campion, inviting her to tea. You are her patron, after all."

Flora's nervousness waned with the arrival of a pair of footmen, one of them bearing a tray of cakes and biscuits, the other a silver urn. To be sure, their liveries were far newer than the moth-eaten ones from the stock wardrobe, but there was a comforting similarity between this scene and those she'd played on the stage. And Julie Forster's fondness for tea parties had accustomed her to the ritual.

"Is this quite as bad as you expected?" Trevor asked softly as he presented Flora with a cup and saucer.

Taking it from him she confided, "It's very much like a play, except that I've got no script to go by. I'm not sure what passes for polite conversation in exalted circles."

"No matter. Aunt Belle would think you a dull creature if you treated her to small talk, and I'd be sadly disappointed."

When Lady Ainsley resumed her interrupted discourse, she asked Flora's opinion of the new houses in the Sion Hill neighborhood. "So much building during wartime cannot be wise."

Leaving the ladies to their discussion, Trevor removed one letter from the pile on the mantel. He ripped the sealed flap, and after a swift but thorough perusal he uttered a sharp curse.

"Bad news?" his aunt asked.

"The worst."

"Do speak freely. Miss Campion, being somewhat acquainted with Hugh, already knows the worst about the Cotterell family."

Trevor handed over his letter, explaining for Flora's benefit, "It's from Linton, my man of business. His clerks continue to search through every church register in London, and as yet they've found no proof of Hugh's nuptials. Could he have used a false name?" he wondered. "But that would make the marriage less than legal and no good to me."

"What about the notice in the papers?" Flora asked. "Did nobody come forward?"

"Oh, yes," he replied bitterly. "According to Linton, two very interesting ladies presented themselves in the Strand. Both claimed to have been secretly married, but only one was in the first blush of youth, and neither could supply Hugh's name."

Lady Ainsley abandoned her inspection of the letter to glance at her nephew. "The Devonshire scheme is still a possibility, Trevor."

This comment indicated to Flora that Lord Leafield had lured her to his aunt's house that they might join forces against her, and the absence of Hugh Cotterell confirmed her suspicion. Curiously, she was not offended by his tactic and could only suppose that she'd become inured.

He had done so much—and might do more—for her and her employer and their theater. But she was less moved by Ben's theater bill or any other practical consideration than by a sudden, insane desire to give this man, so powerful and yet so helpless, what he most wanted.

She said mildly, "My lord, do not look so dismayed. I've already guessed what you are about to ask me."

"How can you, when I'm not sure myself?" he replied, shaking his head as though perplexed by his own words. "First you must acquit me of backing you into a corner, for I never meant to."

A tentative smile flickered at the corners of Flora's mouth. "I won't acquit you, though I might be able to *pardon* you."

"Then I must be satisfied," he told her gravely, "for I am a desperate man. Will you help me, Miss Campion?"

She refused to acknowledge or heed the insistent voice at the back of her mind, which warned her that she would regret her decision. At last she gave him the answer for which he had battled so long, so hard, and so unfairly. "Yes, my lord, I will help. My services are yours to command."

11

She'll not match above her degree, neither in estate, years nor wit.

Twelfth Night, I. iii.

Giving the Forsters no reason for her sudden change of heart, Flora begged off from the trip to Brighton and judged herself fortunate that they neglected to ask about her specific plans. Julie had grown bored—Bath's more distinguished visitors were trickling away—so Ben sent her, his mother, and the two children to the seacoast a week earlier than planned. He and Horatio were so consumed by *Romeo and Juliet* that they failed to notice, as his nosy wife would have done, that Miss Campion was a regular visitor to the Milsom Street shops and a millinery in the North Parade frequented by aspirants to high fashion.

When Lord Leafield had called upon Flora after her visit to Sydney Place, she was dismayed to learn that he expected her to purchase a new wardrobe. "To entice Hugh, you really must achieve a more showy appearance," he explained.

Though he told her to spare no expense, when she visited a Bath modiste she had difficulty overcoming her inborn thrift and the effects of long years of penny-pinching. After one particularly shocking consultation, she returned home moaning about the cost of her many purchases.

Esther Drew refused to commiserate. Eyeing the parcels spread upon the sofa, she asked eagerly, "May I open them and have a look? If you're about to embark upon intrigue and deception down in the country, you must let me share in the fun where I can!"

"Fun is hardly my impression of this afternoon," said Flora with a sigh, wafting wearily into the nearest chair. "My feet ache, my nerves are shattered, and my conscience is giving me fits for having spent so much of the earl's money. Today it was shoes and stockings, scarves, shawls, chemises. Then I gazed at fashion plates and fabric swatches till my head swam. All the gowns will be so dashing and indiscreet—but they may prove useful as stage costumes someday. Tomorrow I'm returning to the milliner's to try on several new bonnets, and my temples are pounding at the prospect!"

She continued to complain about the rigors of shopping until the earl gave her another, far more strenuous assignment.

After an enthusiastic description of Combe Cotterell and its views of estuary and sea, he said he looked forward to showing her around the estate. "I have a steady roan gelding that will make an excellent lady's mount."

"But I don't ride," she told him. Before he could express the astonishment she read in his countenance, she hastened to defend what he obviously regarded as an omission in her education. "A few years ago Horry and I rode donkeys along the cliffs near Brighton, but I don't recall ever being on horseback."

"Never?"

"Does it matter?"

"Well, it's true that long rambles on horseback in Hugh's company would spur on your intimacy," he replied. "And selfishly, I'd hoped you and I might sometimes enjoy a gallop together on the moor. Would you object to having riding lessons?"

"To suit your own convenience or to further your plot?" she wondered.

"Both," was his instant reply. "Bath has a riding academy where you can receive instruction—I'll pay for it, of course."

The riding lessons were impossible to conceal, so she didn't even try. As she expected, Horatio teased her mercilessly.

"Planning to leave us for Philip Astley and his Olympic Pavilion, Florry?" he asked one day. "I never guessed you aspired to perform in equestrian spectacles."

Laughing, she replied, "I'm not nearly ready for Astley's— not yet! I'm learning equitation only, nothing so exciting as bareback riding or acrobatics. Why don't you come to the rid-

ing house with me and see for yourself? This is my last day."
She was determined to mend their rift before he departed Bath.

When her final hour of instruction ended, an impressed Horatio helped her to dismount. "Florry love, you've given me an idea for a new play," he told her as they left the ring together. "An epic history of Lady Godiva. And you, my poppet, shall play the heroine."

"Oh, no, I shan't!" she contradicted him. "It would be far worse than any breeches part I can think of." Fighting the urge to sneeze, for her horse's hooves had kicked up a wealth of sawdust, she tucked the tail of her green broadcloth habit over her arm.

"Don't worry," the actor said with a laugh, "I'll use the same device Sheridan does in *The Critic*, when Tilburina describes the approach of the Spanish Armada, with plenty of 'I see this, I see that.' The property man will be in the wings, clopping away with the wooden blocks. Over the sound of hoofbeats, the good burghers of Coventry will describe Godiva's progress along the street. 'A fine seat she has,' says one. 'Mark you, I like 'em plumper myself,' says another. Although now I think of it," he added wickedly, his eyes gleaming, "mayhap we should let the audience see you ride by—they always appreciate animals on the stage."

"Are you referring to me or the horse?"

"The wigmaker's bill will be exorbitant, because your crowning glory must be fully long enough to cloak your entire figure—more's the pity."

"Lud, you sound half serious!"

"People would come in droves, I tell you. We could puff it off in the papers to make them think female flesh will be publicly exposed. It would be a sensation."

"Ben would *never* stage it, and I would seek employment in a Temple of Hymen before I'd act in your version of the tale," she said with a derisive toss of her head.

The street outside, lit by a July sun, was a blinding contrast to the darker interior of the riding academy. As the actor and actress set out for Westgate Buildings they discussed playwriting, and Flora admitted her desire to try it herself, saying wistfully, "I've a wealth of ideas."

"Someday you'll find time to write them down." Horatio cocked his head at her like a blackbird eyeing a ripe cherry. "I wish you were going to Brighton, if only to keep me out of trouble. This holiday won't be much fun without my Florry."

She prayed he wouldn't ask why she had changed her mind about the trip, for he still harbored a strong resentment of the peer who had taken up so much of her time of late.

With a reminiscent smile he asked, "D'you remember that summer in Portsmouth, five years ago? I'd hoped we might relive those days—another summer by the sea, another production of *Romeo and Juliet* before us."

"I remember how young I was, and also that I'd no business playing Juliet," she said. "This time I'm determined to do better."

Horatio reached for her hand and swung it up and down. "We'll both do better. On the stage and off."

There was no mistaking the deeper purpose behind those confident, carefree words, or his ulterior meaning. Coming to a halt, Flora confronted him. "Are you making a declaration here, in the middle of the street? You might have waited till I was home, with a sofa conveniently nearby to receive my fainting form as I whisper, 'But, sir, it's so sudden!' "

His dark face was still and serious, and he chided gently, "Don't treat it as a joke. I thought you'd be pleased."

"Astounded is more like," she told him with perfect frankness. "But flattered, too." He had been her first love and her last, and she still cared for him, albeit with no more than a vestige of the wild passion he had once inspired. "But Horry," she began, afraid of saying too much but just as determined not to say so little that he would be discouraged, "I don't think we should—"

"We shouldn't," he agreed blithely as they approached her doorstep. "Not here, not now. But think on it. Come September, when we're in London again, I'll come calling on you, a flower in my buttonhole and hope in my heart."

She laughed, but her merriment was but a fleeting thing, and vanished with him as he sauntered down the street.

* * *

While lying in her bed that night, Flora considered the weighty subject her friend had raised so lightly. She knew all too well the troubles she would face by marrying one of her own kind.

Ben and Julie Forster never had a marital squabble that wasn't known and openly discussed by the entire company, for few secrets, particularly domestic ones, could escape nosy, prying colleagues. Romances, infidelities, pregnancies, and quarrels—everyone was conversant with someone else's business. Nor was this uncomfortable absence of privacy confined to the Forsters' troupe. The long affair between Dorothy Jordan and her Duke of Clarence and Mrs. Siddons's estrangement from her spouse were common knowledge. Any player, however innocent or discreet, could become the target of gossip and speculation, as Flora had learned since the night Lord Leafield had first approached her in the green room.

To banish the earl's intrusive and unsettling image, she tried to imagine her future as Horatio's wife. They were incompatible in some respects—he preferred disorder while she was fanatically tidy, keeping her abode clear of the debris of her daily work. Flora stored her playbooks in a bookcase, whereas Horry left them scattered across tabletops and piled them on the floor. She would have to share his lodgings with the favorite stage properties he sometimes carried home from the theater: capes, swords, pinchbeck crowns, and chains of office studded with false jewels. In due course, when Ben relinquished the role of Hamlet to his brother, Yorick's skull would likely find its way into Horry's collection. The grisly but inevitable prospect made Flora smile. Oh, yes, she would know her share of laughter and fun, but would it be enough to make up for the loss of her precious independence or the absence of romance?

Her passionate impulses, which had lain dormant in the years since their early experiments in physical love, were not so very far below the surface—her inward response to the earl's kisses had proved it. Horatio's prowess was legendary, for he'd sampled the favors of nearly every actress and dancer in the company and was reputed to be the most considerate, if inconstant, of partners. But dalliance was an ingrained habit with him, and she didn't expect him to change his ways, not even for her. She couldn't guess how long he might be content with the role of faithful husband. Was she prepared to spend many a night in lonely speculation, wondering whose bed he was in?

After a well-attended final performance, the theater on Orchard Street closed for the season. On the following morning, the Forster brothers bade Flora a fond farewell before following their separate roads, Ben to town, Horatio to Brighton.

She had little opportunity to miss them, for the earl was filling her days with long rides into the countryside. Guiding an unfamiliar horse along city streets and across open land was more difficult than working in the indoor ring of the academy, her mount on a lead and her instructor close at hand.

Prior to his lordship's departure for Combe Cotterell, he took her riding one last time. The day was overcast; an approaching shower scented the air and made their mounts skittish.

The grand new residences springing up in the neighborhood of Prior Park reminded Flora that she must soon find a home of her own, in London. There was no room for a married couple in the Forsters' narrow town house, nor at Mrs. Brooke's, and she had no desire to lodge on one of the crowded, filthy streets of the Covent Garden district. By pooling their incomes and shares of the theater's profits, she and Horry could afford to lease a small house in some attractive rural borough like Hampstead. Chelsea might also be pleasant, as it was so near the river.

Trevor commented on her silence. "You seem entirely oblivious to the beauties around us—that herd of cows, for instance. Are you still so troubled by your impending ordeal in Devonshire?"

"It isn't that. I was thinking of London, and trying to decide where to begin looking for a house. I should have asked Ben's advice before he left Bath, although I daresay he'd have told me to marry Horry sooner rather than later and let him choose where we should live." She had spoken without thinking and immediately regretted her choice of words.

"Is a marriage imminent?"

"Possibly. I'm not entirely sure. Horry has declared his intention of asking me." She had inadvertently given the mare her head, and tugged nervously at the reins. "Five years ago he courted me and I refused him. We weren't children by any means, but ours was a rather childish affair—I'm afraid I was very young at twenty."

"Will you accept him this time?"

"I haven't yet come up with a strong enough reason not to."

"In my experience," Trevor said wryly, "brides-to-be usually simper and blush when they speak of their nuptials. Your face is distinctly woebegone, and I can't help but wonder why that should be—unless Benedict Forster is pressuring you to wed his brother. I know he looks on you as his possession, a rare and precious object which he must guard carefully until he can display you in a way that will most benefit him and his theater."

"He's my friend," she reminded him, putting up her chin. "And so is Horatio."

"Both are businessmen, first and foremost. You would be unwise to let your dependence on them rule your life."

"I make my own decisions," she maintained. "I am entirely independent."

"Are you really?" he shot back so cruelly that she recoiled. "You are a most delightful compound of beauty and intellect, and you possess the talent and sensibility of a true artist, and I detect no vices in you. Your only flaw seems to be a disastrous tendency to be too trusting where Forsters are concerned. Can't you see what is so very plain to me? Your Horatio seeks to continue his brother's theatrical dynasty. If you marry him it will be the most shameful *waste*."

"I'm an actress, not a titled lady with scores of well-intentioned suitors, like your Lady Caroline Lewes," Flora retorted. She was silenced by a bitter envy of the proud man riding beside her, whose long lineage had no blot of shame upon it. "Horry and I share a profession as well as a romantic past, and our marriage will be the most suitable one I can hope to make. If you think I'm ignorant of his wenching and carousing, you're mistaken. He may not be the most faithful of husbands, or the soberest, but he is very fond of me." Ironically, her stalwart defense of her suitor reawakened many of the doubts she'd laid to rest. "For too many years I've been preyed upon by any man seeking a mistress in the green room. At the very least, Horry can provide protection from them."

Trevor said harshly, "You can't deter your admirers by changing your name to Forster."

"Perhaps not, but my husband can depend upon my loyalty." Her cool words were as clear a warning as his had seemed a threat.

"Yet you admit you don't expect similar consideration from him. You must be very much in love."

Flora flinched. "I am a realist. I daresay you expect actors to be guided by lofty ideals, not by a desire for comfort and security. But if we were so completely lost to the practicalities of this life, we'd soon starve. Aristocrats are not the only people who marry for the sake of convenience, Lord Leafield."

After a moment of silent scrutiny, he asked, "Did you tell me of your engagement in the belief that I would release you from your pledge to assist me?"

"Of course not—I would never go back on my word!" Furthermore, she doubted his ability to call a halt: letters had been posted, the necessary travel arrangements were complete, and she'd already packed her new clothes away in their trunks. Within a few days she would find herself in the remote countryside with an overbearing earl, a toplofty countess, and an out-and-out libertine. Only Margery, in her capacity as personal maid, would represent the familiar world of the theater, from which Flora had not intended to stray.

She said waspishly, "For weeks you plotted against me, you've wrecked my peace by involving me in this contemptible charade, and now you insult me. Even worse, you've managed to separate me from my closest friends."

"Not all of them," he interrupted.

"Don't flatter yourself," she said, each word a stiletto. "Margery Prescott will be the only *true* friend of mine at Combe Cotterell!"

*   *   *

Esther Drew returned from a long walk in Kingsmead to find Flora stretched upon the bed, dressed in her riding habit and clutching a damp, crumpled handkerchief that bore all the signs of recent employment. After listening to an impassioned and largely incoherent account of the recent altercation, she commented, "Your anger may be justified, but he's still your patron. And very soon he will be your host."

"He's the most odious, conniving, fiendish person I've ever known," Flora ranted, kicking the bedpost. "I used to have the sense to withstand his blandishments, but since coming to Bath I've been as soft and pliant as a lump of clay, and twice as stupid. In Lady Ainsley's drawing room the other day, he looked over at me, and I wanted to help him so desperately—I would have agreed to anything he asked. *Anything*! Oh, never before have I been such a dunce!" Rolling onto her back, she glowered up at the tester. "Very likely his horrid cousin will compromise me in some hideous fashion, or else I'll break my neck falling from a wild horse."

"I didn't realize it would be so hazardous a mission."

"If Leafield's nonsensical plan does succeed, he'll have no further use for me." Realizing that her last prophecy had more of the forlorn than the furious about it, she took a moment to stoke up her wrath. "He is completely heartless."

Esther sat down upon the bed. "Is the famous friendship over, then? Or will you patch it up, as you always do with Horatio Forster?"

Suddenly Flora sat up, her face transformed by a smile. "At least his lordship won't be able to bully and browbeat me after I'm married. Call me practical and unromantic if you wish— *he* very nearly did—but I've decided to have Horry for my husband."

Esther gave her an impulsive hug. "Oh, I'm so glad!"

"With Miles coming home so soon, there's no better time for a wedding. But you mustn't tell a soul, for nothing is definite. A fine figure I should cut if Horry meets some charmer in Brighton and changes his mind."

"He won't," Esther assured her. "Unless someone warns him about what a termagant he'll have for a wife." Laughing, she ducked as a pillow flew past her head.

12

I have unclasped to thee the book even of my secret soul.

Twelfth Night, I. iv.

Flora, accustomed to the wayside public houses that had sheltered Benedict Forster's players through the years, could appreciate the superior amenities of the Castle Inn at Taunton and the Half Moon in Exeter, where she and the countess spent their nights on the road. But comfortable as the beds were, she slept no better than she had since her parting quarrel with Lord Leafield.

As Lady Ainsley's traveling chaise crossed the South Hams, a prolapse of land between the Rivers Dart and Plym, she contemplated her imminent reunion with the author of her sorrows. Her infatuation with Lord Leafield had somehow survived her discovery of his perfidy, and she feared the effects of his caressing voice and endless capacity to charm. He would hurt her again, it seemed inevitable, but the next time might effect a permanent cure.

Despite her strong determination to find fault with anything and everything connected with him—his cousin, his horses, his taste in waistcoats—it was impossible to disdain his aunt's company and conversation. His country, too, was worthy of admiration. Scattered among green hills and hedged fields were small towns with narrow, crooked streets, their quaint buildings of thatch and stone standing in the shadow of an ancient church in the Perpendicular style prevalent in the shire.

After continuing for a mile or so beyond the village of Combe Cotterell, the chaise swung sharply into a long drive. The earl's property was bounded by an estuary on one side, and its focal point was a substantial dwelling of faded sandstone, roofed in slate. The old-fashioned leaded casements of the Tudor front faced westward; rows of sash windows on a more modern facade overlooked gardens and lawn. The two portions were distinct yet perfectly matched, the grace and simplicity of one age wedded to that of another, and the thorny arms of climbing roses embraced both the old and new wings. This was no blindingly palatial residence along the lines of a Blenheim or a Chatsworth, as Flora had feared, but a handsome manor house, impressive in its antiquity and entirely welcoming.

She had very little time to absorb the ancient grandeur of the timber-vaulted hall before the housekeeper led her past a suit of armor and up an ornate wooden staircase. "Her ladyship wants you to have the Rose Bedchamber," the woman announced, conducting her along a corridor hung with tapestries.

Flora was delighted with her room, which lay in the newer part of the house. Its floral theme was carried out in the chintz bed hangings and several still-life paintings; even the tall mahogany bedposts were surmounted with finials carved in the shape of rosebuds.

With Margery's help, she changed out of her hot carriage habit and donned a new, floating muslin, shuddering at the recollection of its exorbitant cost. Avoiding her servant's shocked gaze, she rouged her lips ever so slightly and unpinned one long black curl to let it fall forward across her breast in an attempt to impersonate a female of dubious virtue.

She went downstairs in search of her hostess and encountered the butler, who stiffly informed her that it was Lady Ainsley's custom to rest after a journey. He then showed Flora to the saloon, where she found an opulence that matched her imaginings, and left her there.

The tall windows were curtained with the same pale blue damask of the giltwood chairs and sofas, and the bright light streaming into the room made the lusters of the cut-glass chandeliers and sconces sparkle like diamonds. The fine carpet under Flora's feet repeated the delicate cockleshell motif of the plasterwork overhead. A self-conscious glance into the massive looking glass showed how dwarfed she was by the size and magnificence of her blue and gold surroundings. Even in the bright afternoon light, and despite her painted lips, she resembled a ghostly figure in her insubstantial gown, with hair too black and eyes too large for her pale face.

She managed to force some color into her cheeks, but the pinched-in roses faded with Lord Leafield's entrance. In his olive coat and buff breeches, he was every inch the country gentleman, with topboots as black as obsidian and just as shiny. The riding crop in his hand indicated that he'd lately been on horseback.

"I wondered if you would come," he said as their eyes met in the mirror world. Holding out his whip, he added, "You may use this if you wish—I deserve to be punished. I was greedy, I wanted your goodwill and your assistance equally. If I sacrificed one to gain the other, I can hardly count it a victory. Can you forgive me?"

Remorse was not what she had expected from him. Less than an hour in his house, only a few minutes in his presence, and already she was under his spell. "You *are* forgiven," she answered, facing him. "And I must beg your pardon for my rudeness at our last meeting."

"I provoked you, and will take care not to do so in future. Now, my dear Miss Campion, may I have the honor of showing you my house?" The twinkle in his hazel eyes belied his formality. After pointing out several objects of note, he guided her into the adjacent drawing room. "The great Robert Adam is responsible for all this rarefied beauty. My grandfather was never satisfied with the wing that his father added, so he engaged the finest of all architects to make improvements."

He took her through the original part of the house, built in the days of the Tudors and scarcely altered. Flora's favorite room was the wood-paneled library, with a door that opened onto a grassy courtyard.

"This is the Queen's Court," Trevor informed her, and he pointed out the marble busts mounted on three of the ivy-hung walls. "Each of the royal ladies represented here is prominently featured in the Cotterell history. The first Queen Mary knighted my ancestor, who wed one of her ladies-in-waiting, and after the victory against the Armada her sister Elizabeth ennobled him by creating the barony of Hopeton. Poor Queen Anne granted the earldom to my great-grandfather a century ago. Come and sit down for a while. It's a long drive from Exeter, and you must be weary."

She let him lead her to one of the stone benches. "Everything is delightful—not only this garden, but the whole of Combe Cotterell."

"You've only seen a small part of it."

"Did you grow up here?"

Shaking his head, he answered, "When not at school, I was most often at Hopeton Hall. It's a fine estate, every guide book extols its beauty, but the house is too large to be comfortable. My grandsire preferred it, which gives you an idea of his character." He chuckled softly. "But he never failed to bring Hugh and me to Devonshire in the summertime. This is my favorite place in all England and the closest thing to home."

Flora was aware of how many properties might have been so designated. In addition to the two country seats, he owned Leafield House in Cavendish Square, a cottage in Leicestershire used only in the hunting season, and that pretty Palladian villa overlooking the Thames. The expense represented by each of these establishments was beyond her ability to calculate or comprehend; she had to accept his wealth as an essential part of him, like the faint cleft that marked his chin. And now, having seen Combe Cotterell, she could better understand why he was so desperate to keep every morsel of his birthright safe from a wastrel cousin. It wasn't the fortune or the title he was protecting so much as the precious property entailed upon the Cotterell heir: the vast acreages and a pair of residences long connected to a distinguished family.

When he excused himself to change his riding dress for dinner attire, Flora remained in the quiet courtyard, watching the robin perched atop the stone wall until Hugh Cotterell passed beneath the arched doorway and frightened it away.

His intrusion annoyed her, but she was mindful of her duty. She smiled with captivating brilliance and invited him to take the place his cousin had lately vacated.

"I might as well," he answered, adding morosely that he'd already ridden to the village and back and therefore had nothing else to do.

Flora couldn't like him; neither did she know him well

enough to dislike him, but she was conscious of his loneliness and boredom.

As soon as Lady Ainsley recovered her strength, the neighbors descended—the squire's wife, the vicar's wife, the doctor's wife. Flora, conscious of her questionable status in the earl's household, learned to escape the house. At the first sound of carriage wheels or hoofbeats she retreated to the ragged cliffs blanketed with wild raspberry, rock roses, and toadflax, or descended to the sandy beach of the cove below.

She soon discovered that her hostess was an avid gardener, as knowledgeable about plants as any botanist or professional horticulturist. "I've had a great deal of time for study," she explained when Flora walked with her through rose beds full of treasured specimens. "I spend the long, cold winter poring over books and catalogs, and in the spring, when the rain falls on Bath, I write out my plans. In summer, Trevor brings me to our Devonshire paradise to carry them out. Hand me the shears if you will be so good. Here's a bloom that wants cutting."

As did the flowers, Flora's friendship with the noblewoman flourished in the warm sunshine. When the afternoon heat drove the countess indoors for her customary nap, Flora withdrew to the shade of the Queen's Court, where she sat upon the grass, her copy of Ben's adaptation of *Romeo and Juliet* open on her lap.

In Bath, Flora had labored while the earl had been at leisure; now it was the other way around. Each morning he disappeared immediately after breakfast to oversee the cultivation of the rich red earth, and he spent hours in his library consulting his bailiff about sheep and cows and other mysteries. Hugh, in his derisive way, said his cousin spent half the day with lazy tenants and the other half with aged pensioners. To Flora's ears it sounded very dull.

The days passed quickly and pleasantly, despite her relative lack of employment. For six years she'd been ruled by the clock, cramming her pursuits into the hours between the end of daily rehearsals and the rise of the curtain at night. Her present wealth of time was a greater luxury than the servants who did her bidding, the silver utensils she used at meals, or the silk-hung bed to which she repaired each night.

One afternoon she went to the drawing room to try out the harpsichord, having already devoted herself to the business of casting out lures to Mr. Cotterell. The instrument was different enough from Esther's pianoforte to present an interesting challenge, and she was wholly absorbed in her music when Trevor charged into the room, his hair wildly disheveled and his face rigid with anger.

Lifting her hands from the keyboard, she asked in alarm, "Whatever is the matter?"

"Horses," he answered cryptically, sinking into an armchair. "And heat. *And* Hugh, whose bad management of my second-best mount has resulted in a strained hock and inspired in me a strong desire to wring his miserable neck. How cool it is here—it's beastly oppressive outdoors. Jem Wallow, my head groom, says a storm is brewing."

"Does that mean we must put off the drive to Plymouth tomorrow?"

"Oh, no, the clouds usually blow over quickly—they should be spent by nightfall. That's my hope, as too much rain would be bad for the corn. Never fear, you shall visit the spiritual home of all seafarers, and I'll show you where Sir Francis Drake finished out his game of bowls before busying himself with the defeat of the Armada."

"Giving you another opportunity to show off your superior knowledge of history?" she quizzed him. "Be warned, I may retaliate by reciting all the pertinent passages about the Spanish fleet form *The Critic*!"

Trevor laid his riding whip on the marquetry-topped table at his elbow. "What were you playing?"

"Nothing but scales; I hadn't yet begun in earnest."

"Please do."

"Would your lordship prefer a sonata or an aria? My attempt at the first would be abysmal, and the latter merely lamentable. I might manage a ballad or a sea shanty, however." When he asked whether her repertoire was suitable for mixed company, she answered, "But of course!"

Grinning broadly, he said, "You astonish me."

"Well, I do know some highly improper songs," she admitted with a naughty smirk.

Trevor stretched out his long legs and regarded the tops of his boots. "Before you entertain me, I wish you'd tell me how your flirtation with my cousin progresses."

"It doesn't."

"Why not?"

"He mistrusts me. He seems to believe that I'm here to seduce you, not him."

Trevor lifted his head. "I wish I had cause to believe that."

To cover her confusion, Flora played "The Seeds of Love," a simple ballad in a minor key.

"You've an excellent voice," her listener remarked when she finished the last of its many verses. "You might earn your living as a singer."

"Not much of one," she said with a sigh. "My voice is sufficient for a drawing room, but not up to the demands of opera or oratorio." Abandoning the harpsichord, she moved to a window and stood gazing out at the dark clouds on the horizon. As she absently fingered a drapery tassel, she said, "I hope the storms in the Atlantic aren't too rough, just enough to make the *Vestal*'s journey home a swift one."

Her wistful words reminded Trevor that the long-absent Miles was the only relative she'd ever mentioned, and he asked curiously, "Haven't you any other family?"

"Not in England. My mother's people are connected with the linen trade in Dublin and I've met them once, during our only tour of Ireland. My aunts and uncles and cousins are most amiable, but there are so many of them that I can't recall their names! And all are quite prolific—I must have fifty cousins."

"And what of your father's family? You are surely acquainted with the Campions."

With simple candor she replied, "There are no Campions. Papa was an orphan, left on the parish when he was but a few days old. His mother died unwed, after being cast off by her protector. We know only her name—not her village or any of her history."

Trevor stared down at Flora, struggling to accept that half of her ancestry was a complete blank. It was incomprehensible to one who could trace his pedigree back to the era of William the Conqueror.

"You look so shocked."

"I'm a little surprised," he admitted. "You've told me that your father was an educated man. How is that possible?"

"He was monstrously clever, and he had a powerful and wealthy patron—Lord Allingham, one of the trustees of the orphanage. You will recognize the name, for he was grandfather to the present baron, and perhaps my own grandfather as well."

"An old gentleman who dandled you on his knee when you were small," he said, remembering something she'd said to him on that long-ago day at Richmond, when he'd questioned her interest in the wild young man who prowled the theater green rooms.

Flora inclined her head. "His lordship's support of my father gave rise to a rumor that he had been responsible for what happened to Susan Campion. Whether or not it's true, he did send my father to a school near his estate instead of letting him be apprenticed to a tradesman. That's the fate of most asylum children—the lucky ones. The rest simply waste away, or end up in a workhouse. Lord Allingham saw to it that Papa went to university and recommended him for the teaching position in Portsmouth. Later he used his influence to secure a commission for Miles. But if Papa was indeed his by-blow, I derived no benefits beyond a few pretty hair ribbons and a spinning top. He never admitted that any tie of blood existed, although Mama, who was remarkably intuitive, chose to believe in it."

So did Trevor, now that he was awakened to the possibility. The symmetry of her countenance was more than noble, it was sublime. From the widow's peak to the delicate chin, every inch had been molded by a master hand. Her colleen of a mother must have been the source of the fair, pure complexion common to the Irish, and the jet-black hair, but there was also a faint resemblance to his crony Allingham. But even if she were the granddaughter of a peer, it was on the wrong side of the blanket. Not only had this child of a humble seamstress and an illegitimate instructor of mathematics been bred in obscurity, she had voluntarily compounded the defects of her lineage by going onto the stage.

When the clock chimed the hour, she said, "So late—and I haven't yet studied my part today. If I'm not more diligent, I'll be sorry later."

"Haven't you played Juliet already?"

"Yes, but so poorly that Ben, fond as he is, admits that he was wrong to give me the role. He says I'm more capable now, yet even if he dresses me in velvets and devises charming tableaux and magnificent processions, the critics will be waiting to pounce. No amount of bribery or puffery or anything else will persuade them to be kind. I might be the greatest Juliet that ever drew breath—I hope I will be—but I'm still the upstart Forster's Juliet, and many will be eager to find fault. All the attention, the notoriety—how I dread it!" This was the first time she had spoken openly of her deepest fears, for she hadn't articulated them to Ben, or to Horatio either, however close their relationship.

"You're being absurd," he told her, smiling. "Forster would never stake his greatest treasure if he had any real concerns about the outcome of his venture."

"You spoke differently at Bath," she reminded him. "And you were correct. He'd risk everything for the chance to retain his license, because keeping the doors of the Princess open is and will ever be his first object. I am but a means to an end," she concluded forlornly.

He placed his hands upon her shoulders and slowly drew her toward him. The moment Flora felt his lips on her forehead, her body quivered and she leaned closer, seeking the consolation he offered. Afterward, when she found the courage to look up, his tender expression lulled her into an utter sense of disregard for plays or parts or problems. His kiss had been as brief as it had been chaste, but it was alarming in a way other more passionate kisses had not been. Horry, she reminded herself, would have comforted her in a similar fashion; it had been a friendly gesture, nothing more.

It was just as well that she put some distance between them, for a moment later Hugh entered the room.

"Ah, Miss Campion, here you are! I was hoping that you

would be so good as to join me in a game of piquet." He turned to his frowning cousin and asked, "Still in a rage about that business down at the stables?"

"What? Oh, that—no, I'd quite forgotten it."

After Flora and the young man sat down at the baize-covered table, the earl watched them for a few minutes before making what she supposed was a strategic retreat.

Presently her adversary looked up from his cards. "Would you mind telling me what the devil you're doing here, Miss Campion?"

"Preparing to best you at this game," Flora replied smoothly.

"I meant what are you doing here in Devonshire, as you know very well."

"My patron invited me to his estate for a holiday, and I accepted."

"Patron?" He narrowed his eyes. "You can't be unaware that he'd rather be your lover."

"If so, he would hardly have brought me to a house where his aunt is also in residence," she pointed out. "He'll seek entertainment elsewhere, I suspect. He may not find any widows in the neighborhood, but he is surely acquainted with some friendly cottage girl or a pretty dairymaid."

The young man threw back his brown head and produced one of his sharp barks of laughter. "*Les droits du seigneur*? Not Leafield! I'd stake my last shilling on the probability that he never diddled a dairymaid in his life. He's not one to take his pleasure amongst the lower orders. So you knew about his Bath doxy?"

"And also about his flirtation with Lady Caroline Lewes."

"It was rather more than that, until something—or someone—changed his mind about offering for her. It wasn't Martha Harris, that much I know."

Flora stared at him, forgetting her discard. "You don't think *I* was responsible!"

Hugh hunched his thin shoulders. "I can't pretend to understand my cousin, especially lately, and most especially in his choice of female companionship."

Ignoring the slight, Flora lowered her lashes. "And you, sir? What manner of lady is your mistress?"

"What mistress?" he asked sourly. "I can't afford to keep one. The last time I was with a woman, I had to borrow money from her. That's a pretty way for a fellow to treat his—" He broke off suddenly.

"His what?"

"His ladybird," was the curt answer. "It's damned uncomfortable, being the poor relation. By God, if I had so much as fifty pounds, I'd book a seat on the fastest coach to London and—oh, never mind."

His burst of confidence ended there, and Flora was unable to draw him out further.

The next day Trevor neglected his estate business in order to drive Miss Campion to Plymouth in his phaeton. He led her around the Hoe, the great Citadel, and Sutton Pool Harbor as scrupulously as a paid guide, all the while striving to stifle yawns born not of boredom, but from lack of sleep.

All night he had tossed and turned in his bed, recalling their conversation in the drawing room. He'd wanted to kiss away all the troubles of the Forsters' making, and any for which he might be responsible, but caution had prevented him from giving her more than that brief, brotherly salute. Nowadays she could annihilate him with one of her cool rebuffs. But that moment of tender communion had revealed a startling truth: his need for her went deeper than desire. A thorough examination of his feelings revealed that this unprecedented yearning was mingled with respect and admiration. He was weary of self-delusion, sick of the charades he had played with his glacial, well-born blondes, and more recently with the widow of Bath. As his mistress, Flora Campion would be more than a convenience. He wanted to cherish and comfort and pamper her as he had no other.

He could not overlook her deflating refusal of him in his overgrown garden at Twickenham and therefore resolved to woo her with greater finesse than he'd demonstrated on that occasion. And when he had won her at last, he would never let her leave his side.

And then, as the sun had risen behind the curtains of his bedchamber window, he also remembered the one impediment to the glorious future he envisioned.

As he strolled with his inamorata along the seawall, he wondered if she was serious about marrying the libertine actor. And however reluctant to introduce his rival's name into their conversation, he had to know her intention, so he asked with studied ease, "Have you heard from Horatio Forster since your arrival?"

"No," she replied. "But I didn't expect to. Esther sees Ben now and again and passes the news along to me, so I know Horry is still on holiday."

"I'd willingly frank your letters to Brighton," said Trevor, although it was far from being true.

"Thank you, but it isn't necessary. If Horry or Madam—and Julie most especially—received a letter with your frank on it, my whereabouts would be secret no more. And if I posted a letter myself, without a frank, it would bear a Devonshire mark, quite enough to damn me. I'll see them soon enough— September is nearly upon us." Flora's bright smile faded and she turned her attention to the gulls gliding above the sparkling water. "How long will you remain here after I return to London?"

"I haven't decided."

During the night he had devised a short play of his own, one that featured Miss Flora Campion in a leading role. In this imaginative work she was installed in a house of his providing in Plymouth, conveniently near the small playhouse where he was certain she could secure employment. It was an easy distance from Combe Cotterell, and yet so very far removed from the distractions of London: Forsters, green-room bucks, and William Shakespeare.

It pained him to think she might not be capable of loving him to the exclusion of all else, but he accepted that she was unlikely to retire from the stage at his request. As long as she consented to receive his private attentions, he would never begrudge her the public attention she was due as an actress. All would be well if only he could convince her that she must break with Horatio Forster, and soon.

13

Fly away, fly away, breath
I am slain by a fair cruel maid.

Twelfth Night, II. iv.

After riding past the villages and mills along the banks of the
River Erme, Flora and Trevor paused for refreshment at Ivy-
bridge, a quaint hamlet on the edge of Dartmoor. They consumed cups of bitter tea and slices of brown bread smeared
with clotted cream, then continued their journey, turning east-
ward. Neither the ominous gray clouds or her fatigue lessened
Flora's determination to explore the changing countryside.

Neatly hedged fields gave way to a vast, bleak landscape
brightened only by the yellow patches of gorse. Rough-coated
ponies, as untamed as their surroundings, lifted their heads to
observe their domesticated brethren but seemed unmoved by
the intrusion.

"I've always been fascinated by the moor," said Trevor
when they paused beside an ancient stone chapel, "but more
than a few consider it menacing, particularly when the thick
mists come sweeping across Black Tor. Storms can whip up in
an instant, with lightning strikes and great crashes of thunder."

Flora envied his knowledge of the land, for she'd never lingered anywhere long enough to have a sense of place.

A misty drizzle fell from the leaden sky as they raced their
horses across the stark terrain. Trevor's swift black thoroughbred easily outpaced her roan, and she followed fearlessly, not
caring where he led her. She felt fully alive and entirely free,
just like the rabbits skipping out of her path. She turned her
head to look at a group of ponies huddled together at the base
of a hill, flicking their scraggly tails and pawing the earth morosely.

The roan gave a sudden, heart-stopping lurch, and to keep

from flying out of the sidesaddle she grasped his mane. He quickly found his footing again, but his gait was so slow that she forced him to halt so she could climb down. Remembering how angry the earl had been when Hugh suffered a similar mishap, she prayed that the horse wasn't lame. Trevor had already turned back; the black stallion was thundering across the soggy turf.

Trevor dismounted swiftly. "When I looked around and couldn't see you," he said hoarsely, "I thought you'd fallen." His face was pale and his eyes unnaturally bright as he approached her. "Thank God you're safe—I love you too much to bear losing you."

She responded to this declaration and the subsequent embrace by clinging to him desperately and unashamedly, returning his kisses as he bestowed them, passionately and with no thought for the consequences.

"My darling Flora," he said at last, "how very *damp* you are."

"And you."

He pressed his lips against her forehead. "I wasn't speaking idly a moment ago—that confession came from the heart."

"I'm glad you saved it until we were here." She sighed, resting her cheek against his shoulder. "I wish we might stay on the moor forever. It seems so far removed from the rest of the world—your world and mine." This comment earned her another kiss.

"We'll come back, I promise, but I must get you home before you're entirely soaked." He knelt down to inspect the roan's forelegs, and after announcing that there was no swelling at the joints, he swung Flora up into the sidesaddle.

She paid less attention to the views during the rest of the afternoon, partly because the moorland was obscured by fog and rain, but also because her senses were too disordered. From their first meeting and forever afterward, she'd been sensible of her escort's charm, his laugh, the way the tight skin crinkled at the corners of his eyes when he smiled at her, which he did for most of their journey back to Combe Cotterell.

Later, when reminiscing about her first and last ride across Dartmoor, she realized that it was by far the longest period in which the theater had been absent from her thoughts.

"Here's a letter for you, Miss Campion," Lady Ainsley announced when the actress took her place at the tea table.

Flora, recognizing Esther Drew's neat script, said hopefully, "It must contain news of Miles." But as she began reading, her face clouded over with disappointment.

"His ship hasn't reached port?" Trevor asked, looking at her over his paper.

"Not yet," she replied in a subdued voice, her eyes focused on the second page. The mantle of joy she had worn for the past few hours slipped inch by inch, leaving her naked and vulnerable.

As soon as she could she found her way to the bench in the Queen's Court and read the letter once more. According to Esther, Horatio Forster had returned to town, and she described his outrage when he learned why Flora was not at the house on Great Queen Street, waiting for him. His very name shamed her, and she was flooded with guilt. London would be a purgatory, for somehow she had to atone for her betrayal of Horry during that insane moment of weakness on the wild moor. He had been her support through many a stormy rehearsal and exhausting performance. He understood her. He intended to marry her.

But all thoughts of Horatio, London, and the theater flew from her mind when Trevor invaded her place of retreat. Watching him make his way across the damp grass, she felt as though the butterflies hovering near the foxgloves were trapped in her breast. He could never be satisfied with a few kisses and caresses, for it was his nature to demand more than she could give.

"Don't run away from me, Flora."

Poised to do that very thing, she remained seated. A clean, swift break, painful though it would be, was her only hope of salvation and self-preservation. In a false, bright voice, she thanked him for a pleasant holiday, adding, "But it is time I returned to town and my work."

"Very recently you were glad that your world was worlds away," Trevor reminded her.

Her fingers crushed Esther's letter in a paroxysm of remorse. How could she explain that she did not belong in this rain-kissed garden, or tell him that he had no place in her life? "I was mistaken!" she cried in desperation. "I realize now that what happened on the moor is better forgotten." After a moment, she said more calmly, "Mr. Cotterell also wishes to leave Combe Cotterell as soon as he can. I don't know if it's in my power—or yours—to stop him."

"His lack of funds will keep him here. Tonight the squire and his lady are giving a ball, and if he doesn't return home drunk and in debt, then I do not know him." Gently, he smoothed the faint furrow in her brow. "Why do you frown?"

"Because you always speak ill of him, and I'm not sure he deserves it. He seems so unhappy that I pity him."

"I, too, am unhappy. Please stay, Flora. You have nothing to fear from me."

"I can't be dissuaded," she told him, "and I'll be packing my things tonight, while you're dancing at the ball."

"I'm not going. I don't feel like dancing, and I have no desire to watch Hugh make a fool of himself." He gazed down at her thoughtfully. "You know, if you were more cunning you could have taken advantage of his greatest weakness. Many a man spills his deepest, darkest secrets when tipsy."

"But by the time he comes home from the village tavern, I've usually gone up to bed."

"Tonight you'll wait up for him," Trevor instructed, "and you must wear the most beguiling of the costumes you bought in Bath." When she objected, he cut her off by saying bitterly, "If you can persuade him to admit the truth about his marriage tonight, you can be on your way to London tomorrow morning."

Her strong desire to do exactly that compelled her to follow his suggestion. When changing for dinner, she selected a gown of crimson silk with a tight bodice and a décolletage that Flora, no prude, considered excessively low-cut. The rich color threw her skin into pale relief, making her hair appear blacker and more lustrous.

"You look like a Jezebel, ma'am, and no mistake." The dresser sniffed, handing Flora a pot of rouge. "I suppose you'll be wanting this, just as if you was going on in the play tonight."

"Very amusing," she said mirthlessly. "You needn't wait up for me tonight."

"Which is as good as saying I probably should!" the older woman shot back.

Throughout the meal, Trevor's eyes were continually drawn to the tempting expanse of bosom on display. As soon as the cloth was removed the ladies retired to the drawing room and he followed them, choosing the chair nearest the harpsichord. A branch of candles cast a golden light upon Flora's face, and he noted the faint shadows the downswept lashes made against her cheeks. He drank several glasses of port as she played on, apparently oblivious to his presence.

On the moor, in his arms, she had been everything he had dreamed—warm, ardent, responsive. Afterward, when she'd done her dispassionate best to convince him that she regretted her actions, he had refused to believe that she meant it. But however frustrated he was by her determination to escape him, he dared not forget the lessons of the past. Each victory over her resistance and her scruples had been costly; he couldn't afford an error of judgment now, with so very much at stake.

He was surprised when his aunt, who had been plying her needle on behalf of the parish poor, sought her bed earlier than usual. One look at her wan face told Trevor that she was feeling unwell, but when he expressed his concern, she said tartly that she merely wanted to prepare herself for a busy day of gardening on the morrow.

Flora regarded him warily, as if afraid he might pounce now that they were alone together. Hoping to calm her, he blandly suggested a game of cribbage.

Her share of the ensuing dialogue was devoted to her professional concerns, and the important role that posed so many difficulties. He suspected that she'd raised the subject as a barrier against more intimate topics of conversation. "Juliet has become your obsession," he commented, moving his peg forward several paces on the board.

"Yes, I know," she said apologetically. "But it's worrying, the knowledge that the success of our theater rests on my shoulders."

"There's more to a season than a single play." Abandoning the game for a moment, he said, "I hope Forster doesn't plan to turn you into a tragedienne—his own version of Sarah Siddons."

Shaking her head, Flora reshuffled the deck of cards. "He couldn't even if he wanted, for Mrs. Siddons and I are worlds apart in age and experience."

"True, but in my opinion your talent far exceeds hers. You have that delicate touch she lacks, a quality of lightness that enables you to excel in comic as well as weightier roles."

"Comedy is more difficult to play than tragedy," she admitted, "because timing is so important. But no matter what the play, a first night is always the same—instinct and training take over. As soon as the curtain rises, I'm like any other cart horse when it's put into harness."

"You always manage to shatter my most romantic illusions about your art," he said lightly before inspecting the hand she had dealt him.

"I always notice the most inconsequential things during a performance," Flora continued reflectively. "A rent in the curtain, or an actor whose false beard is askew. But whatever my eye may see, my mind and body are engaged with the words and stage business." Her fingers fell slack and her opponent might have read every card she held, had his eyes not been fixed upon her rapt face. "It's so difficult to describe. Haven't you ever felt a strong sense of heightened excitement, a moment of exhilaration that's somehow physical and mental and spiritual and earthly, all at the same time?"

Trevor had known many such moments with the unnumbered, faceless partners in his amours, yet none of them had held so great a promise of fulfillment as the lady gazing back at him. He murmured daringly, "Yes, I've known that feeling, although not for some time, now. Too long, I think." But his dread of offending prompted him to add a plausible elaboration. "It has been many months since my last address in the

House of Lords, the closest *I've* ever come to performing in public."

"Then you do understand."

The glow in her eyes was not in reaction to his bold words or anything else connected with him, and the cold, unreasoning jealousy that gripped Trevor was stronger than he'd ever felt for Horatio Forster, his human rival. He battled the urge to fling down his cards and prove to her then and there that there were other joys in life, a greater passion than the one performing had inspired. Had no other man tried to seduce her from her absorption in her work? As always, he shrank from acknowledging the unpleasant possibility that the theater would always be her greatest love.

She was calmly adding up her points when the sound of carriage wheels outside caused her to exclaim, "He's here!"

Trevor held one finger to his lips. "Quietly, now. After you've put away the cribbage board and the cards, sit down at the harpsichord and begin playing. I must leave you, but I'll return later." He extinguished the candles in the wall sconces before exiting through the double doors leading to the saloon.

The faint strains of a minuet lured Hugh to the drawing room, and he paused on the threshold, grasping the door frame to steady himself. "A delightful performance as always, Miss Campion."

The actress looked up from the keyboard. "Did you have plenty of pretty dancing partners?"

"I didn't go to the ball to dance, and the only partners I had were at the gaming tables. And what d'you know, that fickle creature Dame Fortune sat in my pocket all night."

He lurched into the room, seeking drink, and took up a decanter from a console table. "Claret," he sighed mournfully. "Dismal stuff, fit only to wash down dinner. I suppose Trevor has drunk up all the port, greedy fellow." After presenting Flora with a full glass, he filled one for himself and held it high. "To my good luck, to my one hundred pounds, to my journey to London—to your fine eyes, m'dear!" He downed half his wine in a single gulp.

Flora sipped hers tentatively. "Your decision to leave

Combe Cotterell seems rather sudden." Her eyes were already accustomed to the semidarkness, and she had no difficulty judging just how inebriated he was. She feared she would never be able to manage Hugh as well as she could Horry in a similar state. The actor, however much he drank, never lost his endearing affability, a quality this young man had never possessed to begin with.

"I told you I'd be only too glad to brush off, if only I had the money. Now I've got it."

"But what if the earl—"

"The earl can go to the devil! He can't keep me here, and he ain't your jailer neither. I'll want some con—congenial company on the road, something sweet to warm my bed. Come with me, why don't you? Let's run off tonight!" He stumbled toward Flora and slipped his arm around her waist. "I'll show you a grand time, it'll be my last fling. For we must part when we get to town—someone is waiting for me there, and she's my love. My gypsy, my enchantress," he sang, slurring the sibilants. When Flora tried to free herself from his partial embrace, he tightened his hold. "Jealous of my Em, are you?" he taunted. "She's a dear, delightful witch, but you—why, you are a fairy, my fair Flora." He squeezed her. "Won't you fly away with me?"

There was enough strength in him to alarm her, but her protest was stifled when his mouth covered hers. The kiss was punishing, his breath was so potent that she reeled, and when she could endure it no longer she kicked his shins.

Muttering curses, he released her. "What the devil was that for?" When she wiped her lips in a gesture eloquent of distaste, he let out a sharp, humorless laugh. "Do I disgust you? Well, that makes us even. My little Emmy is worth ten of any woman who offers herself for public sale. You're destined to become Trevor's doxy, though I can't think why he'd want soiled goods."

Flora slapped his contemptuous face so hard that her eyes watered and her hand stung from the impact. "How dare you slander me! I wish to heaven I'd never met you—*or* your cousin!"

Hugh rubbed his cheek and looked down at her, frowning.

The blow must have acted as a restorative, for none of his words were slurred when he said, "I shouldn't have said that—it was the drink talking. I've no more interest in dalliance than you, and I know you're not a slut, because you've succeeded in eluding Trev. If you do come with me, I swear I won't lay a hand upon you." With a lopsided smile, he added, "We might as well share a carriage to London, don't you agree?"

Flora was tempted, but she would not repay the earl's good faith and hospitality by running off with his cousin, however innocently. "I can't," she said on a note of regret. She looked toward the window, her attention caught by the faint glow of lamps. "A carriage is coming up the drive—who could it be at this late hour? It must be past midnight."

Hugh took out his watch. "So it is, but not by much. They're on time after all." He crossed to the window and unlatched it.

"What are you doing?"

He repocketed his timepiece. "Escaping. Did you think I jested when I said we could leave for London tonight? I arranged my journey on my way to the squire's party—I had a feeling my luck was about to turn!"

Flora went to stand beside him, her fingers closing on the fabric of his sleeve. "But you can't go now!"

"Watch me," he retorted. "I'll leave it to you to express my farewells to Aunt Belle and Trev, and my thanks for such a *delightful* visit." With a mocking laugh, Hugh leaped over the sill, landing in the shrubbery below.

"Wait, please," she begged him, leaning out of the open window. "Stay until tomorrow."

"Trust me, it's better this way. Be a good girl now, don't raise a hue and cry." He grinned up at her and said, "Best of luck, Miss Campion, in all things."

She watched helplessly as he loped toward the waiting post chaise. He turned to wave at her before climbing inside, and the moment the door closed behind him the postboys spurred their horses.

Flora gasped as a warm hand covered her own, still resting upon the sill.

Trevor whispered, "Don't be startled, it's only me."

"Go after him!" she cried. "You can chase him down!"

"It's hardly worth the trouble of throwing a saddle across my horse," he said, calmly fastening the window and drawing the curtains.

He seemed not to care about the failure of the scene he had staged, the culmination of so much plotting and persuasion, and ironically she found herself in the position of trying to convince him not to give up so quickly. "He mentioned a woman, and might admit to being married if we persevere! You *can't* let him get away from you now!"

"I admit I'd like to thrash him for the things he said to you," Trevor said grimly, "but it's less messy this way."

Her eyes widened. "Did you hear—were you in the next room eavesdropping?" His nod confirmed it, and her bosom swelled with her wrathful intake of breath.

"I'm glad you didn't go with him." He smoothed her tumbled hair.

"Don't touch me," she said through clenched teeth.

He took a small backward step. "You didn't object earlier today, on the moor. Don't you know how much it meant to me, holding you close to my heart? That's where you belong, Flora."

"You've fallen into the habit of being with me—actors and actresses almost always fancy themselves in love with each other by the end of a season, but it's a fleeting emotion. You'll find that the recovery comes very quick."

"What a rake you are, breaking hearts with your warm kisses and your cool words. Someone should put a stop to you."

"Someone is going to," she said, lifting her chin.

"I hope it will be me."

Her laugh stuck in her throat, and when it finally emerged it was a feeble sound. "Not a chance of it. Why must you make it your habit to want what you can never have?"

"Because I usually get it. Remember, not so very long ago you swore you'd never come to Combe Cotterell."

"I wish I hadn't," she declared. Not to hurt him, which she obviously had, but because she couldn't come up with a more discouraging reply.

14

No wit nor reason can my passion hide.

Twelfth Night, II. iv.

Flora, waking from a troubled sleep, began the new day as she had ended the last one, berating herself for her failure to discover Hugh Cotterell's exact relationship to the female named Emmy. Was she his lawful wife or a favorite mistress?

The young man's flight was discussed by his relatives over breakfast. Lord Leafield, outwardly unruffled, said he did not despair of uncovering the truth in time.

Lady Ainsley, whose hands shook as she poured out the tea, advised him to inform his London solicitor of Hugh's abrupt departure. She had eaten only half of her boiled egg when she rose from the table, her face deeply flushed, and admitted that she was feeling a trifle weak.

"Don't let Trevor send for the doctor," she said a few minutes later, when Flora tucked her into bed. "He already has so many patients and is busy night and day—there's a fever running through the village."

After trying to make the countess comfortable, Flora hurried back downstairs and found the earl in the library, writing a letter.

"How is she?"

"I can't say," she answered helplessly. "I'm not familiar with her constitution, and I know next to nothing about illnesses."

"Well, Dr. Snell does know." Trevor continued to guide his quill across the paper. "I'm sending a message to him at once."

"She'd rather you didn't."

"And I'd rather she hadn't fallen ill here, so far away from her Bath physician. But because she has done, she must submit to Snell's authority."

"And yours?" she couldn't resist asking.

"And mine."

Dr. Snell arrived within the hour and was inclined to take an optimistic view of her ladyship's case, saying she had succumbed to the trifling malady presently making its rounds of the neighborhood. He prescribed bed rest and sustaining broths, and told the earl he would return the following day.

When Flora wasn't needed in the sickroom she retreated to the gardens, where she dead-headed the roses with great enthusiasm. She was thus engaged one afternoon when she heard the unmistakable sound of carriage wheels and hoofbeats crunching along the drive.

She stepped out from behind the bushes expecting to see the doctor's gig or the barouche belonging to the squire's wife, not the mud-splattered post chaise that had halted before the door. She held her breath in anticipation, wondering if Hugh had returned, but the gentleman who climbed out was a stranger of middle age. Because he carried a valise in one hand and a long black box in the other, she surmised that he was an illustrious medical practitioner summoned from Bath or London.

Flora had not seen the earl all day; since early morning he had been in the fields, overseeing the final stages of the harvest. She went down to dinner wearing the most flattering of her new gowns, a pale silk the color of young leaves, and found him in the saloon with the owl-like gentleman.

Her entrance marked the end of their discussion, and that it concerned her was made clear when Trevor observed cheerfully, "Here is the lady now. Miss Campion, allow me to present Mr. Linton, my man of business."

She was troubled by the censure she read in the sharp gray eyes; the solicitor had evidently drawn his own conclusions about her relationship to his noble client. Unable to refute them by word or action, she was therefore extremely self-conscious throughout the ensuing meal. As soon as the last course was over, she excused herself.

Trevor, with a nod at Mr. Linton, suggested that they remove to the library.

When they were settled in comfortable leather armchairs by the fireside, each with a full glass of wine, he said, "Well, I can't be other than satisfied with the outcome of your investigation, though it took far longer than I imagined. You are perfectly sure Hugh's marriage is legal?"

"My clerk found the proof at St. George's Church in Whitechapel last week, and the officiating parson verified it. Your cousin married Emily Marsh, spinster, in the last week of February, and she expects to be confined in a month's time."

Trevor added up the months in his head. "Then it is as I suspected—he married her under duress."

Mr. Linton lifted his shaggy brows. "It seems not, my lord. When Mr. Cotterell learned of the young woman's unfortunate situation, he was willing to wed her."

"Really?" Trevor sipped his wine thoughtfully.

"He admitted it to me, and the lady has shown me her marriage lines. When I received your lordship's letter informing me of his flight to London, I put Bow Street on the case with instructions to search for the Marsh dwelling. Within a day they found your cousin living over a butcher's shop on Batty Street—St. George's Parish—his father-in-law's establishment. Very outspoken the old gentleman was on the subject of the Runner sticking his nose into people's private affairs."

Frowning, Trevor said, "Undoubtedly a misalliance of this sort would have infuriated my grandfather."

With a grim smile, the older man said, "Mr. Marsh is also concerned about the match being an unequal one. He is willing to pay out his daughter's dowry, which is modest but respectable, but he had the effrontery to demand that you provide Mr. Cotterell with an allowance suitable for a married couple."

Climbing to his feet, Trevor said agreeably, "He'll also need a home for his wife and child, and some form of employment."

His attorney, taken aback, said ponderously, "That is hardly a punishment for the young man's transgressions."

"You may be sure that if I put him to work, he'll regard it as such." After a pause, Trevor asked, "Have you already drawn up the necessary papers?"

The older man opened his black tin box to remove several rolled-up documents, which he untied and passed to the earl.

Without even glancing down, Trevor ripped the sheets in

half, then held them up to the branch of candles on the mantel. When the flames began to lick at the fragments, he dropped them into the empty grate. Looking toward Mr. Linton, whose face registered shock and anguish, he said, "I have no further need of them."

"But the codicil to the late earl's will states clearly that if Mr. Cotterell marries without your knowledge and consent—"

"He has my consent," Trevor said inexorably. "You have faithfully discharged your responsibilities, Linton, and for that I am grateful. But that codicil doesn't *require* that I disinherit my cousin."

"That is true," the solicitor acknowledged reluctantly. "I hope you won't regard it as an impertinence, my lord, but I should like to know what made you change your mind so suddenly."

"I doubt you would understand—I scarcely do myself. Don't think you've come all this way to no purpose, for I need to review the monies I intend to settle on Miss Campion."

"Very well, my lord," said Mr. Linton in a voice heavy with resignation, and once again he reached into his document box.

Flora was sitting with Lady Ainsley when the housekeeper announced that the earl wished to see her. Going downstairs, she made her way to the older wing of the house and found him waiting for her in the library.

Before she could guess his purpose, he hurried to meet her, enfolding her in his embrace. After kissing her with considerable thoroughness, he laughed and said, "Don't be angry, I simply couldn't help myself and didn't even try. You look so beautiful tonight, and that perfume is too, too tempting. What is it?"

"Scent of bluebell."

"You must never wear anything else."

With a glance at the open door, Flora disentangled herself. "One of the servants might have seen," she reproved him.

"By this time everyone will be at the Harvest Home." He picked up a decanter from the table. "This ought to be champagne, but we had none on ice. Will you take a glass with me?"

"A very small one." She watched silently as he poured out the wine.

Replacing the crystal stopper, he said, "Poor old Linton, he must have thought my wits were addled. For the last hour I attended to no more than half of what he told me, and I'm afraid some of my replies shocked him very much. You've bewitched me," he accused her.

"I must have done," she said, striving for a light tone, "because you haven't yet told me what you learned about Mr. Cotterell."

Trevor handed her a wineglass, half filled in obedience to her wishes, and raised his in toast. "To the happy couple—my heir and his six months' bride."

"I'm glad, for your sake—and your cousin's. But what will become of him now that he's been disinherited?"

His joviality gave way to seriousness when he admitted, "I couldn't do it, Flora. When I learned that Hugh married a Whitechapel butcher's daughter to give their child a name, it occurred to me that he possesses honor enough to be an Earl of Leafield. I've undertaken to provide them with a town house and an income. And Hugh can take the position of land agent, which has been vacant for several years, in order to familiarize him with the management of my various estates."

"It may be that your show of good faith will steady him as much as the marriage and his other new responsibilities," Flora hazarded.

"I hope so. I was always so eager to think the worst of Hugh that he was afraid to come to me with the truth. I must have put him through hell by separating him from his wife—clearly he kept silent so long to protect her. I not only understand that, I have to admire it."

She was pleased by this speech, and favorably impressed by his change of attitude. The magnanimity he was showing to Hugh and the girl he'd married would have been out of character for the proud, unyielding man who had visited her at Mrs. Brooke's house so many months ago.

"And when you hear what else I have to say," he continued, smiling at her, "you'll find that we have still more to celebrate."

This remark raised hopes she hadn't dared to acknowledge until now. But his acceptance of his cousin's marriage didn't mean he would go down on his knee to a lowborn actress beneath the very noses of his Cotterell forbears, whose portraits lined the walls.

"I must not stay," she said nervously.

His voice was low and sonorous as he replied, "I know. Our present situation is painfully awkward, but we can begin making plans. I want you to live with me, Flora. For some time I've been thinking that my villa at Twickenham will answer perfectly—I always thought it would be the perfect setting for you, as I said on the day I took you there." He stroked the nape of her neck. "To set you up in some town house, to visit you discreetly between the hours of two and five, or after the play—no, that would never do. I know you haven't had a real home for years, and I'm not sure I have either, however many houses I may own. Linton and I have just concluded a lengthy conversation about settlements—you can depend on me to be generous. I'm not asking you to give up the stage, either. You'll have a carriage of your own, so you can come and go as you please, to rehearsals and—"

"No—oh, no!" she protested. "I will not be your mistress." She wouldn't take the first step on the path to sorrow and shame, however great the temptation. "It is impossible."

"I'll do anything to make it possible," he persisted. "Before I knew you, no woman was ever more to me than the plaything of an hour. When we first met and for a while afterwards, I hardly remember how long, I didn't guess you could be different. But you are. You surpass every female I've ever known—you are my friend and my love and my whole desire. And you're mistaken if you think I crave only your body. I want your heart and your mind and your soul, in exchange for mine, which you already possess."

"You ask too much," she said sadly, "you always do. Although no man ever asked so beautifully."

His sun-bronzed face wore a grave expression. "Have there been other men? No, don't answer that," he said swiftly, "I won't pry into your past. What matters is that you will share your future with me."

Flora pressed the backs of her hands to her hot cheeks to cool the flame his question had kindled. "You are mistaken," she began, but before she could explain that she had no sordid past to conceal, he gripped her shoulders.

"Don't you love me even a little?" he demanded.

She'd never told him an untruth and couldn't do it now. "I must, or my heart wouldn't ache so. But however much I might *want* to live with you, there are a thousand reasons why I cannot."

"So many as that?"

"How would your relatives receive the news that you and a play actress were living together without benefit of clergy? Lady Ainsley would be greatly distressed, and also your uncle—isn't he a parson?"

"That needn't concern you."

"I have a brother whose feelings I must consider," she went on. "And I couldn't bear to disappoint Ben and all the Forsters."

"Surely you aren't still planning to marry that actor?"

"My mind is such a muddle I can't plan anything. Poor Horry," she sighed. "When he learns how badly I've treated him, he may not want me."

Lifting the point of her chin with his forefinger, he chided gently, "Always so quick to offer your pity to others, when I am the one who most deserves it. Forster can seal his vows to you with a marriage ring, I cannot. I won't lie to you, or hold out any false hopes, though if I ever thought you could—'" Here he paused, and whatever words he'd intended to utter died a premature death.

"I never intended to be any man's wife," she told him frankly. "Except Horry's."

"If you do marry your Horry, he'll be unfaithful in time—as I could never be—and I presume he has designs upon your earnings, which naturally I do not. But only he can ensure that respectability you crave, whereas I, loving you and wanting only to make you happy, must destroy the reputation you guard so carefully. There is no way I can prevent gossip, though I will do my very best to shield you from it."

Of all that he'd said, one thing lingered in her mind. "You

would never be unfaithful to me? Yet one day you will want some highborn lady for your wife. When Lady Caroline Lewes or her like becomes Countess of Leafield, what happens to your fidelity to me?"

"Like you, I can't think of anyone else now," Trevor responded savagely. "I'm as reluctant to wed a giddy, unformed aristocrat as you are to enter into one of those plague-ridden theatrical unions you've described to me. And perhaps, with you at my side, I won't ever care to marry. I have an heir. It's you I want more than anyone or anything." He reached out to her again, and she backed away from him. There was an unpleasant edge to his voice when he asked, "Will you stubbornly fling away your happiness—and mine? Does my love mean so little that you can refuse it outright? To speak your own language, that is cruelty of the cruelest sort, Flora."

"How dare you lay such a charge against me!" she cried. "You don't know how I feel, how much I hate hurting you. It isn't easy to reject so tempting an offer, for I've no home, almost no family, not even what you consider to be a normal life—only my independence. And just because I live in a world where such liaisons are accepted doesn't mean—has never meant—that I would enter into one myself. I don't say that it is wrong, only that it's wrong for *me*, and I've always known it. Otherwise, I might have given myself to you that day at Twickenham. It would have been so easy—then, and many times since."

He didn't appear to be gratified by this painful confession. "Do you intend to live as a nun for the rest of your days? Or will you marry a man you don't love for the luxury of building a reputation no one will believe in? Don't bother to reply," he said, having by now worked himself into a rage. "You want to run back to that precious world of yours, more dear than any human except a Forster. You think yourself independent, yet you refuse to unravel the rope of dependency tying you to that family! And if you are so misguided as to wed your Horatio, you won't be marrying a man, just a rickety theater and an empty respectability."

"That can't be worse than becoming your lordship's whore!"

Trevor's tanned face turned a sickly white. A moment later he turned his back upon her and moved toward his desk. Sinking heavily into the chair, as if all strength had been drained from his body, he said quietly, "Many months ago, when I said you could name your price if only you would come to Devonshire with me, I never dreamed that our association would be so very costly."

"It's late," she said in a distant, detached voice, "and I promised to read to Lady Ainsley. May I go to her?"

"Still running from me, Flora? It has grown to be a habit with you. Oh, very well, but at least have the fairness to consider my offer more carefully before you decline it."

It was imperative that she leave Combe Cotterell, if not that very night, which was impractical, then early the next morning. She must hasten to London, where she would begin the painful task of trying to forget she had ever been desired by such a man. If he had the power to draw from her unwilling lips the admission of love she'd never wanted to make, what else might he not win from her in time? One possible answer to that question sent her running blindly along the dark corridor and up the staircase of carved oak.

15

Get him to bed, and let his hurt be looked to.

Twelfth Night, V. i.

Although Trevor was in no mood for the harvest revels, he owed it to his laborers to make an appearance at the great barn where the common folk were making merry. By the time he arrived, the food tables had already been cleared, but the home-brewed ale and potent cider still flowed freely. While he quaffed a brimming mug, he watched the young men and their sweethearts perform a lively reel and regretted that he couldn't teach it to Flora, with whom he'd never danced.

How could he change her mind? He'd never once been able to move her with clever arguments or soft kisses. She was answerable to no one; she had no parents whose feelings she must consider and no husband—not quite yet. She was free to take a lover or refuse one as she wished.

When Trevor returned to the house, he went directly to his aunt's bedchamber. Her face was wan and pale, etched with lines of weariness and something else he couldn't define until her first words told him it was pity.

"Oh, my poor boy—come and sit down so I can talk with you."

He sat down upon the armless chair which Flora occupied when reading aloud. "She told you everything, didn't she?"

"No, only that she must go away tomorrow, and that was enough. My traveling chaise will take her to the Royal Oak at Ivy Bridge, for the mail coach to Exeter and London."

"No doubt she's grateful to you for helping her escape my wicked snares," he said dryly.

"What else could I do? I admit, I'm surprised she turned you down, which I gather she has done."

"In no uncertain terms. But she isn't an ordinary creature,

Aunt Belle, as I have discovered to my delight and despair."
After a moment of silence, he remembered to tell her about
Mr. Linton's success. "He found proof of the marriage, though
I've chosen not to make use of it, and says that my cousin will
shortly become a papa." He clenched one hand into a fist, then
slowly released it. "To think that I should envy Hugh, of all
people. It seems I've fallen victim to one of fate's crueler
jokes."

His aunt smiled. "I don't object to your being in love with
an actress, but I really must draw the line at remarks like that
one. You sound like the hero of a very poor play. If you can't
have Miss Campion as your mistress, you might consider making her your wife."

"Even though her father, however wise and worthy a man,
was the bastard child of a peasant woman? Perhaps sired by a
noble lover, but just as possibly by the village blacksmith."

Said Lady Ainsley tartly, "You won't convince me that her
parent's illegitimacy, or even the fact that she was reared in a
playhouse, are obstacles to you."

"Perhaps not," he confessed. "But if I had asked Flora to
marry me, her answer would have been the same. I can't imagine she would willingly sacrifice what promises to be a brilliant career merely to become a countess, even mine. Not that
she'll remain single forever—she wants the respectability a
husband can provide. If she marries her actor, she can have
both her work *and* her good name."

"She'll find no joy in either one if she weds someone she
doesn't love," said Lady Ainsley. "A convenient marriage
isn't always the best one."

"Yet you encouraged me to dangle after Lady Caroline."

"Only because I didn't realize you'd already lost your heart
to another," she said in defense. "Well, whatever happens, you
may always count me as your friend—and hers."

He leaned over and kissed her thin cheek. "Thank you for
that. I'm sure that in time she'll understand that my proposal is
the best and only one I can make, given our circumstances."

*   *   *

Flora, who was at that moment frantically opening drawers and removing her belongings, understood only the necessity of immediate flight.

Margery Prescott, when informed that they would be leaving Combe Cotterell at daybreak, accepted the lack of explanation without a blink. Seeing that her mistress wore the wild expression of a rabbit fighting to free itself from a snare before the gamekeeper comes to dispatch it, she said soothingly, "You may leave everything to me, ma'am." Then she moved to the tall wardrobe and began taking down bandboxes in an unhurried, methodical fashion.

The garments Flora had purchased in Bath hung on their pegs, a rainbow of colors: crimson silk, blue cambric, green broadcloth, summery pastel muslins. All had been bought with his lordship's gold. A collection entirely suitable for a mistress, she thought with a pang, and he must have known it all along. To keep them would be to give the impression that her principles were variable—and vulnerable.

"Pack only my own gowns," she said with apparent nonchalance. "I'll leave the rest behind—they don't really suit me."

"I'll ask the laundress to press your gray traveling habit for tomorrow," Margery offered.

"Yes, it will do very well." Flora thought bleakly that the color would suit her mood to perfection. She removed her elegant gown and tossed it aside. After putting on her nightshift, she sat down at her dressing table and reached for her reticule. "Here are vails for the servants," she said as she sorted through a selection of gold and silver coins. "A half-guinea each for the housekeeper and the butler, and a pair of sixpences for the chambermaid and the laundry woman."

Margery promised to distribute them for her.

Flora unpinned her coiffure and raked the comb through her long curls. With her hair down she looked young and lost, not at all the twenty-five-year-old actress who should have known better than to let herself fall in love with an earl. But she mustn't think of him now, or she would never sleep; she'd have an excess of time for reflection on her way to London.

Her eyes fell on the battered trunk Margery was pulling out from under the bed, the companion of many a long journey and a symbol of her profession. Each scratch in the leather and dent in the lid marked a move—from one town to the next, from one theater to another. Someday, she vowed, she would stay in place for more than the length of a season. With maturity had come a dwindling of her resiliance, and a fitful longing for a life that was less public and more domestic. Her would-be lover had known exactly how to tempt her, with his promise of a shared home, a peaceful refuge from the hustle and bustle of her workaday world.

After years of practice, Margery was efficient and thorough, and she didn't take long to finish packing. "Is there anything more I should do?" she asked, turning down the bed.

"No, I think not."

"Good night, ma'am. Don't sit up, now, if you mean to make such an early start."

When Flora finished combing her hair, she bent forward to blow out the candles affixed to either side of the mirror. The money she'd intended to dole out to the household servants still lay beside her purse—Margery had inadvertently left it behind.

She shrugged into her paisley dressing gown, loosely tying the sash, then scooped up the coins. She tiptoed out into the stone-flagged hallway, and after making several wrong turns she finally found the narrow wooden stairway leading to the garret and Margery's quarters. The older woman scolded her for wandering about a drafty old pile without her slippers when she should be in bed.

Because Flora had left her room in darkness, she was surprised to see a light beneath her door. When she stepped inside, she saw a wax taper on the mantel, which cast a soft glow over the curtained bed and the figure standing by the window.

She let out a startled exclamation when Lord Leafield turned to face her. He wore no coat or cravat; the collar and cuffs of his shirt were unfastened. "Did you mean to go without bidding me a fond farewell?"

"You shouldn't be here." Drawing her dressing gown more closely about her, she fumbled for the sash, only to discover it was missing. She watched with increasing alarm as he moved closer. His expression was a compound of gentle amusement and something she didn't feel comfortable meeting in her bedroom so late at night.

"How lovely you are." Placing one hand over the inverted triangle of brown flesh revealed by the gap in his shirt, he recited, "And yet 'tis not your inky brows, your black silk hair, your cheek of cream—you see I've been studying the Bard, the better to woo you."

"My lord—"

"Use my name, Flora. That is a simple means of pleasing me, and costs you nothing."

"My lord," she repeated firmly, "there is nothing more to be said. I am departing early tomorrow."

"Wilt thou leave me so unsatisfied?" When she stared back at him, he smiled and asked, "Don't you know your next line, my sweet Juliet? You're supposed to reply, 'But what satisfaction canst thou have tonight?'"

"I haven't forgotten, it is only that I do not relish your jest," Flora replied, not altogether certain it had been one.

"Flora." He reached out for her, pulling her so close that the short, curling hairs on his chest tickled her cheek. His lips touched her hair and lightly brushed her temple before avidly claiming her mouth, and the hot kisses melted her resistance.

He pushed her wrapper away from her shoulders, and it slid to the floor, pooling at their feet. As he touched her breast, now covered only by the thin fabric of her nightdress, she felt her nipple contract and harden beneath his hand. Pressed against him as she was, she sensed the tension in his lower body and was aware of a liquid softness in the corresponding region of her own anatomy.

"I know how to chase all your doubts away. Let me love you—I can show you how it will be." His tone was restrained, reassuring, but his eyes burned with passion.

Flora knew that if she rendered the secrets of her body she would never be free of him—but was that what she really wanted? Confused, half faint with desire, she did not protest when he guided her toward the bed with the rosebud finials.

Trevor removed her gown slowly and deliberately, savoring the first, ritual unveiling of her white body. She was a thing of beauty, with contours so graceful that she resembled a piece of marble statuary, an artist's idealized conception of woman-hood. With increasing urgency his hands explored the straight back and tapering waist, moving ever downward. He curbed his impatience as best he could, for although it had been many weeks since he'd had a woman, this one was far too precious to take a single moment before she was ready to receive him.

Gradually it dawned on him that she wasn't responding as eagerly as she had been a moment ago. Her eyes were tightly shut; her expression was one of resignation, not rapture. "Don't be afraid," he murmured.

"I can't help it," she said feebly. "Isn't it natural—the first time?"

His hands stilled, and he stared down at her, his voice hoarse with shock as he asked, "Have you never lain with a man?"

She buried her cheek in the pillow. "You'll have proof of it soon enough."

There was no mistaking her meaning, and Trevor was too astonished to say or do anything. Flora, who had trod the boards for half a dozen years, and had lived among actors for most of her life, had somehow managed to retain her virginity. And that, he realized, explained her characteristic elusiveness and her oft-stated reluctance to become his mistress.

"You might have told me," he chided gently.

"Perhaps I would have done," she replied, "if I thought you'd believe me."

"I'll always believe you, Flora." Taking her bare and trembling body in his arms again, he said, "My past behavior has made you doubt my ability to be patient, I know, but you have my word that I won't rush you. I can wait, and my consolation will be knowing that I'll be your first and only lover. You must go to London as we discussed last night, to my villa at Twickenham, and I will join you there as soon as I can."

He hadn't really changed, Flora thought miserably, he still had that old habit of backing her into a corner and trying to rule her as it pleased him. Was he going to ordain her entire future? It was a fearsome prospect.

"I will not live with you," she declared. "I'm returning to London because my duty lies there, but I shall never, ever go to Twickenham." She freed herself from his embrace and went to gather up her dressing gown from the floor. "There's more to life than lying together in a bed," she said, covering herself. "Suppose you got me with child? I know you, you'd shut me away, you would make me give up acting. What a slur it would be upon your lordship's dignity if your child—even your bastard—were born in some backstage corner! I don't want a protector, and even if you did make love to me it wouldn't persuade me to accept your offer."

As Trevor stared at her wild, white face, he fell prey to that persistent fear that he would always be the lesser of her loves. "Go to London, then," he told her harshly, for there was nothing else he could say.

He left her without a backward glance, and closed the door behind him.

Late in the afternoon a stage coach, heavily burdened with baggage and passengers, brought Flora and Margery to the cathedral city of Exeter. They took rooms at a quiet inn, and the actress ordered tea while her dresser visited the post office to book seats on the next mail coach to London.

"It leaves at dawn," Margery reported when she returned. "We'll make London by six o'clock the next morning, provided the coachman can keep to his time bill," she announced.

"A twenty-four-hour journey—what an exhausting prospect." Flora sighed.

She went to bed early, for she hadn't slept at all the night before, and all too soon Margery was shaking her awake again. Half conscious, her temples pounding, she scrambled into her clothes and tried to revive herself with a cup of tea. She and Margery arrived at the post office in time to watch the guards load the sacks of Royal Mail. A handful of bleary-eyed passengers had gathered in the yard, most of them still yawning; some stared at the sad-faced beauty in drab gray.

During the first stage of the journey, Flora spoke scarcely a word. Her headache worsened, and just before the coach stopped at Honiton to take on the mail, she felt a twinge of pain in her lower back.

When they stopped at Salisbury for dinner, she asked her companion how much time was allowed for the meal.

"Thirty minutes, according to the time bill, but we won't go till the cross-mail comes in from Shaftesbury," said Margery, who had become friendly with the older of the two guards during the course of the journey. "Sometimes it's as much as twenty minutes late," she added. "And if you're ailing for the reason I suspect, you'd do better to stop here and spend the night."

"I own I don't relish traveling today, but the journey will be over by morning."

"When the cross-mail comes in, then we'll see if you feel like being jolted around all night long," the dresser replied. She cast a knowing glance at the wan face, and a short time later slipped away to request that the guard remove their baggage from the coach. After speaking to the landlord and engaging a room, she led Flora upstairs and tucked her into bed with a hot brick and a glass of wine, her standard and infallible remedies for the onset of menstrual cramps.

"It's come a week early," she observed dourly, as if it were Flora's fault. "And you are regular as an old clock all these years. Well, they do say as how a shock can sometimes bring it on." And she sat down to bend her gray head over the tatting she had begun in the country, where her duties had been so limited.

Flora, buried under the covers, held her body immobile in the hope that by doing so the next wave of pain would pass her by.

For a day and a half she'd kept regret at bay, but as the wine took effect she could no longer avoid thinking about Trevor Cotterell. He loved her and she loved him, even if he seemed unable to accept her dedication to her work, and her dread of scandal and disgrace. She was unable to hover in the background of his life in some equivocal position, more than a mistress but less than a wife. It might have a certain romantic appeal, but in time that would be overshadowed by her shame.

In the morning she felt sufficiently refreshed to continue her journey by post chaise, a more expensive mode of travel but one which permitted her to call a halt if she wished. And consequently she reached Great Queen Street at a more civilized hour than if she'd remained on the mail.

Her arrival was unexpected but timely, or so Esther said as she lured Flora to the back parlor with the promise of a surprise.

Two gentlemen were waiting there, both so tall that their heads—one black, one golden—nearly brushed the low ceiling.

"Miles!" Flora cried, casting herself into the arms of one tanned giant. She shed a few happy tears onto the front of his blue coat, and it was several minutes before she regained her composure. "I'd forgotten you might be here, but how glad I am to see you—and you, dear James!"

Captain James Drew tossed his young son into the air, his laugh booming disconcertingly in a house that had long been the preserve of soft-spoken females. "She *forgot*—that's hardly a sisterly welcome!"

Miles Campion, as black of hair and green of eye as his sister, said, "Esther hasn't removed her arms from her husband's neck long enough to pen the happy news to you, Florry."

"I'm glad I saved her the trouble. Oh, Miles, how brown you are." Flora laughed, reaching up to touch his cheek. His complexion, once as fair as her own, was ruddier than ever from the harsh sun of the tropic regions.

Mrs. Brooke took her squealing grandson from his proud but unhandy papa. "How do you come to be in London so soon, Flora dear?"

"Indeed, you weren't due to arrive for another week, or so you said in your last letter," Esther observed. "That's what we told Master Horry when he dined here last night."

Flora blushed to hear Horatio's name but replied serenely, "Lady Ainsley's fever broke, so there was no reason for me to remain in the country. Perhaps I had a premonition of our sailors' return!"

As always after one of their long separations, Lieutenant Miles Campion was alert to changes in his sister, but he supposed her long journey was the reason she looked pale and tired. He was more disturbed by the fact that her former bright gaiety had been tempered by time, and the discovery that two years had made her so much older.

16

Some are born great, some achieve greatness,
And some have greatness thrust upon 'em.

Twelfth Night, II. v.

Flora hoped her brother would be an antidote to sorrow, but he
was not completely free to devote himself to her.

The morning after she returned to London, he and Captain
Drew departed for Portsmouth, where their ship was undergo-
ing refurbishment, and Esther chose to go with them. After
two long days on the road, Flora had little interest in another
trip, and let Mrs. Brooke take her place in the carriage.

She was in the nursery, watching young Hartley toddle
about on his sturdy and inexhaustible legs, when the manservant announced that Mr. Forster had come to call. Flora
jumped to her feet. "Which Mr. Forster?"

"Master Horry, ma'am."

"Tell him—" She hesitated, fighting her craven desire to
plead a headache. "Oh, tell him I'll be down at once." Abandoning the child to his nurse, she made her way to the parlor.

After kissing her cheek in his usual fashion, Horatio commented that the air of Devonshire seemed to agree with her.

This was a kindness, for Flora knew better; her looks had
suffered in recent days. "I'm sure any bloom will fade quickly
enough, from the combination of London living and company
rehearsals." Thinking it best to cover the highest hurdle at
once, she said, "I'm sorry I concealed my whereabouts from
you, Horry—I was afraid to tell you beforehand, for fear you'd
misunderstand. Are you terribly angry with me?"

"I was furious," he declared. "Just ask Esther Drew, who
witnessed the explosion. To be sure, she wove a convoluted
tale about evil cousins and masquerades, all the while swear-
ing up and down that your sojourn in the country was the most

innocent thing in the world. Do you know what disturbed me most about her muddled explanation? The fact that Lord Leafield's aunt was there. I could no longer assume he intended a seduction, but rather, a serious courtship. So I've been practicing saying 'yes, your ladyship' and 'no, your ladyship' ever since."

"You go too far, Horry," she said crossly, for this was not a subject she cared to be teased about.

"So he didn't ask you!" Horatio crowed triumphantly.

"How could he? He's an earl, and I—well, we both know what I am."

"A simpleton. Dukes have taken wives from the playhouse, though none lately. As for earls—why, only think of Lord Derby and his high-nosed countess, who used to be plain Elizabeth Farren of Drury Lane. And Louisa Brunton has been heard to say that she would wed the Earl of Craven if he asked her."

"If you seriously believe that I could be party to so unequal a match, then you don't know me, Horry."

"I know you well enough to suspect that you haven't returned to London as heart-whole as you'd like me to believe," he shot back. "Come here, love, and give us a kiss," he invited her, holding out his arms. When Flora scurried out of the way, the spark of mockery went out of his brown eyes. "I suppose," he said at last, "that if you can't bring yourself to kiss me, then you'll find it much harder to marry me. Did your noble patron make you forget my last words to you at Bath?"

This was close enough to the truth to make her flinch. "Just because I don't indulge in the sort of slap and tickle you delight in doesn't mean—" But she hadn't foreseen into what murky depths she was plunging until it was too late to save herself.

"It doesn't mean what? That you don't care for him? That you won't marry me? Don't toy with me, Florry! You owe me the complete truth, I've a right to it, as a friend and suitor." He sat on the sofa and patted the seat cushion invitingly. "Now be a good girl and confess all, for however naughty you've been, I'm hardly the one to look askance."

Flora knew he was right. Her wicked Horatio was the only

person to whom she could unburden herself without fear of censure. And perhaps by telling her troubles, she might be able to lay them to rest, which she'd been unable to do by keeping them to herself. "You're too perceptive for comfort, Horry, or else I'm not the actress I was trained to be." She sighed.

"Poor lass, doesn't he love you back?"

"He does, that's the whole trouble," she said miserably. "He asked me to be his mistress, but I said no. Even so, I didn't stop him from—that is, I didn't stop myself. I should have, I meant to, and now I'm afraid he thinks that someday I'll say yes." She pulled out her handkerchief, having discovered that the dangers of confession lay in not knowing what would come out, or how. She resisted the strong impulse to weep all over her confessor, and after a brief dab at her eyes, she continued more coherently. "He won't wed me—my birth and background are unacceptable. There was nothing to do but part. And oh, Horry, I can't marry at all, not anyone. Not now."

"Oh, my God." If the substance of her revelation was more than Horatio had bargained for, he nevertheless responded gallantly. Taking her hands in a firm grip, he said, "I'll marry you. Whatever he did to you, no matter what results from your—your liaison, I'll stand by you."

"I'm not *ruined*," she told him, blushing.

He digested this, then said firmly, "We can be married anyway."

"You are a good friend," she murmured, giving his hand a grateful squeeze, "and though I love you dearly, I refuse."

He asked quizzically. "Must I wait another five years just to round out a full decade from the first time I asked? I've been pining for you, Florry."

"That may be, but I doubt you lived the life of a monk while you were in Brighton."

"It never mattered to you before."

"Perhaps not, but loving someone else does matter. I couldn't be comfortable in a marriage of convenience now, not even with you." She turned the full force of her green eyes upon him, silently pleading for absolution. "I don't want to risk spoiling the affection we have for each other."

"What a wise woman adversity has made you," he commented.

"I'm an arrant fool," she contradicted. "And one who appreciates your not saying, 'I told you so.' Because you did warn me. You were jealous of Leafield, and I think it was that, and a kind of nostalgia for the sort of love we once shared, that prompted you to propose marriage."

"That may be true. It makes no difference now." His jaw clenched, and then he said, "Call me jealous if you like, but I wish your first lover had been worthy of you."

"He *wasn't* my lover," she said firmly, "and you've no cause to speak ill of him."

"Don't I?" he retorted.

But he was smiling again by the time he left. Kissing her on the forehead, he said gently, "You're a brave girl. I'm sorry about everything—not just for you and myself, but even for Leafield, little as I like him. I can guess how he must feel."

Though her conscience was clearer, Flora continued to experience an unprecedented malaise of spirits. Her long stay in the country had left her rested in body, but definitely not in mind. She reminded herself that suffering built character, but what good was strength of character when one repaired to bed each night to speculate on what might have been, if she'd been able, if he'd been able—but what was the use? Denied marriage to the one man she loved and unable to love the only man she could marry, she must prepare herself for a solitary but productive spinsterhood.

When Benedict Forster came to see her in the afternoon, she seized upon the legal papers he brought like a drowning victim taking hold of a towline, and signed her name to her bond with a flourish. "I'm yours to command," she told him with a false smile.

Within a few days she was back at the theater, but even there she couldn't forget Trevor. In Bath he had often met her at the stage door to walk her home, listening patiently to her litany of professional joys and sorrows.

Her brother guessed that a deeply troubled soul was hiding beneath the mask of contentment. To Miles she seemed altogether different from that Florry of furloughs past, who had gushed and giggled about her colleagues and her conquests. Although she demanded the names of all the flirts he'd left behind in the port cities of the Caribbean, she hadn't disclosed the names of her admirers. He was aware that her present salary was handsome, but money was evidently not the source of delight it had been earlier in her career. She seldom laughed, and the songs she played on the pianoforte tended towards a minor key. And the fleeting, wistful expression that crossed her face sometimes when the Drews billed and cooed together led him to suppose that something crucial was being withheld from him, probably a failed romance.

One night she returned from the theater to find him the sole occupant of the back parlor. "Is everyone abed already?" she cried in dismay. "Never say it's *that* late!"

He folded his paper and laid it aside. "Not quite. James and Esther and Aunt Tab are dining across the street with Julie Forster. Poor girl, she never sees her family any more than we do you, so she imported some company. That was her excuse, but we all suspect her of wanting to show off the talents of her new French chef." Two pairs of green eyes met as brother and sister exchanged smiles. "You were a long time at the theater," he said. "Have you dined?"

Flora gave him a lopsided smile. "I recall Margery pushing something foodlike in front of me during a lull, but whether I finished it, I can't say."

"Poor little Florry, was your day so bad as that?"

"Worse!"

"Tell big brother all," he invited.

"Well, first there was the riot. Someone—probably Sheridan—orchestrated a nasty little demonstration outside the theater this morning, so Ben postponed rehearsal. Then I had to stay late because he arranged for one of the scene painters to make a sketch of my face. He thinks I'm going to be the rage as Juliet, and wants to sell my portrait to the booksellers and printshops. As always," she concluded, "he won me over by saying it will benefit the theater. Tell me about your day— didn't you and James call at Somerset House again? What news from the Navy Office?"

"Nothing definite," he answered, going to the fireplace to add a few more coals against the late September chill. "The *Vestal* is still being refitted for battle, and James and I may go to Portsmouth again to mark the progress. I was scanning the war reports in the paper just now, until I was diverted by the libelous descriptions of Ben in the back pages. Why doesn't he bring a suit against the publisher, for damages?"

"Controversy is good for business," she explained. "I suspect him of writing half of what appears in print and submitting it anonymously. The trick must work. Horry told me there's hardly a place to be had for the first performance, except in the one-shilling gallery. He peeked at one of the seating ledgers."

"Aren't you nervous, knowing there will be a crowd?"

"I would be if I'd the time to consider it!"

But on the day of the opening she had something more than the prospect of a full theater to overset her, and that was the news she had been dreading: Lord Leafield had returned to London.

Horatio, her informant, had attended the grand dinner he'd given for the theater's managing committee. "If Julie's new cook is true-born French, then I'm a Chinaman," he said sourly. "The food at her table is nothing like what was served last night in Cavendish Square! I lost all count of the courses—we had a different wine with each one. Oh, I should've told you at once—Leafield asked about you. I wonder he had the nerve." He reached into his coat pocket and pulled out a packet tied with a red ribbon. "*And* he bade me give you this, which I was sorely tempted to toss into the gutter."

She took the parcel without a word and carried it to her new dressing room, a refuge from well-meaning friends and curious colleagues. One of several benefits she'd derived from her promotion to leading player, it was large and had easy access to the stage, but in her opinion it was too near the noisy green room for peace. She also missed having a window. But for Margery's sake she was pleased; the dresser presided over their prestigious new quarters with a pride that far exceeded her own.

Flora sat down, her fingers shaking as they untied the gay

ribbon and tore at the paper wrapping. The object that fell into her lap was familiar: Trevor had found and returned the missing sash from her paisley dressing gown.

The sight of it revived the memories sweet summer had left with her, the strongest and most recurrent being the night a man had taken her in his arms, proving that she was capable of passions more real than those she simulated on the stage.

As she tucked the sash into her reticule, she pondered the significance of its return. Was this a sign that Trevor accepted her decision and had forgotten her, or did it symbolize his determination to win her?

On that all-important day, the Princess was a small city possessed by a frantic population as everyone from the lowliest scene shifter to Benedict Forster himself made the final preparations for the first performance. The utility players raided the stock wardrobe for trimming and lace to make themselves stand out in crowd scenes. Aproned workers swept out vestibules, planting virgin tapers in the brass sconces in the saloon and the box lobby, while the coffee-room attendants did the same in their humbler domain. At midafternoon several of the actors and stagehands left the premises in search of dinner or to down a mug or two of sustaining spirit; others ordered food and drink from a nearby tavern and ate at the theater.

A full two hours before the doors would be opened, a crowd began to form outside the pit entrance. Within, an expectant hush fell over the building. In the lamplighting room, the workers poured oil into the globe-shaped footlights. The chandeliers over the pit were lowered and their candles lit; the liveried footmen from the great households, admitted early to guard their employers' seats, gossiped together as they watched this ritual.

Flora dined in her dressing room with Sally Jenkins, whom Ben had promoted to the roles left vacant by Louise Talley. As always on a first night, the redhead was restless and talkative, and she chattered away uninhibitedly.

After clearing away the plates, Margery withdrew.

"How lucky you are to have your own dresser!" Sally sighed enviously. "I should have asked her to rearrange my hair, but you've got clever fingers, love—can you help this poor mop?"

Flora sorted through her finery and produced some silk flowers to match her friend's costume. As she tucked them into the cluster of copper curls, Sally glowered into the mirror and muttered, "Devil fly away with Ben Forster!"

"What's he done now?"

"I had my heart set on a new short crop, but he says I must keep my ringlets. They're such a bother to dress."

This complaint was a familiar one, and Flora nodded, adding another sprig to the elaborate coiffure. "I've been dressed and undressed, curled and poked and pulled about so often this week that I feel like some stupid, helpless doll."

"But a beautiful one—that's all Ben cares for." Sally took up a hare's foot and tapped it against the edge of the table to remove the residue of rice powder from the fine hairs. With studied indifference, she announced, "Fred Stafford and I have parted."

"Oh, Sal, why?" But Flora understood only too well her friend's probable state of mind and possible reluctance to dwell on the rift, and she added gently, "Or would you rather not talk about it?"

"I think I must tell someone or go mad," Sally declared. "A week ago he asked me to marry him—that's how all the trouble began. Lud, Florry, can you believe it? I know he's hard-working, and that any musician is worth two actors, but I won't be fettered. And then last night I told Fred my secret." Her great blue eyes clouded over.

With grave delicacy Flora asked if she was increasing.

"No, and that's what set him off. I've been taking certain precautions. And you needn't pretend to be shocked, because you know perfectly well that they exist."

Indeed, Flora and every other actress knew a variety of preventive measures, and so did the bawds and the prostitutes of the district. In murky alleyways near the theater, wizened crones hawked foul nostrums which were guaranteed to cure the pox or pregnancy, or both. But it was also common knowledge that these concoctions could have worse effects than inducing miscarriage.

She said fearfully, "Not drugs? But they can do more harm than good—it's not worth the risk. Oh, please don't say you've been taking something dangerous!"

"Nothing so chancy, I swear. I used—well, never mind what, but it's a harlot's trick. Eliza Ellis began doing it after her last confinement, with some success, and I went to her a year ago when Fred and I began living together. I never told him—I didn't dare—till our row last night. But he was so damnably smug when he said if I were breeding I'd marry him quick enough. And I said not bloody likely." The freckled face screwed into a mask of pain. "He called me such names, Florry. Unnatural, unwomanly, depraved—I wanted to die."

"You did as you thought best."

"And you don't disapprove?"

After a moment's consideration, Flora gave the only possible answer. "I'm a woman too, Sally, and can't find it in myself to condemn you. But men are very different."

The other actress acknowledged the truth of this with a nod. "He and I had some jolly times, and I'll miss him—till the next likely chap comes my way. So tell me, how does that dashing brother of yours feel about ladies of the stage?" Sally had asked this in a jesting tone and was therefore startled to see that Flora was rather damp about the eyes. "You mustn't cry, love—I've always been too careless and selfish to keep a lover for very long. Here, take this or you'll spoil your face." And the comforted became the comforter as she pressed her handkerchief upon her distraught friend.

Using the edge of the white square, Flora carefully soaked up her tears before they could splash onto her painted cheeks. When she was done, she gave Sally a tremulous smile. "Why are all the unfairnesses in the world heaped upon actresses? Eliza Ellis and Mrs. Siddons must make room in their busy lives for everything other females take for granted—a husband, children, managing the household. Anyone who goes into keeping, like Dora Jordan or Mrs. Logan, gains an everlasting reputation of easy virtue no matter how faithful she may be to her protector."

"Well, all I know is that I want to live my little bit of life away from the theater on my own terms. And you must feel the same," Sally hazarded, "if you've turned Horry down again. He's already dangling after that little dancing girl, the one with the lisp."

"Is he? I hadn't noticed."

"That nor anything else."

Flora shrugged, offering no explanation or excuse.

"That's how I knew he'd proposed to you again—every time he does you refuse him and he has to find a new flirt." The redhead rose and shook out her frothy blue skirts. "I really must go, or your dragon Margery will give me a scold for imposing too long. You're a dear to listen to my troubles, and if I can ever return the favor—" There was no glimmer of response in Flora's still face, so Sally said brightly, "Remember that wager we made at Bath? I have it on good authority that Mrs. Jordan is engaged at Drury Lane for the season, so you owe me a guinea. And mind, don't you and Horry eat all of the first-night supper while we comedians slave away in the farce."

On her exit she nearly collided with the callboy, who stuck his gray head through the door to say respectfully, "You're wanted, Miss Campion, Miss Jenkins. 'Tis time for His Majesty's hymn."

The two actresses immediately joined the flock of players hurrying toward the stage. Through the curtain they could hear the last frantic cries of the orange women out front, calling, "Apples! Oranges! Bills of the play, good sirs, a penny apiece!" When the orchestra struck up, the green draperies began to rise slowly, and the assembled company sang "God Save the King." The audience chimed in, more or less reverently, and afterward the stage was cleared of all but Horatio Forster, who spoke a lengthy prologue on behalf of the players, begging the indulgence of the audience.

Flora waited in the wings on the prompter's side, drawing deep breaths to calm herself. Her feelings were, as ever, contradictory: she was impatient to begin acting the part she had studied so long, and she wished she might turn tail and flee the premises. And then there was no more time for rational thought because Madam Forster, as the Nurse, was calling for Lady Juliet. Flora's entrance inspired an approving murmur

punctuated by a few catcalls from the partisans of the royal
patentees, but these protests were quickly hushed.

She had studied the part all summer, had lived and breathed
it during the rehearsal period, and now the legacy of her own
impossible love gave her new insight into her role. She had a
strong empathy for any lovers who struggled to overcome the
odds stacked against them by an unkind fate, and because her
own personality was many-faceted, so was her Juliet's. As the
play progressed, the character matured before the eyes of a
captivated audience, which saw first the winsome child, then a
trusting adolescent in the throes of first love, and finally the
strong-willed woman, capable of fighting for her happiness
and doomed to fail.

At last came Ben's great moment, the funeral procession.
The focal point was Juliet's flower-bedecked bier, carried aloft
by mourners and followed by grieving Capulets, the Nurse, the
Friar, and lesser characters. Bringing up the rear were three
dozen utility players decked out as priests, monks, nobles, and
Veronese peasants, all singing mournful dirges. This magnificent display received a thunderous ovation; even John Kemble's supporters, inured to spectacle, were greatly impressed.

The volatile groundlings demanded to see the entire parade
a second time, shouting boisterously, "Again! Again! Give us
the funeral!"

The manager, fearing some damage to his theater if he
failed to appease the mob, stepped forward, bowed once, then
ordered his players to begin the scene again.

Afterward the pit settled down, and the play continued on
toward its melancholy end. The suicides of the lovers evoked
sobs and sighs, and all but the most case-hardened wept as
Flora, clutching her happy dagger, made her final speech, and
sank to the ground. She did so thankfully, although Mr. Warren, on whose bony form she had fallen, was a most uncomfortable resting place. Never before had she been so glad to
expire: her entire body throbbed with weariness, and the oppressive heat made her feel faint. The oil-filled footlights, can-
dle-lit chandeliers, and roomful of tightly packed bodies had
turned the theater into an oven. When the curtain fell on the

final tableau, a unified sigh of relief went up from players and public alike.

The corpses sprang to life and Flora faced her next trial, speaking the epilogue. She stepped past the curtain and walked out to the stage apron to begin the rhymed speech Ben had composed, but she could scarcely hear her own words.

The gentlemen in the pit shouted her name; the ladies wept and waved their handkerchiefs. Those few souls brave enough to contradict the consensus of opinion found themselves in danger of being attacked. Flora curtsied as they heaped their noisy adulation upon her, and as her ears grew accustomed to the din, she could hear Ben hissing from the wings, "Make your obeisance to the boxes. The pit be damned, woman—curtsy to the *boxes*!"

Obediently lifting her heavy crimson skirts, she presented herself to the boxes on her left and sank downward, rose, and turned to the right. And then she saw him.

He sat in the forefront of his stage box, the man who filled her thoughts, the one she had last seen when he had left her bedchamber. As the Earl of Leafield leaned slightly forward, his face was the only recognizable one in that sea of hundreds. Assailed by paralyzing memory, she scarcely heard Ben's next command—he was telling her to curtsy again. Although she tried to obey, her legs failed to respond to her will.

The roar of the crowd was more deafening than ever; it seemed that the mob was about to hurl itself at the stage. She turned a beseeching face toward the prompter's box.

The two Forsters rushed forward to take her by the arms. As they led her off the stage, she cast one final, fleeting glance at Trevor.

Suddenly Ben was kissing her and Horry was kissing her. Strangers approached her and addressed her in reverent tones, as though she were some royal or divine being, while she wondered vaguely who they were. The mob had chased her down, right into the green room, and she forced herself not to shrink as it pressed closer. Not even Margery Prescott could fight her way through to drape the shawl across Flora's shoulders, and Miles was trapped on the far side of the room, with Esther and James beside him.

Ben squeezed her waist. "Ah," he said gleefully, "Dick Sheridan and John Kemble will be green when they hear of this night's work. My beauty, you have conquered London in a single night—not since Siddons's appearance back in 'eighty-two has there been such a debut. We are made, Florry, *made*!"

Her answering smile was weak, for nothing that had occurred since the fall of the curtain seemed real to her. The crowd's approval had been gratifying, but its animal intensity had frightened her. Now she felt isolated from everything and everyone around her, cast adrift in a sea of well-wishers. It was as if she still played a part, albeit an unfamiliar one; she knew none of the lines and was wholly unprepared for her next cue. She wasn't Juliet any longer, but she wasn't Flora either. While the foppish Mr. Skeffington fluted his extravagant praises at her, she told herself that this was a dream and tomorrow everything would be as usual.

Only Trevor, who finally forced his way through the crush of bodies, seemed real to her. Or was he? Because when he bowed over her hand, his handsome, golden face was inscrutable, his voice detached.

"My felicitations, Miss Campion."

"Your lordship is kind," she replied in a wooden voice, thinking that his kindness was of the cruelest sort.

"I wish you joy in your great success." And with that he moved on to speak to the Forsters.

Her unconscious hopes had gone unanswered: she'd received no smile, not a glance, no proof whatsoever that she still held the preeminent place in his heart. In the very moment she had counted on him to put everything in its proper perspective, she was made to feel more alone than before.

And it was his coolness, not weariness, not her frayed nerves, not even joy in her great triumph, that caused Flora Campion to cry herself to sleep many hours later on this, the most important night of her career.

17

How the hours have racked and tortured me,
Since I have lost thee!

Twelfth Night, V. i.

"Your trick, Trevor," said Mr. Rupert Harburton, announcing what was perfectly obvious to the rest of the gentlemen at the card table.

Lord Edgar Fleming commented, "Well, one does visit Brooks's Club fully expecting to be fleeced."

"The game isn't over," his mentor reminded him gently.

"Faith, it might as well be," huffed the viscount who was Trevor's partner. The most rotund member of the foursome, he was seated in the place that had formerly belonged to Charles James Fox, leader of the Opposition. A substantial portion of the baize-covered table had been cut out to make room for the late Whig's ample belly.

After inspecting his remaining cards, Trevor led with a trump.

The Great Subscription Room of Brooks's was lit by a single chandelier hanging from the center of a curved ceiling. The pale green walls were almost bare of ornamentation, save for an intricate plasterwork border and a tall mirror above the plain mantel of marble. Four oval frescoes of gods and goddesses were situated high above the doorway and windows, in order that the gamesters should not be too much distracted by Zucchi's artistry.

When the rubber was played out, the gentlemen ordered another bottle of claret and discussed the news of the day.

"Did any of you invest in the new gaslight scheme?" Lord Edgar wanted to know. "Every soul in London has put his money in Mr. Winsor's Light and Heat Company. I heard that twenty thousand shares have been sold."

Said Mr. Harburton, "Perhaps someday Trevor will illuminate the interior of his theater with gaslight."

"It would be an expensive undertaking," Trevor replied, "and Benedict Forster has talent enough for spending my money as it is."

"The Prince of Wales is a fond playgoer—has he visited your theater?" asked the Viscount.

"Not yet. He's been too busy amusing himself with Lord Hertford's wife."

Trevor's companions laughed.

While they continued talking among themselves, Trevor's thoughts returned to the theater—indeed, these days they seldom left it.

Last month he had attended the initial performance of *Romeo and Juliet* in a fever of excitement that had nothing to do with the play. And that night he discovered that fortune had turned her back upon him, being so busy showering her bounty upon the Forsters and Flora Campion.

Still smarting from the blow London's new darling had delivered in Devonshire, he had no choice but to watch helplessly as she was buoyed up out of his reach by the tide of fame. When the reviewers praised the purity of her speaking eyes and crystalline voice, or acclaimed the natural spontaneity of her performance, or said that the pathos of her playing made butchers weep, he felt equal parts pride and pain. Whenever he walked to his club, her likeness gazed back at him from the bow windows of the print shops in Oxford Street and St. James, and the serenity of her painted smile wounded him.

He wondered if she was haunted by the memory of the brief time they had lain so close that their hearts had beat as one. Or was she too busy congratulating herself on her near escape from an entanglement that would only be a nuisance to her now?

From the night of her debut she had been the latest sensation. She was mobbed on the streets. Nobles and nobodies alike fawned upon her. She had only to be seen wearing a particular color for it to be immediately seized upon and sold by dressmakers as Campion Blue or Pink or Yellow. A variety of portraits and flattering representations of her as Juliet sprang up in shop windows, and London's most reputable artists lined up to limn her newly famous face. Tributes from the conservatories and hothouses of the elite found their way to her door. Flower markets did a brisk trade in the campion; the humble wildflower had risen to sudden prominence, and was cultivated for the adornment of the buttonholes of the beaux and bucks who professed themselves in love with the actress.

Richard Sheridan reportedly coveted her for his theater, as did John Kemble, and both had made overtures in the belief that the contract binding her to the Princess Theatre was only as durable as Benedict Forster's disputed license. Drury Lane and Covent Garden were suffering a period of artistic sterility; their offerings were mediocre at best, for their famous actresses had grown older and stouter by the year and increasingly improbable in youthful roles.

Each time *Romeo and Juliet* was announced, the long lines outside the Princess Theatre attested to its popularity; everyone wanted to view the theatrical triumph that was on all lips. Trevor went there every time Flora performed and always visited the green room to pay his respects. Her manner was polite but stiff, and there was always some other gentleman at her side, usually Ben Forster, often Horatio. Sometimes her brother was in attendance, a tanned seaman whose resemblance to Flora was startling.

Lord Edgar's piping voice cut across his thoughts. "I say, Trev, did you know the rich Miss Drummond was married to Peter Burrell a fortnight ago, in Edinburgh?"

"Was she indeed? I thought it was a settled matter between her and William Beckford."

"It quickly became unsettled," the younger man reported. "He wrote a letter which she considered impertinent."

"Marriage is most definitely in the air," said Mr. Harburton in his dry way as he poured another glass of wine. "I've heard of half a dozen betrothals this week. The betting book lists Frederick Byng and Lady Harriet Cavendish, as well as Lord Henry Petty and Margaret Beckford."

"Wish I'd laid a few guineas on the chance that Allingham would become engaged," said the viscount glumly.

"It's not too late to bet on the marriage, Reggie," Rupert

Harburton comforted him. "The odds are against his ever getting to the altar."

Trevor, who had been tracing his finger across the green baize, looked up to ask, "Has Allingham got himself engaged again?"

"To Lady Caroline Lewes," his friend replied.

The viscount's fat face puckered in a grin. "I want to know what'll become of his ladybird, the bosomy little actress at Drury Lane."

In a proprietary voice, Lord Edgar announced that Miss Louise Talley had availed herself of his protection.

This development surprised Trevor far less than the news of Baron Allingham's betrothal. The whole world was pairing up, he thought gloomily, and before long he would be the only one alone.

Leaning closer to Trevor, Lord Edgar muttered, "Don't look now, but Sheridan has just wandered into the card room. Louise tells me he's vexed by your partnership with Forster."

A few minutes later Mr. Lumley Skeffington delivered a similar warning when he emerged from that room.

"You here, Leafield?" he cried, throwing up his hands in an extravagant show of dismay. "Be forewarned—old Sherry may cut you dead, he's that annoyed over this third theater business. Not that he thinks such a bill could ever pass," he concluded, patting his scented tresses with a slim white hand.

Knowing the dandy to be a good source of theatrical anecdotes, which interested him far more than society gossip these days, Trevor invited him to join the party.

Mr. Skeffington confirmed the persistent rumor that John Philip Kemble was interested in Miss Campion. "He knows he can have her if Forster loses his theater—unless Sherry and Tom King snap her up first. They desperately need to boost the profits of Drury Lane. Mrs. Jordan has been ill lately. At least Kemble can rely on Grimaldi the Clown—his decision to repeat *Mother Goose* at Covent Garden has brought the crowds, as I'm sure you know."

Trevor did know, for Benedict Forster had been very careful not to play his triumphant tragedy on the same night as the popular pantomime. "And how does your playwriting proceed?" he inquired politely.

"Very well indeed," Mr. Skeffington replied. "I'm hoping the piece will be acted at Drury Lane in the New Year. It's called *The Mysterious Bride*." He turned his perfectly coiffed head as a party of gentlemen passed through the doorway linking the card room and the Subscription Room. "Here comes Sherry. No offense intended to your lordship, but he mustn't see me talking with you." He rose from his chair with ludicrous haste, and Trevor watched his spindly form mince across the carpet toward the manager of Drury Lane.

Richard Brinsley Sheridan, his face flushed from drink, his clothes disheveled, grasped Mr. Skeffington's frail arm. Before making his exit he cast his eyes toward the table where his old friend Fox had held court until a year ago.

A hush fell over the tables as the gamesters waited to see how he would react to the Earl of Leafield's presence.

"Damned meddlesome fellow," the illustrious playwright and politician declared in a loud voice before permitting Mr. Skeffington to lead him away.

"It might have been much worse," Rupert Harburton commented as he and Trevor descended the iron-railed stairway leading to the entrance hall. "By tomorrow he won't even remember that he insulted you."

Laughing, Trevor replied, "I wasn't offended, for he spoke the truth—I *am* a damned meddlesome fellow. And I wouldn't challenge old Sherry to a duel even if he had been sober."

"I'm glad to hear it," his friend said seriously, "for I hardly think this new hobby of yours worth risking your life."

While waiting for the porter to fetch their greatcoats, Trevor expressed the hope that Mr. Harburton would support the bill he intended to sponsor. "I already have an ally in the House of Commons who has agreed to introduce it, but I rely upon you to help him win votes from other members. Sheridan's position is strong, for even those who dislike him most won't want to alienate him. He's close to the Prince of Wales and is still a power in the Opposition."

"I'll do what I can," Mr. Harburton assured him. "But you must know how unlikely it is that such a bill will pass on the first attempt. The Theatres Royal have held their patents since the time of Charles the Second, and their proprietors are far better known than your friend Mr. Forster."

"I never said he was a friend," Trevor protested. "But I do share his belief that another legitimate theater would benefit the public. The success of the Princess thus far has proved that London can and will support one."

"Save your arguments for the House of Lords," the other gentleman advised him. "You'll need every one of them."

It was Trevor's painful duty to attend the meetings of the theater's governing body, where virtual strangers erected barriers that would forever close Flora away from him. As much as he resented it, he had no right to protest their methods or their motives. By allying herself with the Forsters, Flora had empowered them to organize her life.

Wild-eyed Horatio brandished her name like a weapon, treating Trevor with a coolness that told him Flora had confided the most pertinent and personal details of her weeks in Devonshire. The actor's churning resentment was palpable, but Trevor empathized; they stood on common ground now. Although his former rival currently shared his lodgings with a ballet girl, there was no evidence that Flora's pride was hurt by his defection. She remained on the best of terms with her friend and seemed not to resent the fact that he'd found consolation elsewhere.

Trevor sought no consolation. He'd made his bed; it was an empty one, and he knew why. "Noblemen don't marry actresses," he'd said once to Lord Edgar Fleming. Those lofty words, spoken so many months ago, constantly echoed in his mind. If he had offered matrimony to her at Combe Cotterell she might have accepted, and though theater-going London would be the poorer for it, his own life would be complete, not the empty, aching thing it was without her. The irony was that if he could wed the lady he loved, which he was now so desperate to do, the scandal would be far greater than if he made her his mistress.

Trevor began meeting Flora socially at parties to which they had each been bidden, he as guest, she to provide entertainment. The same elegant ladies with whom he had danced and dallied for so many years were eager to receive Miss Campion into their homes, for she lent a cachet to the genteel parties of the autumn's Little Season. Benedict Forster, forever at his protégée's side, showed her off proudly, accepting compliments on her behalf and seeing that she exchanged a few words with the most influential persons in the room.

At one particularly lavish soirée in Hanover Square, Flora, exquisitely gowned in white silk, delighted the assembled company with a heart-wrenching recitation of Portia's "Quality of Mercy" speech. Afterward she was so besieged by admirers that when Trevor approached her, she looked toward him in desperate appeal.

Pushing his way past the crowd, he placed his hand beneath her elbow. She recoiled at his touch, but he paid no heed and conducted her out of the crush before releasing her. "I think you'll be more comfortable in the supper room," he said. "It is quieter."

As she accompanied him downstairs, Trevor kept his eyes on her profile, which still looked as if it had been carved from the purest, whitest marble. Her fine eyes were faintly shadowed by fatigue—Forster was working her too hard. Or was it some other trouble that disturbed her? he wondered, guiding her to a refreshment table. Flora rejected all of the many delicacies there, but he persuaded her to try a strawberry ice.

They sat down on an empty sofa in an alcove, and he watched her toy self-consciously with the dessert. In hopes of easing the constraint between them, he embarked upon an uninspired commentary on the various notables present, but she cut him short to ask how Hugh Cotterell was faring.

Taken aback by this unexpected query, Trevor replied, "Mrs. Cotterell presented him with a fine daughter several weeks ago, and Hugh's besotted with both. I had a letter from my aunt today," he went on. "Bath has heard of Miss Campion's great success, and she counts herself fortunate to have met the lady whose name is on all lips. She hopes you enjoy your good fortune." After a short pause he asked, "Do you?"

"The money is agreeable," she told him. "Miles has been very provoking—he won't let me share a bit of my new wealth with him. But I did make a contribution to the orphans' asylum at Portsmouth in our father's memory."

Trevor knew her salary down to the penny—and her share of profits—and marveled that she should judge them sufficient for her own support, much less a pet charity's. "Rumor says that the Prince of Wales has become the latest of your admirers, and without yet having seen you perform. Ben Forster must be elated by the prospect of receiving support from that quarter."

"I don't refine too much on the possibility." Flora shook her head, and the silk flowers woven among the dusky curls trembled. "If His Royal Highness should visit our theater, it would be a slap in the face to his papa, by whose authority Drury Lane and Covent Garden hold their patents."

"Ah, but our prince is known to show favor where it will most displease the king. He's a byword for filial opposition. Forster had best refurbish his Royal Box—I'm sure it will soon be filled with Prince Florizel's portly person."

With an unexpected show of humor, she laughed. "More fodder for the caricaturists, then! I can just imagine what they'll make of it: 'Prinny at the Princess,' or 'Florizel visits Forster's Folly,' or some such. It's worrisome enough to see my face peering back at me from shop windows, but the satiric cartoons are the worst aspect of success. No," she said meditatively, lapsing back into her pensive mood, "that's not true. *This* is the worst by far."

Surely, he thought in anguish, she wasn't alluding to his presence. How much of this kind of torture did she think he could bear? "This?" he repeated hollowly.

Looking him full in the face for the first time, she explained, "These dreadful parties."

Trevor was caught off guard by this hint that her experience as a public figure had not been as roseate as he believed it to be. "Come now, you must like being the rage."

Waving an agitated hand, she said, "In some ways it has been gratifying. But—oh, I don't know how to explain."

"I wish you would try," he prompted.

"Uncivil as it sounds, I'd rather be at home with Miles. Now that England has declared war on Denmark he expects his sailing orders to come through, and time is precious. But Ben must drag me out to put me on display like some tame beast in a menagerie. People stare and exclaim and all but pat me on the head—it's the whole Master Betty phenomenon all over again. He was another nine days' wonder, and where is he today?" she asked, her voice filled with anxiety. "Playing in the provinces, basking in the fading glow of a former fame. He, who had the advantage of youth, cannot hope to retrieve his position in the London theaters. Sensations have a very short life here."

He said soothingly, "You do yourself a great disservice, describing your success as a nine days' wonder. The whole of London agrees that you are a Siddons and a Jordan combined, and those ladies have enjoyed a lasting reputation in their separate spheres of tragedy and comedy."

Flora shrugged. "I'm hardly human any longer, I'm just a— a creature, a draft horse, plodding along in harness, working for my supper and a kind word at the end of the day."

Once he had been amused by her favorite analogy; now it saddened him.

"Last week I attended a party much like this one," she continued, "and after I sang my songs and recited my speech, Ben led me around the room to curtsy and smile. He introduced me to Lord Dartmouth, the Lord Chamberlain, and presented me to our hostess. She handed me a purse with such a condescending air that I wanted to shrink, one so heavy that I knew it held a great deal of money. Fifty guineas—an outrageous sum for a few ballads and a poem! But against a fee twice the size, I'd have chosen a quiet night at home with my brother." She glanced down at her plate to find that the strawberry ice had melted away entirely, so she swirled the pink liquid with her spoon.

"I never guessed this was so difficult for you," Trevor confessed, wondering how he could have been so mistaken as to believe she reveled in her fame. "I might have known. I *should*, knowing you as I do." Determined to cheer her whatever the cost to himself, he said bracingly, "You'll grow accustomed in time."

"I hope I won't have to. Every day I wake with the expecta-

tion that all this fuss will come to an end. It's so distracting—
although very good for business," Flora added, catching sight
of her mentor on the other side of the room. "Ben is beckon-
ing—pray excuse me, but I must go to him." They both rose,
and she smiled up at him uncertainly.

"Thank you for rescuing me. And you've been very kind to
sit here and listen to my troubles. It seems I hardly have time
for any of my old acquaintances these days, there are so many
new ones."

Acquaintance, Trevor repeated to himself as she drifted
away. It was the unkindest cut of all, for with that remark she
had driven the knife in, and twisted it, too. But remembering
the strain she had exhibited, he was inclined to forgive her.
Her face had pleaded for assurance that she was something
more than a curiosity to be viewed by anyone who paid the
price, be it a shilling for a gallery seat or fifty golden guineas
for a ballad. Look at me, her eyes had mourned, I am that
thing I refused to be for you. I have prostituted myself, and for
what?

The party had dwindled down to a few conversation groups
when Flora noticed her employer's absence. When she went in
search of him, a footman informed her that Mr. Forster and
Mr. Skeffington had departed a quarter of an hour earlier.
Concealing her displeasure at being abandoned, she asked him
to secure a hackney for her, that she might go home.

She was standing in the vestibule fastening her velvet opera
cloak when the Earl of Leafield materialized at her side for the
second time that evening.

"Forster has already gone," he told her. "When Skeffington
invited him to a tavern to discuss his latest play, I offered to
escort you home. My coach is waiting."

Flora's hand trembled as she worked the silken frog at her
throat. "That won't be necessary," she replied, instantly suspicious of his knowledge of Ben's plans.

"But it is," he declared triumphantly, "because I intercepted
the servant and said you'd changed your mind about the hackney. The famous Miss Campion must ride in style and comfort, you know, and my carriage offers both."

Flora experienced a familiar outrage, but she permitted him to lead her out of the house and down the front steps.

As soon as his footman closed the carriage door upon them, she loosed her pent-up fury. "You *arranged* for Mr. Skeffington to lure Ben away, didn't you?"

"Yes. I needed to speak with you once more, in private."

"I've nothing whatever to say to you," she warned him.

He reached for her hands, gripping them tightly as he said, "I don't care a damn for your foolish attempts to give me the cold shoulder—did you hope they would keep me away? You act as if you despise me, when not so many weeks ago you were lying naked in my arms." She gasped, but he continued ruthlessly, "I've noticed that you're not entirely yourself, and I want to know the truth. Are you regretting the decision you made that night?"

Her rigid control dissolved. Pulling her hands away, she hid her face in them, her shoulders shaking as she gave way to sobs. She'd never wept in his presence and feared he would think the worse of her for it. In a broken voice she said, "I am not pining for you, and there's nothing wrong that a good night's rest won't cure."

"Is it Horatio Forster? Are you so unhappy because he deserted you?"

Flora lifted her head so swiftly that the hood of her cloak slipped back. "Horry did *not* desert me. He offered for me, even after I told him how I had compromised myself. But I refused," she said on a sigh. "I would have been wrong to marry him."

"Because you still love me."

"Please don't make me say that." She ran her tongue over her lips nervously, then said, "I don't belong to you and never will, there is no lasting connection between us. I thought I proved that by leaving Combe Cotterell."

"And were you trying to prove it to yourself or to me?" he wondered aloud.

It was a question she dared not answer; if she told the truth he could twist it around to his advantage. "I don't have the strength to fight you any more, honestly, I am so tired of—of troubles and tribulation. Please, Trevor, lay the past to rest. If you care for me, leave me alone."

"To stand aside and let you ruin both our lives seems to me a very poor way of demonstrating my love."

"My life isn't ruined."

He leaned back against the cushions and said thoughtfully, "No, not in the same way as mine. You have your work, after all. I have nothing."

Flora very nearly cried out that there was no consolation for her either, that she loved him desperately, that she was sorry. But it would be most unfair to push him away with one hand and cling to him with the other, although that was precisely what she wanted to do. "I think," she said faintly, "that you should consider leaving London."

He did not reply at once, and appeared to be thinking over her advice. "Perhaps so," he said as the carriage turned sharply into Long Acre.

Flora reached for the leather strap, but not in time to prevent herself from falling against him. His arm closed around her waist, and even as she asked that he release her, her treacherous body thrilled at his touch.

Dipping his head down to hers, he said, "If I must go, at the very least you owe me a proper good-bye kiss."

But it was a most improper kiss he had in mind, as Flora discovered an instant later. She might have expected that, if he'd given her the opportunity to think at all before he drew her into his embrace. She felt dizzy—whether from his passion or her own, or from the odd sensation of being made love to in a moving carriage, she knew not. The certainty that she was better off apart from him evaporated at his touch; there was no happiness except within his arms. And when his caresses grew even more intimate, her response was stronger than her strongest vow not to be swayed by them. Unable to evade his insistent hands, she sighed as they stroked her into a welcome state of oblivion. When his fingers teased the bare flesh of her neck and shoulders, and the portion of her breasts exposed by her low-cut gown, she murmured softly, but not in protest.

Suddenly, with no warning, he pulled away. "Are you playing games with me, fair cruelty? How can I believe you really want to be rid of me when you offer such eloquent encouragement?"

Flora was too ashamed to reply. Now that she was separated from the heavy warmth of his body, she felt cold again despite the thick cloak she wore. Looking toward the window, she saw that they were on Great Queen Street; she could see Mrs. Brooke's house.

The conveyance came to a full stop, and without even waiting for the liveried footman to open the door, she wrenched the handle and pushed with all her might, uttering a wretched jumble of good nights and thanks and apologies.

During his solitary drive home Trevor leaned his head against the velvet cushions, inhaling the faint scent of bluebell that lingered in the air. He smiled when he recalled Flora's sighs of pleasure at his kisses, then frowned over her suggestion that he leave town. Not now, not yet—and never alone, he vowed.

A tiny white object lying on the seat caught his eye: one of the silk flowers she'd been wearing in her hair, which had been dislodged by his roving fingers. He picked it up and held it gently between his fingers, careful not to crush it. It was as pale and vulnerable as the lady he loved, and like her, it belonged to him.

18

A solemn combination shall be made of our dear souls.

Twelfth Night, V. i.

At the weekly meeting of the management committee, Lord Leafield had taken a firm stand against the manager's plan to stage *Hamlet* and had prevailed upon him to revive *In Praise of Parsimony* instead. Ben Forster agreed, saying that would whet the public's appetite for Flora's next portrayal of a tragic heroine. When she heard the story, it confirmed her suspicion that he would do anything to appease the earl, his powerful and noble ally.

The demanding repertory, particularly *Romeo and Juliet,* had left her depleted and depressed, and how Trevor had guessed it was a mystery to her. But she was grateful to him, and welcomed the respite from the rigors of Shakespearean tragedy.

The managers of other theaters, with Sheridan overtly luring them on and Kemble doing so covertly, had declared open warfare on the Princess Theatre. The furor was so great that Lord Dartmouth had been heard to say publicly that until the Forsters closed their Folly and left London, the city would know no peace.

Controversy swirled around Flora yet somehow never touched her. Her sense of isolation was exacerbated by the very people on whom she depended to cure it. Horatio, now that he had his dancing girl, was the most casual of cavaliers. Esther Drew was wholly occupied with her James and their child. Miles might have been her greatest solace, but with the outbreak of the very real war against Denmark and Portugal, he expected to return to his ship at any moment, and she didn't like to burden him with her problems.

After a considerable period of soul-searching, she finally

admitted to herself that all joy in her work had been taken away, bit by precious bit, by her fame.

The critics admired her in comedy but cried out for her to essay Desdemona or Cordelia, or heaven forbid, Cleopatra. If she must act Shakespeare, she countered whenever Ben raised the subject, let it be Kate the Shrew, or feisty Beatrice, or wise Portia. Certainly the adoring public cared not what she did so long as she appeared on the boards regularly. Her cult of worshipers came from all walks of life, and included the Prince of Wales. Before dashing down to Brighton, he had attended one of her performances with Lady Hertford, the latest in a succession of middle-aged royal mistresses.

Success had shaken up her quiet, ordered existence like nothing else had done since the night when Lord Leafield entered her life, changing it so dramatically. In reaction to her present lack of peace and privacy, she looked back fondly on the nineteen happy years she had passed in comfortable obscurity in Portsmouth. Before embarking upon a stage career she'd lived quietly and contentedly with her parents and Miles, looking to her friends and her books for fulfillment. And because her present was so distasteful and her future uncertain, she tended to regard her uneventful youth with nostalgia.

One night, after a well-attended performance of *In Praise of Parsimony*, Ben Forster called his actors and actresses into the green room and announced his intention of purchasing the Orchard Street theater in Bath.

Groans of dismay went up from the assembled company, and Mr. Warren, a young firebrand who had won modest accolades as Flora's Romeo, jumped to his feet. "Bath!" he cried scornfully. "Well, I shan't be going back there. It would be demeaning for me—for *all* of us—after our great success."

Madam Forster eyed him with disdain. "There is nothing demeaning in honest work, sir. And if you would take a walking part in a London theater over a leading role in the provinces, I think very little of your ambition."

Her son Ben stood in the middle of the room, observing the disappointment in the circle of faces. "There's no cause for alarm," he said, "for the Lord Chamberlain hasn't yet decided about our license. But even if he rules against it, I pin my hopes on the third theater bill which our illustrious patron, Lord Leafield, will introduce after Parliament's Christmas recess."

Flora, who had not intended to speak, suddenly looked up to ask, "If we go to Bath, what will become of the Princess? You do still own it, after all."

"And I'll retain my ownership of the property, in the expectation that we will return after the theater bill passes. Another manager has expressed an interest in leasing it for his productions of burletta and pantomime."

Flora accepted Madam's usual offer that they share a hackney, and as it traversed the fog-shrouded thoroughfares, she reflected on her earlier sojourn in the spa town and reminded herself that she had found it exceedingly pleasant. But would she like it so well in gray wintertime, without Trevor there to make her laugh?

When they reached Great Queen Street, Ben helped the two ladies out of the carriage. Flora hurried toward Mrs. Brooke's front door and had reached the area railing when she heard Ben Forster say, "Just a moment, Florry—I'd like a word with you."

Pausing on the pavement, she waited for him, shivering in the cold.

"I forgot to explain earlier that the lease of the playhouse will be drawn up to include the stock wardrobe, to save us the expense of transporting everything back and forth. If, as I suspect, our company will be somewhat diminished by the first of the year, we won't need it: leading players provide their own costumes. I know you and Sally and Eliza store your personal properties in the wardrobe room, so you'll want to be sure they're removed before the theater closes."

"Oh, Ben, I'm so sorry about everything."

In a valiant approximation of his confident manner, he replied, "It's only a temporary setback. Now listen, my dear, for I have some advice for you. I think you should make a tour of the provincial circuits before joining us in Bath so you can reap the benefits of this season's success. Mrs. Siddons and her brother Kemble make their progress every year to keep themselves solvent, and you would do well to follow their example. A tour to the Birmingham, York, and Edinburgh circuits, and some smaller towns would be lucrative, and I want you to consider it."

"Oh, very well," she replied, immediately shoving the unwelcome notion to the recesses of her already troubled mind.

One Sunday afternoon Flora set out for the theater dressed in a serviceable gown of faded kerseymere, ready to take on the difficult task of sorting through her belongings. The timeworn building wore a deserted, shuttered look on this day of rest. The elderly doorkeeper, who also acted as custodian, shook his grizzled head when she stated her purpose.

" 'Tis a sad thing when a body is forced from home, Miss Florry." He patted her shoulder, adding, "But Mr. Forster will find us another one, eh?"

As she made her way to the topmost level of the building, she was struck by the echoing silence. She missed the sound of hammers from the carpentry shop and the gentle swish of brushes in the scene-painting room. This was the Sabbath, of course, but those who labored high above the stage weren't overly assiduous in their observation of the holy day. Nothing could have said more clearly that the season was drawing to a close.

She went directly to the musty loft where many of the costumes and stage properties were stored, and found the usual jumble of court gowns and doublets heaped upon the floor. Crowns and scepters were piled unceremoniously in a corner, and a few stray pieces of furniture—beds, chairs, chaises, and plaster statuary—were scattered among the mounds of clothing. Her own costumes were hung neatly on pegs in one corner; Margery had wrapped some of the rich velvets and brocades in holland cloth as protection against dust and sunlight. And there she found a pair of wooden trunks.

Flora knelt down on the floor. Taking a key from her reticule, she unlocked the first one and lifted the lid.

On top lay her fans, covered in tissue. One had sticks of ivory, intricately carved; the other was spangled silk. She laid these aside and burrowed deeper through a collection of shawls, too threadbare to be worn in company but acceptable for stage use. Next she found a ballgown that she'd recently acquired from a dealer in secondhand clothing. It was almost new, a shining russet tabby; Margery hadn't altered it yet. Working her way through to the bottom of both trunks, she reviewed every scrap of lace, each petticoat and set of whalebone stays, with a view to what could be discarded.

But not even a pair of cheap, gaudy buckles with paste brilliants could be cast aside, for Horry had given them to her in the heyday of their affair. Something else that should have been rubbish was the sunshade with a broken ferrule. Long ago she had almost destroyed it in a fit of pique, but it might be mended. And how could she throw away the lovely, hand-worked apron she had worn so often as Miss Hardcastle in *She Stoops to Conquer*? There was a rent down the front, not even Margery's nimble fingers had been able to repair it, but it was a precious reminder of one of her favorite roles. Each item, however battered or useless, was a treasure. These trunks held memories, which had outlived the applause at the end of long-forgotten performances. Their contents were tangible proofs of her unremarkable, unalarming past.

When she had replaced all of her keepsakes, she climbed nimbly to her feet. The light was fading—it was December now, and the days were as short as they were chilly.

She had intended to return home, but instead she wandered around the room, picking up some of the familiar props. She unsheathed a dagger and stabbed the air several times, then tried on a pinchbeck crown. She wrapped herself in robes of office and tried on wigs, wistfully recalling the childlike joy she had known at the outset of her career.

The sound of footsteps along the corridor was thunderous in the sheer silence of the place, and she looked up from a stack of playbooks expecting to see the custodian.

Trevor stood in the doorway. "I came seeking you," he explained, looking about curiously as he entered the loft, "to discuss a subject of considerable importance. I went to Great Queen Street first, but the manservant seemed to think you'd come here. That old fellow downstairs let me in. Have you a fancy for gloom today? This place is a tomb."

"I know," she said. "I had to see to a bit of packing—a necessary evil when one faces a move."

"Ah, yes, Forster's return to Orchard Street."

"But have you heard the latest? He's encouraging me to undertake an extensive tour of the provinces before joining the company at Bath. According to him, I should journey the length and breadth of England, and enrich myself in the process."

"And will you?"

"I haven't decided what to do. I'm afraid my choices are rather limited."

"So it seems," he agreed. "If you don't return to Bath with the Forsters, you must desert them for the endlessly insolvent Sheridan of Drury Lane, or those tragedy-loving Kembles of Covent Garden."

She shook her head, saying adamantly, "I won't turn traitor. Anyway, Ben has spoiled me so, I'd never be comfortable with any other manager." How strange, she thought, that she was able to talk to him so candidly, without any constraint. Was it because they were at the theater, where she felt most at ease, or simply because all this time she had shunned him she had also missed him terribly?

He was a constant in a changing universe, and a certain source of comfort. "Help me, Trevor," she pleaded. "Hold me." And when he gathered her close, she hid her face in his chest.

"I wish I *could* help you, Flora, because I want you to be happy. But having learned the unwisdom of meddling in your life, I know you'd oppose any remedy I suggested."

At that moment she couldn't remember why she had been so perverse. Sorrow had softened her, and loneliness compelled her to reach out rather than close herself off from him. Whatever else he might have wished her to be, and however often his actions had disappointed her, he cared for her. And curiously, the man who had so often wrecked her peace was now giving it back to her.

Contact with his solid, familiar form changed her despair into a desire for greater intimacy, and she wound her arms around his neck, melting against him. He kissed her deeply, and she parted her lips for him, permitting his tongue to brush hers. And when he shifted his hands from her waist to her hips, drawing her still closer, she felt the proof of his arousal through the fabric of his breeches.

He looked down, his voice a rough, urgent whisper when he asked, "What am I to do now?"

She glanced uncertainly toward the jumble of furniture against the wall.

"You are sure, Flora?"

"Yes—oh, yes."

Sweeping her off her feet, he carried her over to the one un-obstructed piece, an ancient bedstead. Its mattress seemed to contain more dust than down, for as they lay down upon it a great cloud rose to choke them.

Flora helped him remove his coat. He pulled off her slippers, then untied her garters, slowly peeling away each stocking. He unfastened the cloth-covered buttons at the neck of her gown with agonizing deliberation until he had bared her breasts.

All sensation seemed to reside wherever his lips and fingers moved across those parts of her body that were exposed. She felt no shyness or shame, and gloried in his appreciation of her as he lifted her long skirt. His hands caressed her legs, trailing their way to the place where her desire was centered.

Tugging at his hair, she forced him to look up. "Promise me," she begged him.

"Anything, dear heart."

"No expectations, Trevor. No demands this time."

"As you wish," he assured her.

The gentle stroking ceased while he unbuttoned his breeches.

She gasped when he entered her, her muscles tensing invol-untarily as he eased his way past the barrier nature had raised against his sex. Murmuring endearments, he rocked against her, and her discomfort gave way to new, increasingly pleasant sensations. She arched upward to meet him, until, at the mo-ment of his violent release, he drove himself against her.

She supposed he would turn over and go to sleep—that was what the dressing-room chatter had taught her to expect—and she was elated when he continued holding her. It seemed so

natural to lie so close, to feel the furious pounding of his heart
and rise and fall of his chest beneath her cheek. Soon she slept,
her head pillowed against his shoulder.

Flora woke with a start to discover that the wardrobe room
was completely dark.

When Trevor looked over and she smiled at him, he required no further encouragement. Her pain was less this time,
and vanished completely in the heat she felt deep within her as
he urged her into that mystical rhythm once more. The tiny
flame leaped and danced, growing higher and hotter, and she
cried out as a powerful tremor rocked her body.

Afterward she lay beneath him, stunned, and he murmured
against her ear, "You make me very happy, Flora, even when
you most confound me."

Her fingers plucked the damp fabric of his shirt, separating
it from his warm skin. As she held her sated lover in her arms,
she thought that her favorite poets had been too restrained in
their descriptions of fulfillment, and her female friends too
matter-of-fact. In the past she had believed that to give herself
to him would be nothing short of ruinous, but she didn't feel
ruined. She felt more serene than she had for many months. If
he should beg her to live with him as his mistress now she
would say yes, and gladly.

Her rapturous expression faded when she became aware of
peculiar sounds coming from outside—tramping feet, shouts—
and she lifted her head. Then, in fearful recognition, she sat
up, saying, "Listen, do you hear? It's coming closer all the
time—they're coming *here*!"

"Who?" he asked, perplexed, when she left the bed. "Who's
coming?"

Looking down from the window, she saw that a crowd of
people was marching down the dark street, slowly but purposefully. Many of them brandished cudgels; some carried
torches. "It's a mob," Flora announced woefully.

As soon as he discovered that she spoke the truth, he
grasped her arm and dragged her back, saying furiously,
"You've no business standing there—they might throw stones
or bricks. Has this happened before?"

"Last spring some hirelings threw rotten fruit and vegetables. And we were disturbed again just before the first performance of *Romeo and Juliet*. But these men are carrying torches, and they must know the theater is deserted on Sunday. Do they mean to burn it down?"

"They're making a token protest against Forster, nothing more."

"But why now, when he is about to have everything taken away from him? It's too unfair!"

Running his fingers through her tangled curls, he murmured, "There, there, I'll go down and—"

"Don't leave!" she begged, clutching at him.

"Only for a moment, just long enough to send the old man to Forster's house to warn him." Trevor led her back to the bed, and gently forced her into a sitting position. "Stay here—and don't you dare go near that window again. I'll be back before you can finish putting on your stockings and shoes."

When she heard him vaulting down the wooden steps, she swallowed past the lump in her throat and began to look for her discarded garments. But her hands were shaking so badly that she could hardly tug her stockings up, and tying her garters with nervous fingers was a nearly impossible feat. She was almost done when a brick sailed through the window, shattering the pane. It landed with a thud on the wooden floor, only a few feet away.

When Trevor returned, she was standing near the door. Pointing at the brick, she said ferociously, "See what they've done—the knaves!"

"I sent the doorkeeper for Forster and some reinforcements—officers from Bow Street, I hope. The crowd is fanning out around the building, from the front entrance to the back courtyard. I took the precaution of barring the stage door."

"So we're trapped. Oh, I do hope Ben comes soon." She was startled when he suddenly reached out as if to fondle her breast. "Trevor, not now!" she cried in admonition, before realizing he had done so in order to fasten her bodice. She pushed his hands away. "I can do it myself. Try to find my shawl and my bonnet."

He returned with the requested articles. As he shook them, a glistening shower of glass shards fell to the floor. "There must be some other outlet from the building that our visitors don't know."

Thinking quickly, she said, "Downstairs, the machine room beneath the stage. There's a door to the side yard. The scene shifters go there to drink and smoke during the performance. The yard is connected with a back street, and it leads directly to Drury Lane."

"I think we should at least make an effort to get away," he said, holding out his hand. "Come along and show me how."

She gripped his hand tightly as they descended the three flights of rickety stairs to the stage level. The auditorium was an empty cavern, and her whisper seemed loud in the black silence when she told him, "We'll have to climb down through the stage floor, it's the only way. The large trapdoor must be pushed open from below, but the grave trap lifts up by a cord." She showed him the smaller of the two doors in the planking.

A slight tug was sufficient to lift the trap, and they gazed down into the seemingly bottomless pit. "How much of a drop is it?" Trevor asked.

"Only a few feet. Just a short jump for you, your legs are so long." She watched him ease his body into the narrow opening, and begged him to hurry. "There's a ladder lying on the floor somewhere," she said, peering down at his disembodied face.

"I can swing you down more easily than I can find a ladder in the dark."

Flora sat down at the edge of the hole in the floor, and was about to push off when she cried suddenly, "My trunks! I can't leave without them!"

"You most certainly can," Trevor told her sternly. "Come along now."

She took a deep breath as she pushed off the edge, as if plunging into water. His strong arms closed around her, and her feet grazed the floor. She couldn't see him—her eyes had trouble adjusting to the greater darkness beneath the stage—but she felt his breath on her cheek when he asked her, "What about those damned trunks is so important that you would risk your neck?"

"Only my whole past." She sighed.

"Which way to the door?"

"It's in the far wall. But go carefully—heaven knows what machinery and stage pieces lie between here and there." Together they groped their way past pulleys and gears, canvas flats and coils of rope, making a tentative progress until at last they stood on the other side of the door. The world was dark and damp, and a freezing drizzle fell from the sky.

With a shaky laugh, Flora said, "I feel as if we've escaped from the Tower of London—or the Bastille."

"You *look* as if you have," he retorted. "What a pair we make. Ah, here come the reinforcements—it seems Forster is depending on his brother and the navy for assistance."

She looked around and saw Miles and Horatio running down the alley toward them.

"Flora—thank God you're safe!" her brother exclaimed.

"But where's Ben?" she asked.

"He and the Runners went 'round to the pit entrance," Horatio told her. "You shouldn't be here, Florry—best let Miles take you home."

When Trevor offered to escort her, Miles glowered at him. "What the devil are *you* doing here? My lord," he added belatedly and with scant respect.

"I have made a substantial investment in this theater, Lieutenant Campion," was the nobleman's calm reply.

The feeling of communion Flora had known when she and Trevor had lain together was slipping away. Other men who loved her had closed around her, cutting her off from him. "Perhaps it would be better if I go with Miles, Lord Leafield," she said, her eyes pleading for his understanding. "You and Horry will both be needed here."

He bowed, his courtly gesture at odds with the state of his attire: his cravat was in wild disorder and his dark coat defiled by dust and grime. Watching his and Horatio's retreating figures, Flora regretted not giving him some small token of assurance—a parting glance, a tender smile—so he would know how reluctant she was to be separated from him.

"What *was* he doing here?" Miles repeated as they proceeded down the alley.

"I was sorting through my trunks and—and he helped me."

"You had an assignation," he accused.

"We did not," she defended herself. Chin high, she said, "You've spent the whole of your life on the seas, and very soon you will sail away again. Do you feel you have a right to dictate to me during your few weeks on shore?"

"You're my sister, Florry, and you can't be so muddle-headed as to think I'll let some damned nob seduce you right under my very nose!"

"Really, Miles, there's no cause for histrionics." Not yet, she added silently, knowing how outraged he would be when she found the courage to admit that she intended to live with the earl.

When they reached the house on Great Queen Street, Flora evaded Esther's and Mrs. Brooke's questions and closeted herself in her room, refusing Margery's offers of tea or toast or hot bathwater. She changed her petticoat and carried it over to the washstand, knowing she would have to remove the rusty stain her innocence had left upon it. The dull ache between her legs was another reminder of her initiation, but she suspected it would soon subside.

The dresser eventually coaxed her out with the news that Horatio Forster was downstairs and wanted to speak with her.

"The theater still stands," he informed Flora when she joined him in the parlor. "Some windows are broken and a door or two will have to be replaced, but otherwise the Princess is in one piece."

"What do we do now?"

"Continue our work. Would you expect my brother to do anything else? Business as usual tomorrow—we'll begin with the reading of Jones's new play. Ben intends to have it ready for Christmas week. An armed watchman will be posted at the theater for the remainder of our stay in London, at Leafield's expense. I must say your admirer has his uses."

"You mean he has money," she said bitterly.

"His high and mighty lordship is damned officious where you're concerned," he continued. "You should've heard him—

wouldn't let me go home to my dinner till I'd promised to bring you those blasted trunks. They're out in the hall, and I had the devil of a time getting them in and out of the hackney."

"What a good, sweet Horry you are," she declared, standing on tiptoe to kiss his swarthy cheek. "Your errand is accomplished, and now you may go home to your supper—and your pretty dancer."

But before the actor departed, Miles Campion demanded a private audience.

Flora was in the hall instructing Frank about where to stow her treasures when the two gentlemen emerged from the back parlor. Their serious faces and heavy, portentous tones warned her that something was amiss, but they left the house before she could demand an explanation.

19

Be not amazed. Right noble is his blood.

Twelfth Night, V. i.

Flora hurriedly buttoned her thick, fur-trimmed pelisse, an extravagant purchase and a necessary one. The weather was typical of early December, gray and cold, it was Monday besides, and the morning would be devoted to the first reading of Mr. Jones's new play. Only the deeply ingrained habit of half a dozen years of punctual attendance prevented her from sending a message that she was ill. She picked up her muff, and after a swift glance in the mirror to be sure her furry hat was on straight, she left her room.

Miles was waiting for her in the vestibule, his large figure obscured by a greatcoat. Drawing on his gloves, he announced that he was escorting her to the theater, his tone indicating that he would not yield to any argument.

As they followed Great Queen Street toward Drury Lane, she essayed a laugh and said, "Lord Leafield is hardly likely to abduct me between here and the theater, Miles."

"I mean to make quite sure of that," Lieutenant Campion told her, each angry syllable a puff of vapor hanging in the frigid air.

What could he mean, she wondered, trying to keep up with his brisk stride. Knowing that gentlemen held strict notions about protecting the chastity of their female relations, she could only hope he was too prudent to resort to violent measures. She hated concealing the full truth of her relationship with Trevor Cotterell, but if she chose to enlighten Miles while he was in such a disagreeable mood it wouldn't be a question of a gentlemanly duel, but out-and-out murder.

The green room was less crowded than usual; several players had already sought places at other theaters. When Ben

Forster and the playwright entered, the actors and actresses took their places at the table. During the scramble for seats, Flora asked Horatio what he and her brother had discussed the night before.

"Nothing that need concern you," he answered dismissively.

"Don't try to bamboozle me," she whispered furiously. "I realize Miles is suspicious of Tre—of Lord Leafield—and if you reveal a word of what I confessed to you upon my return to town, I'll never speak to you again! A duel would be the ruination of his career, you know that. Trust me to tell him what he needs to know in my own good time."

For the rest of the day her recurring vision of her brother— or her lover—felled on the field of honor made her insane with worry. As soon as she was home she sat down to pen a hasty and only marginally coherent note to Trevor, begging him to come to her. Perhaps if they faced Miles and admitted their attachment, a dangerous and potentially fatal confrontation could be averted.

Miles would simply have to accept her decision to become Lord Leafield's mistress. And if he accused her of depravity, she would simply point out that as an officer in the Royal Navy he had no cause to look down his nose at her, for corruption and cruelty were by far more prevalent in his world than hers. He might be surprised by her choice to live in sin, but she couldn't believe he would be shocked, especially when she convinced him that Trevor would be a kind and generous protector. Everything a woman could ask would be hers—except a marriage ring.

Mrs. Brooke's manservant carried her letter to Cavendish Square, but he brought back no reply.

"Surely you gave it to someone," she said impatiently.

" 'Twas the porter took it, toplofty as he could stare," Frank grumbled. "His lordship is leaving town, and granted most of the servants a holiday."

There was nothing to do but thank her messenger and dismiss him. Staring into the fire, she wondered where Trevor might go, and why. Her first fear, that he had discarded her now that he'd finally seduced her, was foolish and had to be discounted. He wouldn't, he couldn't cast her off after what had happened yesterday, and certainly not if he loved her as much as he professed.

Honesty compelled her to acknowledge that she had given him no clear signal, and had even imposed silence upon him. Had her own foolish words driven him away? She had confused him time and again by her unpredictability—and her seemingly endless rejection of his love.

At the end of the week she played the Countess Olivia in *Twelfth Night*, always a reminder of the first time she had seen Trevor's golden face. Her mood was one of despondency and forboding, and she left the theater as soon as she could, hoping the long-awaited message had come during her absence.

The street was lined with town carriages. One highly varnished door bore Lord Leafield's crest, and she approached it in the expectation of finding him inside. But the brown head that emerged from the window belonged to a different Cotterell.

"Trevor let us have his stage box tonight," Hugh explained, climbing out to greet her. "And his coach as well." He looked very fine in his evening clothes, and there was no trace of his sullen expression when he spoke of his cousin. "You must let us take you home—I'll be most disappointed if you refuse. And Mrs. Cotterell is eager to meet you."

Flora was surprised to discover that the lady who had enslaved Hugh was no beauty, and the recent confinement had left her a trifle plump. Her accent was unrefined but not unpleasantly so when she said shyly, "Every time my husband sees your name in the papers, Miss Campion, I must hear all over again how greatly he admires you."

Flora felicitated them on the recent happy event and asked the name of the new addition to the family.

The proud young papa described his Arabella as the most beautiful child in all England. "My cousin stood as godfather. He has been most generous—we've got a snug house of our own, and he even offered us his carriage while he's away, thinking Emmy would like it. Which she does, I can tell you. And he said we might use his box at the theater."

"Do you know when he means to return?" Flora asked.

Hugh shook his head. "He paid us a call on his way out of

town, but never even said where he was going. He drove off in his phaeton—I remember thinking it was frightfully cold for an open carriage. He left on Monday, didn't he, Em?"

"Monday," Flora repeated blankly. The day after their encounter in the deserted theater. She wondered if he'd left London before or after receiving her letter.

When they reached her house, Hugh escorted the actress to her door. In a low voice he said, "Truly, I'm glad to see you again, Flora. I suppose you know that Trev and I have made our peace, and I wanted to do the same with you—I was so rude to you at Combe Cotterell. At the time I regarded you as an enemy because you distracted him from that Lewes chit. But everything turned out for the best. Have you heard? Lady Caroline is engaged to Baron Allingham."

"Is she?" Flora smiled to think of that volatile nobleman, possibly her kinsman, as a husband.

Before saying good night, Hugh told her, "Trev said your success hadn't changed you a bit, and I see that he was right."

She chose not to dispute the allegation, false though it was. Her three months of fame had altered her beyond description, and she continued to feel cut off from the mainstream of activity, increasingly an observer, seldom a participant.

With the arrival of December, the weather took a turn for the worse. The accumulated snow made Flora's walk from the theater seem longer, and as she trudged toward Great Queen Street she hoped it would not last.

The morning's rehearsal of the new play had ended abruptly when Ben had been called away, and unlike her fellow players, she'd been sorry. Everyone else seemed to have someplace to go, some pressing business to take care of—even Sally Jenkins, who had declined an invitation to tea. Flora, wishing that she had some useful occupation, paused at a linendraper's establishment on the way home, but none of his wares tempted her. It wasn't long before she left the warmth of the shop to continue her journey through the snowy streets.

When she entered the house, she could hear laughter from belowstairs, and she envied the servants their daily tasks. And because this was one of her nights off from the theater, she had no hope of alleviating her ennui.

She was therefore delighted when Sally appeared on the doorstep later in the day, her cheeks rosy from the cold and her blue eyes bright with excitement. "Such an afternoon as I have had," she exclaimed as she dropped into a chair in the parlor. "I'll have a cup of tea, love, if you're still offering it."

"Of course," replied Flora, before going to tell Mary to heat the kettle. She returned to find her friend resting her feet upon the grate, her skirts bunched up to reveal a pair of bright yellow stockings. "And what have you been doing with yourself?" she inquired, taking a seat.

"Paying calls. Our acquaintance Miss Talley has a new lodging, you know. Her current paramour, who has neither the wealth nor the title of the one who cast her off, has provided a modest set of rooms in Bolton Row. You should hear her complain of having to take a hackney from there to Drury Lane! Well, I predicted her slide down the social scale months ago," said Sally with satisfaction. "Lord Edgar Fleming may be the son of a duke, but he's still a commoner. She'll throw him over as soon as she can, you mark my words—she'd rather be a nobleman's doxy than anything."

"I suppose so," said Flora, wondering if she would be so described in future.

Frank appeared with the tea tray, and Sally's flow of gossip ceased until Flora had poured two cups and passed the cakes.

"But I didn't spend the whole afternoon on Bolton Street," she went on. "I also went to have a look at Louisa Brunton's trousseau—you do know she's to marry Lord Craven in a week's time?"

"Yes, I heard that."

"Oh, the gowns she has! So fine—the sleeves of one of 'em cost all of five and twenty guineas! Lord Craven has settled five thousand pounds a year upon her, as though she were a lady born and not a Drury Lane actress. He's not a bad sort, though I've heard that Harriette Wilson was bored to tears when she lived with him. I say, love, these cakes are grand—I make do with stale biscuits and a scrap of toast, now that I'm living alone in my hovel. That reminds me, would you like to share rooms when we're in Bath?"

"If you don't find someone else," Flora said diffidently.

Sally chuckled. "A gentleman, you mean? Mr. Warren *has* been attentive lately, but I'd have to convince him to stay with the company and I'm not sure he's worth the effort."

She chattered on for some time, seeming not to notice or care that Flora had little to contribute.

When Sally was gone, Flora determined to study her new part in the privacy of her bedchamber. Halfway up the stairs was a landing with a window seat, presently occupied by the gray house cat. Feeling the need of physical contact, Flora sat down to cuddle the dozing feline.

She watched the occasional carriage pass along the street, and the people huddled in their heaviest garments, trying to keep from slipping. The flakes were falling thick and fast, and soon darkness would cover the city; the lamplighter and his assistant were already at work.

Absently stroking the purring cat, she noticed a town coach moving through the dense haze of snow and fog. As it came closer, she recognized a crest that was as familiar as her own signature. Had Hugh and Emmy Cotterell come calling?

Her hand stilled when the vehicle came to a stop before the Forsters' house. Horatio climbed out, followed by Trevor, and Flora watched in bemusement as the two men shook hands in the middle of the street. The actor moved toward his brother's front door, while the nobleman—suddenly she bounded up from the window-seat, not even bothering to lay the cat down on the cushion where she'd found it.

She dashed down the stairs to the hall, and without even waiting for his knock, she flung open the door. A blast of cold air struck her, blowing her curls into disarray.

"Do come in," she invited him breathlessly, as the creature in her arms struggled to break free. In order to take his lordship's hat and stick, Flora had to let go of the cat. "Daft moggy," she muttered, as it dashed outside.

"Shall I chase after her?"

"No, she'll come back for her supper." Leading him into the parlor, Flora said, "How glad I am to see you—it seems an age since I sent my note, though of course Mr. Cotterell told me you went away."

"What note?" His startled question cut across her excited greeting.

"Last week I sent a message to Leafield House. Isn't that why you're here?"

"Not exactly," he admitted. "I haven't been to Cavendish Square yet and don't employ a secretary to redirect my letters when I'm out of town. I've been at Twickenham."

"Oh."

"Is Lieutenant Campion here?"

"He and James took Esther and Aunt Tab to an exhibition." She noticed that her visitor wore a campion bloom in his button-hole, proclaiming him one of her admirers, and many of her concerns faded.

"So I find you quite alone and unprotected. Fate is kind indeed, but I can't rejoice—actually, I came here seeking your brother."

Flora tried to conceal her agitation, but it crept into her voice when she said, "My lord—Trevor—if you love me, or have ever loved me, *please* don't do it."

With a laugh, he said, "I hope you mean to tell me what has unsettled you so much that you continually speak in riddles."

"I saw you with Horry just now," she explained. "And I'm asking you not to be angry at Miles, whatever he's done. I couldn't bear it if he—if you—if either of you should be wounded, perhaps killed, and all because of a stupid misunderstanding." She was astonished when her caller began to laugh even harder. His flippant response unnerved her, and she reached out to shake some sense into him.

"Stupid misunderstanding indeed!" he crowed, holding her off. "You think I have come here to issue some kind of challenge—or to accept one? Calm yourself, Flora, there's nothing in my business with your brother to alarm you, but yes, you are concerned in it. His presence will be considered necessary at some point. Have you any idea when he will return?" She shook her head. "No matter. You're of an independent spirit, I know it all too well, and as a grown woman you hardly require his consent, just his blessing. For I have come a-wooing," he said tenderly. "Will you do me the very great honor of becoming my wife?"

"Your wife," she repeated on a choking gasp. "But I thought—that is, you once said it was impossible."

"I was mistaken. Be assured that it is very possible, so long as you are willing."

Her heart lurched in the most peculiar fashion, for he appeared to be serious. "Are you doing this because we—because of what happened at the theater?"

"I intended to ask you then, though I never had the chance. Is my proposal unacceptable?"

"No—that is, I don't think so, but—oh, dear, I was prepared for the other offer, never this one," she wailed.

"You know how greedy I am," he said lightly. "Each time I told you how much I wanted you, you fought back, saying no, and no, and no again. In Devonshire you used your innocence as a weapon against me. Then you tortured me by leaving me for the theater and the Forsters. When I chased you down to London, you battled me with silence and avoidance. Haven't you realized love is impervious to such tactics?" He extended his hand to stroke her cheekbone, then buried his fingers in the black curls.

"But marriage! Trevor, it would be a scandal."

"I don't give a damn for any opinion but yours."

She read the truth of it in his face.

"I came to town with the intention of making you my wife, but as soon as I set eyes on you again, you became a public figure. For a time I thought you happier in that than you could ever be with me. And then you made it quite clear that you weren't happy at all." He was about to claim a kiss when Flora placed her forefinger over his lips.

"I'm not the stuff of which countesses are made," she said simply. "Not so much because I'm an actress, but because my father was baseborn."

"Your father's father might have been a Baron Allingham or a stone picker, or anything in between. I am determined to marry you, Flora."

"But our children—"

"You will be their mother, and that is all the pedigree I re-

quire for my heirs. Now, what is there to amuse you in that?"
he asked quizzically when she smiled. "Don't you believe
me?"

"Yes," she replied. "And I just realized that ours would be a
most equal marriage despite the differences in birth and status,
because of the concessions each of us must make. You are prepared to accept my mongrel children, and if I accept your proposal, I must give up the stage."

"I can't pretend that you will find the same sort of fulfillment in the many things that I can provide. You aren't tempted
by the title and fortune, or the houses and carriages and servants. I won't promise you an easy adjustment, either, or approval from my family—though Aunt Isabelle and Hugh will
be delighted. My Uncle George and Aunt Grace will be cool at
first, though they'll also be endlessly civil. But we'll have
each other, and tears and tantrums and laughter—everything
else we've shared already, although not enough. Never enough
for me, Flora."

"Nor for me," she whispered, for she had realized it long
since.

She knew she would willingly sacrifice her work and anything else to ensure that he would continue to hold her close
and whisper such gratifying things into her ear. Her eyes were
beacons of pure emotion when she lifted her face to his. "Here
is your answer, Trevor—yes, and forever yes." Anything else
she might have said was lost in his kiss, so she gave him the
balance of her reply in an uninhibited response to his ardor.
When he nuzzled the column of her neck, she closed her eyes
and a beatific voice in the back of her mind told her never to
look back with regret. All promise of happiness lay in the future, and she left nothing behind her but a triumph that had
been hollow because he'd had no place in it.

When he interrupted his explorations of her face and form,
it was to ask if she was quite sure of her decision. "For if you
abandon something so important only because I have pressed
you, you'll resent me again, and that I could not bear."

"How could you ever think I delight in this horrid, lonely
life?" she wondered. "I hate it. I'm not even an actress now."

"Only a cart horse," he said, turning the words into a caress. "But a very beautiful one."

"On Sunday I made up my mind to be your mistress after all. But I probably shouldn't admit it, lest you retract your marriage proposal!"

"Never," he murmured.

"And then after we—afterwards, you left town and I was in agony."

"I was encouraged to absent myself," Trevor explained. "Horatio Forster called at my house on Monday and interrupted my breakfast to warn me that Lieutenant Campion is as hotheaded as his lovely sister. He promised to do his best to keep Miles at bay, but I saved him the trouble by retiring to the country. Theater business kept me in close communication with the Forsters all week; I assumed one of them would tell you where I had gone, and why."

"Damn Horry," Flora moaned. "He might have told me he was trying to soothe Miles, not stir him up."

"And how, mistress mine, will your brother accept the news of our engagement?"

"With relief, I should think, for he probably expects the worst. My only real qualm is on poor Ben's account. He won't like my leaving him."

"I wondered how long it would be before you'd recall poor Ben." He sighed.

"Trevor, is there any hope that he can keep the Princess?"

"None in the world. He knows it now."

She gripped his arm. "Where did he go when he left the theater this morning?"

"The committee was summoned to Lord Dartmouth's house. The Lord Chamberlain has apologetically but firmly denied Forster's petition for a renewal of the license. He was already opposed to it, and the mob action last Sunday was the final straw." Looking down at her, he said sternly, "I don't want to hear about your obligations to *poor* Ben, who will benefit more from our marriage than if you remain in his employ. He depends on me to promote a third theater bill in Parliament, so he'd better not oppose me when I demand that he release you from your bond."

Flora had forgotten that her tie to the theater was a legal one. "And if he refuses?" she asked hollowly.

"Where you are concerned, pure selfishness is my watchword. I'll present him with an ultimatum: only if he sets you free will I introduce his precious bill after the Christmas recess. If he won't let you go—and I wouldn't blame him, for you're more valuable to him now than ever before—he'll regret it. What chance is there that your friend Horatio will join my cause? Wouldn't he support your happiness over his brother's ambitions?"

"It won't come to that," Flora replied positively. "Winning a permanent license is more important to Ben than any actress."

When Trevor sat down on the sofa, his betrothed perched upon his knee and declared, "When I'm ancient and infirm, with a dozen grandchildren gathered 'round my skirts, I daresay I shall make much of my days on the wicked stage and sigh over how I was bullied into respectability by one very determined gentleman."

"Yes, you had my measure from the outset, didn't you? But I was altogether mistaken in my judgment of you, that first time you received me in this room. Little did I suppose then that on my next visit I'd be so intimate with the aloof Miss Campion." He tweaked a curl.

"And when are you going to make an honest woman of me?" she inquired.

"As soon as you let me. Why not today? In fact, it's the perfect solution to our dilemma. We'll present Ben Forster with a *fait accompli*. I acquired a special license weeks ago, and it's waiting at Leafield House. All we need is a parson. And witnesses, but that will be simple enough, for you'll want your brother and your friends—and Margery Prescott. I don't imagine our union would be quite legal if she weren't there to see the knot tied. The more I think on it," he said with a broad smile, "the better I like the notion. You need only decide whether the deed will be done in this parlor or at a church."

"Church, if you please, preferably my own. St. Giles-in-the-Field is where my idol, the great David Garrick, was wed," she informed him, swinging her legs back and forth.

"I require no further recommendation. St. Giles it must be.

Will you be content with my signet for a makeshift marriage ring until I can purchase a proper one? It might take considerable time to find something suited to your exalted station, and I'm too impatient to embark upon a shopping trip just now."

Flora, in spite of being pleased by her bridegroom's impatience, made a great show of being put upon. "I do hope you'll give me time to change my dress."

Trevor kissed her forehead. "I'm prepared to take you as I find you, but I accept that I must let you have your way once in a great while. Run along, then. I'll fetch the license and visit your church to arrange the ceremony. Be sure to tell your good Margery to pack whatever you need for a visit out of town—I intend to spirit my wife away from London as soon after our wedding as is decent."

"Combe Cotterell?" she asked hopefully, scampering down from his knee.

"Alas, too far." With a devilish smile he said, "I am admittedly eager to make love to my bride, but not in a roadside inn. The beds are so ill-aired." He continued in a more serious vein, "I would happily install you in Cavendish Square, but that might give rise to a worse kind of publicity than has already been inflicted upon you."

"Where do we go that is neither too close nor too far from London?" she wondered, following him to the front door.

"To a place I know," he said with so mysterious an air that Flora instantly took umbrage. "No quarrels today, if you please—wait until we're safely married."

"I must be mad to consider spending the rest of my days with a—a marble-breasted *tyrant*!"

Laughing, he retrieved his hat from the hall table. "Your experience of my ruthless methods should have led you to expect something of the kind. But I shall strive to be a better, more reasonable husband than I've been a lover."

When he was gone, Flora ran up the stairs, her slippers barely skimming the risers, and after giving Margery the happy news asked her to press and lay out a white gown sprigged with forget-me-nots. Then she sat down at her dressing table to reflect as calmly as possible on her drastic and delirious decision to exchange her present lowly status for that of Lady Leafield.

Much better that she leave the stage as quietly and unobtrusively as she had found her way there six years earlier; there was a pleasing symmetry about it. A gala farewell performance held no appeal, nor did laudatory verses composed in her honor; that sort of parting from the old life would be too public and too funereal to suit her. Her final night before an audience had been uneventful, hardly memorable, but it was tucked away in a corner of her mind and that was sufficient.

The stage, once her only home, had become a platform where she displayed herself to the curious in an increasingly mechanical and joyless fashion. She had given up Trevor to tilt with fame, but had found no consolation for her heartache. Sacrificing a potentially brilliant career might not be a painless prospect, but it wouldn't destroy her peace. She had found a more comfortable, more private home within the circle of her lover's arms.

The throngs that had flocked to see her perform had set her on a pedestal, declaring her to be a goddess, a nymph, a genius. Flattering but quite untrue, she thought, emptying her drawers in search of a lace veil to lend a bridal touch to her best bonnet. The noble Earl of Leafield had spent the better part of a year proving to her that she was all too human, just as she had shown him that she was a woman of integrity and independence. She'd argued with him and thwarted him in ways no other person, male or female, had done before, and he'd angered her beyond reason. She had laughed with him and teased him and told him things she had never admitted to another soul. She had run away from him more than once, only to discover in the end that she had been running toward him. And through it all his love had been unwavering.

The occasionally tempestuous nature of their relationship and the unorthodox way she'd earned her living would ensure that theirs would be no ordinary union. And Flora, whose experience of the truly ordinary was limited at best, knew she would have it no other way.

20

Here comes the Countess. Now Heaven walks on earth.

Twelfth Night, V. i.

The night was still young, but the Earl and Countess of Leafield had already retired to their bedchamber, where the mussed bedclothes and general disarray of the great fourposter testified to what had lately occurred there. A cravat draped negligently upon a chair bore the appearance of having been hastily removed, as did the lacy chemise lying upon the floor.

Now the newlyweds, clad in their dressing gowns, sat at the fireside. Trevor occupied a wing chair, his brown head bent over the newspaper, and Flora reposed at his feet, her legs tucked beneath her.

As her husband's fingers played with her tousled curls, she gazed thoughtfully into the flames.

They had exchanged their marriage vows a fortnight ago in a hurried ceremony at St. Giles-in-the-Field, in the presence of her brother and the Drews, and the moment the register was signed the wedding party had returned to Great Queen Street for an impromptu celebration. Before Flora's eager lord had carried her off to Twickenham, she'd composed a note to Benedict Forster, crammed with explanations and apologies.

Upon arriving at his Palladian villa on the Thames, Trevor sat down to write out the formal announcements for the London papers, but the task of folding and sealing them was abandoned for other, more pressing matters. His subsequent preoccupation with his bride made him forget the notices, still gathering dust on a writing table downstairs.

Flora displayed very little interest in the world beyond their wintry, snowbound retreat. When it occurred to her that her days would never again be regulated by the familiar round of rehearsal and performance, she didn't repine; her husband was taking great care to fill her time and her thoughts.

He heaved a deep sigh, and the newspaper crackled as he folded it in half. Reaching down to hand it to Flora, he said, "I believe you will want to read this."

There was no doubt about which paragraph he deemed worthy of her notice, for it was embedded in a column generally devoted to theatrical gossip.

LONDON'S LOST ACTRESS

Public curiosity, excited by the disappearance of that ornament of her profession, MISS CAMPION, has been gratified. MR. BENEDICT FORSTER has announced that the Lady's retirement is as certain as the imminent closing of his Theater, where she delighted playgoers this season. Never again will her like be seen upon the London stage. Her portrayals of Juliet, of Ophelia, of Letty Loyal, and her brilliant execution of Comic and Tragic roles, will not soon fade from the memories of those who were privileged to view them in London or at Bath.

In the wake of Lord L——'s absence from the Metropolis, rumors of an Alliance are rampant amongst the lady's former colleagues. If she has joined the rank of the countesses, she follows the example of both LADY DERBY and LADY CRAVEN, who formerly trod the boards.

The Managers of the Theatres Royal, Messrs. Sheridan and Kemble, assuredly regret their failure to steal the esteemed Actress from FORSTER, their Professional Rival, and will be saddened to learn that a Nobleman has plucked this fair flower from the stage.

"It sounds as though I was buried, not married," said Flora when she finished reading. "Ben wrote it, of course. He eulogizes me most handsomely, but shows his hand in that last bit about Sheridan and Kemble. Such spiteful stuff!"

"You might have known he'd find some way to discomfit

them, but certainly you deserve the praise," said her husband with fond pride.

"Poor Ben, even though he expected to lose the license, he has suffered a terrible blow. And only a few hours later he received the news of my desertion." She shook her head in regret.

Trevor reached down to stroke the white shoulder peeping from her dressing gown, which had slipped. "I daresay poor Ben is already planning his next assault upon Bath. And the campaign for the third theater bill will keep him busy."

"I know, but it's sad to think of the Princess closing her doors."

"Do you miss the theater so much? We've shared a great deal during this brief, glorious time, but never your feelings on that subject."

Flora searched for the best words to communicate the mix of emotions she experienced, determined to give the truthful answer he would expect of her. "Of course I'll sometimes miss my friends, and all the excitement of a first night, and the camaraderie of benefit week. And the acceptance—actors are so open-minded, they care nothing for background or breeding, and base their judgments on talent alone. But I won't miss the quarrels or the petty jealousy or the lack of preparation for a new play, or the endless packing and unpacking during a tour. At Combe Cotterell I discovered I could be happy living away from the theater—*and* the Forsters."

"I wish you'd told me at the time," he said, running his hand through his shaggy brown locks.

"I didn't know it myself until I returned to London," Flora replied. "But in Devonshire I think I began to suspect what I now know, that my stage career was an interlude, the curtain-raiser that comes before the main piece. And though I was on the stage for more than six years, the whole time I was but standing in the wings waiting for the real play to begin. And it finally did, Trevor, at St. Giles."

Smiling down at her, he said, "For the past fortnight I've wondered what we ought to do next, and you've just supplied the answer. Our stay here has been delightful, this is the perfect love nest and will always be, but we can't stay here forever."

"Are we going to Hopeton Hall?" she asked, concealing her trepidation at the prospect of meeting his clergyman uncle and saintly aunt.

"Eventually. First, however, I want to see you acting the part of mistress at the Combe, especially now that Christmas draws near. Would you like to travel to Devonshire?"

Jumping to her feet, Flora flung her arms around his neck and pressed her lips to his cheek. "Yes, please," she breathed, "as soon as possible." She spent some time convincing him of her delight, to his immense satisfaction and her own, and afterward she found herself seated upon his knees, her head on his shoulder.

"Trevor," she murmured, her eyes half-closed, "I don't yet miss my work, but I can't help worrying sometimes that one day I will feel a void. And I've already decided what I'll do, so don't object too strenuously."

"And what is that, dear heart?"

"I think I might like to write a play," she confessed, suddenly feeling shy. "Horry and I always talked about trying it, but we never had the time, being busy with other people's plays. Which were usually so stupid that I ached to improve them." She turned her earnest face toward him to judge his reaction, and was puzzled and a little hurt when he gave a shout of laughter.

"But of course," Trevor agreed, to her great relief. "For you must have some outlet for those creative fires, and I can't expect marriage to quench them. Why should I object, Flora? I can see that you might require an endeavor that is your very own, some accomplishment that is quite unconnected with me. I have made a firm vow not to stifle the very quality that is so attractive in you."

"My independence? Why, Trevor, have you been reading tracts on the emancipation of females from the tyranny of males, on the sly? I never guessed that you, of all men, could be an admirer of Mary Godwin and her ilk," she teased.

"To be honest, I never gave the subject much thought, but I

think I'd better if your ladyship is going to be the next Aphra
Behn or Joanna Baillie."

"Or Mrs. Inchbald," Flora added thoughtfully.

"As your patron, for so I still consider myself, perhaps I will
commission a play from you." But Trevor's bride apparently
hadn't heard his playful suggestion, and he recognized that familiar, fervent light in her lovely green eyes. She was leagues
away from him already, and he almost regretted his foolhardy
words about cherishing her creative impulses.

But by this time he knew perfectly well how to recall his
presence to her with only the slightest exertion on his part, so
he tightened his hold on her waist and let his free hand slide up
and down one of the shapely legs draped across his knees.

His tactic was eminently successful; Flora abandoned the
discussion of her playwriting scheme. But something else occurred to her, and she drew back from her ardent spouse.
"Trevor, you asked me if I had regrets, and it's only fair that I
ask the same question. Are you disappointed in me?"

"After two weeks of living with you, my dearest love, and
becoming more intimately acquainted with your finer points, I
can say with great certainty that you could never, ever disappoint me," he told her, his hazel eyes gleaming.

She pinched his earlobe. "I didn't mean in that way, and you
know it. I meant because I'm not a dignified lady, only a common play actress whose dresser is her personal maid. I brought
you no lands or dowry."

"I care nothing for the dignity of the Countess of Leafield,
as I have been proving to you this fortnight," he replied, "nor
do I give a snap of my fingers for land, having quite enough of
my own. Your first play can be your dowry, if you feel the
lack of one. I regret nothing, Flora. If you had accepted me as
your protector when you were the toast of the town, I might
never have discovered which had the greater share of your affections, the stage or my humble self. No, don't interrupt, I'm
not done yet," he said, despite the fact that she hadn't spoken a
word.

For Flora had simply turned her melting eyes upon him, giving him a loving look that thus far in their marriage had resulted in her being stripped of her garments and chased

mercilessly into bed. She might have forgotten this, or she might not, but she continued to gaze at him in just that way. "Why, Trevor—"

But further speech was prevented by his eager kisses. Already his hands were gently working at the sash of her dressing gown, and she permitted him to untie it. She sighed with anticipation, for he was granting her yet another opportunity to prove to both of them how very little she blamed him for enticing her away from that other world to make her queen of his.

Historical Note

A third theater bill was introduced in the House of Commons but was defeated during the Parliamentary session of 1808. Later attempts in 1810 and 1813 met with similar failure.

The theater in Covent Garden burned to the ground in the autumn of 1808, and reconstruction took place soon after. John Philip Kemble's decision to raise the admission charges for the 1809 season sparked the "Old Price" riots and forced a temporary closure. Early in 1809, Sheridan's Drury Lane playhouse was destroyed by a blaze that lit up London, and until the costly rebuilding was completed three years later his company used the Haymarket Theatre and the Lyceum. The patent privileges granting the Theatres Royal exclusive rights to produce "serious" drama were abolished with the passing of the Theatre Regulation Act of 1843.

One particularly enjoyable aspect of my research for The Toast of the Town was studying the collections at London's Theatre Museum in Covent Garden and attending performances in provincial theaters.

Bath's Theatre Royal of 1805 has been painstakingly restored to Regency splendor. Its predecessor on Orchard Street was long ago converted to other uses, but the structure still stands.

The neighboring city of Bristol possesses the oldest working theater in Britain and an auditorium virtually unchanged from what was typical of the Georgian age. I hereby express my gratitude to my friends Margot and Robert Pierson for taking me there regularly.

Abundant thanks to my parents, who had to endure my youthful preoccupation with the stage, and to Christopher, my companion during so many hours spent in "box, pit, and gallery." M.E.P.